EMPTY VESSELS

Meet Inspector George Bartlett and Constable Archibald Boase in their first investigation together. In the closing months of 1921, Bartlett and Boase have a missing girl on their Falmouth patch. Before long they find themselves drawn into a murder investigation when another girl is found dead on a local beach. We meet the Pengelly family, unwittingly drawn in through their daughter's involvement with the prime murder suspect and find ourselves involved in mysterious goings-on at Penvale Manor. Deception and disguise come together in the final spectacular and surprising showdown when the killer is revealed.

EMPTY VESSELS

EMPTY VESSELS

by

Marina Pascoe

Magna Large Print Books
Long Preston, North Yorkshire,
BD23 4ND, England.

British Library Cataloguing in Publication Data.

Pascoe, Marina
    Empty vessels.

    A catalogue record of this book is
    available from the British Library

    ISBN   978-0-7505-4228-9

First published in Great Britain in 2014 by Accent Press Ltd.

Published in Large Print 2016 by arrangement with
Accent Press Ltd.

Magna Large Print is an imprint of Library Magna Books Ltd.

Printed and bound in Great Britain by
T.J. (International) Ltd., Cornwall, PL28 8RW

In memory of
Peggy Russell 1996-2010
and
Sydney 1995-2004

Chapter One

November 1921. The small town of Falmouth, which nestles on the Cornish coast and dips into the English Channel, was shrouded in a cloud of damp, clinging November fog typical for the seaside town at this time of year. The houses, tall, narrow and close to their neighbours, seemed almost to huddle together against the damp night air. Few people lingered about in the thickening fog, which was threatening to remain all night, and the town was quiet, with only the distant sound of men mooring boats by the pier, having been caught out by the rapid descent of the weather. The old, narrow streets were stranger now and uninviting; the darkness of this winter evening had come quickly.

There was talk of murder in the town following a local girl's mysterious disappearance nearly a month before and everyone seemed to be suspicious even of people they knew quite well – 'you never could be quite sure, even when you thought you knew someone' was the general uneasy feeling in Falmouth at the moment. One or two of the old cabbies who still worked in the town had decided to take their horses home and stable them up for the night; they wouldn't get much custom now. Most of the 'new' people that visited the town wanted motorised transport. For now, though, the cabbies survived with the help of their old regulars. Soon this way of life would change, and most thought not for the better.

Rose Pengelly tightened the old black woollen shawl covering her head and made her way along Webber Street, a small, narrow, shop-lined road, now dimly lit due to the worsening fog creeping in from the sea. The dampness chilled her right through, and she felt pain in her knees as she walked; she hurried as best she could to keep warm. It was becoming difficult to see much now as the fog closed in but, as she reached the corner which gave onto the road known as High Street, she saw a small person, head down, walking in her direction. Rose was pleased to see her daughter.

'Kitty, Kitty,' she called loudly.

As her voice seemed to melt into the lingering fog, it was apparent that the girl, walking quite slowly down the hill for fear of slipping on the damp pavement, had not heard or seen anything. Then, as Rose peered through the gloom, she was horrified to see, moving swiftly behind her daughter, a tall figure clothed in black. Closer now, very close.

'Kitty, KITTY.'

Rose felt a soreness in her throat as she screamed her daughter's name. The larger figure stopped and looked up and down the street and Kitty, hearing her mother's voice, began to run towards her. Rose reached out and hugged the girl to her.

'Didn't you 'ear that man behind you?'

'No, Ma,' the girl replied, turning around to look back up the street. 'No, I never 'eard nobody. Look, there's no one there.'

'I thought I'd better come and meet you; that shop of yours shuts at six o'clock, now it's nearly five to seven. What've 'e bin doin'?'

'The money was short, Ma. Mrs Williams made me and Mabel stay behind to try an' sort it out. Then she started on Norman for mixing the tobaccos up wrong an' I tried to 'elp 'im. You know 'e's not very bright an' all – she's always on at 'im.'

'Mrs Williams this, Mrs Williams that, she don't know what she's doin' 'alf the time. She should 'ave give up that shop years ago but she's too mean, just like the rest of that family.' She drew her shawl tighter and mother and daughter linked arms and quickened their step.

'I was waiting there,' the older woman continued, 'on the corner of Webber Street and I saw that man behind you – when I called out 'e disappeared down the opening. I worry all the time about you an' your sister,

13

especially since that dear Berryman girl went missing – three weeks now and not a sign of 'er.'

The women made their way back along Webber Street and, on reaching the open expanse known as the Moor, made their way up Killigrew Street to the basement rooms the family rented there. Down the steps they went, feeling for the rails in the darkness and entering the small courtyard below. Kitty opened the large door and they both entered into the hallway on the other side. The warmth was welcoming after the damp night air and they were glad to have arrived home. They were greeted by Jack, who, at seventeen, was the youngest member of the Pengelly family. He beckoned them into the kitchen.

'You found 'er then.' He grinned at his mother as she made her way through into the scullery. He looked at Kitty as she took off her coat. 'Ma was worried about you, especially with that Norma Berryman murdered an' all, she thought...'

'Jack, that's enough, I won't 'ave talk like that, do you 'ear me? We don't know what's 'appened to that poor girl, we've got to 'ope for the best,' Rose clasped her hand to her forehead in despair, 'an' 'er poor mother so unwell too – it must all be too much for 'er. I don't want any talk of murder in this 'ouse. I don't even want to think about it.'

Jack wasn't to be done down;

'Well, ev'ryone's talking about it down the docks – they all say she's bin murdered. One of the apprentices who knows all about life on other planets and things like that, 'e says she might 'ave been abducted by creatures from another planet, like Mars or the Moon. It's bin 'eard of before, 'e knows someone who 'ad a brother an' 'e was taken away by these people an' they never saw 'im again. The last time anyone saw 'im there 'e was goin' up in an airship. It's true. It 'appens all the time in America.'

Rose looked irritated. 'Well, they might all be talking about it down the docks but we're not talking about it 'ere, and that's that. They stupid boys you go round with, Jack, well I think it's time they grew up – s'posed to be young men now, coming up to seventeen, eighteen and still reading they daft comic books, they'll rot their brains, you mark my words.'

'They already 'ave, Ma,' interrupted Kitty.

At that, the front door slammed shut, and slow, heavy footsteps walked up the passageway to the parlour. The little group congregated in the kitchen stopped their bickering. Bill Pengelly entered the room, filling up the doorway as he did so with his six foot one, sixteen-stone frame.

'Sorry I'm late, all,' his voice was loud yet soft, 'thought I'd do a couple of hours over

15

tonight.' He came into the kitchen and hung his hessian bag on the back of the door. Rose scowled at him.

'You don't need to do any extra – it's gettin' too much, 'ow many times 'ave I got to say it?'

'Stop moanin', Mrs Pengelly, you want us to 'ave a 'appy Christmas this year, don't you? We'll be able to get a turkey if we're lucky, a drop o' beer, a nice bit o' fruit, an' some nuts...'

His wife interrupted him sharply. 'If you're six feet under by then, I won't want Christmas at all. An' I don't want gallons o' beer, neither – it's only you that drinks it. Jack isn't old enough.'

'Aw, Ma, I'm nearly eighteen, all my friends drink,' came the protest.

'You're just a boy until you're twenty-one.' His mother ruffled his hair and looked at her hand. 'What is that muck in yer 'air?'

Jack looked embarrassed.

'It's hairdressing actually – lots of men my age wear it.'

Bill winked at him;

'Yer mother said yer just a boy until the age of twenty-one and I agree. What do you want with that sissy stuff anyway? You tell me what young lady'll want to run 'er fingers through yer 'air with that tripe on it?'

Jack looked fed up.

Bill sat down at the table. 'I enjoyed that

16

pasty in particular today, Mrs Pengelly, just the job.' He squeezed his wife's waist as she walked past his chair.

'Oh give over, you old fool, it's only a pasty, 'ardly fit for a king,' came the reply. Rose could relax a bit now; she never relaxed until all the family were home together.

'You know no one cooks like you, Mrs Pengelly,' replied Jack giving his mother a squeeze in an attempt to imitate his father. Bill pointed his finger, 'You find yer own lady to go squeezin' – she's mine.'

Jack laughed, he liked it when his parents called each other Mr and Mrs and thought it was rather quaint.

'That'll do, you two, and I 'ope you made the most of my cooking, because I got fish 'n' chips tonight. I 'ad some money left in the tin so I thought I'd treat us all – mind, I'll 'ave to warm 'em up – they'd still be 'ot if it weren't for yer sister. Good job I went to meet 'er – there was a man following 'er down 'Igh Street an' she never even 'eard 'im – 'eaven knows what might 'ave 'appened.'

'I already said sorry, Ma.' Kitty was indignant. 'Anyway I didn't see no one – it was probably the ghost.'

'What ghost is that, Kit?' asked Jack who had a taste for all things strange and supernatural.

'I'm bein' serious, Jack,' his sister replied. 'Don't tell me you've never 'eard of the man

17

that 'aunts 'Igh Street – thought you were interested in all that.'

'You're right, I am – tell me about 'im, Kit, go on.'

'Well, apparently, loads of people 'ave seen 'im – all in black 'e is. They say 'e walks up an' down looking for 'is wife who was murdered in one of the 'ouses about two 'undred years ago...'

'All right, dear, never mind now, sit down while I butter some bread.'

Rose cut this conversation short – she didn't like tales of dead people and ghosts.

'Now, anybody who's still got boots an' shoes on, take 'em off, all of you, go on. You know I don't like you ruining me floor.'

The family obeyed then took their places around the vast wooden table, which, smooth and clean, bore testament to the work that went on daily in the heart of their home. The table was scrubbed daily – Rose couldn't abide dirt and was up early every morning to make a start and prepare everyone's food for the day. She lived by her late mother's standards. Rose had been born fourth of nineteen children and had grown up in poverty. Even so, her mother always kept a spotless house and everyone had had to do their share. The Pengelly household, although much smaller, lived by the same rules. Every morning, by the time the rest of the family awoke, a most wonderful smell pervaded every room. As they all prepared for work, Rose would be bringing trays of hot pasties from the oven, sometimes a cake or even a rice pudding. Bill and Jack always had bacon, eggs, hog's pudding and fried bread on a work day, but not the girls; there would never be enough money to pay for that so they made do with some bread and dripping or jam. And not one of them could even begin the day without copious amounts of strong, sugary tea.

Rose Pengelly was a small, frail-looking woman with a quiet voice, but she could put the fear of God himself in anyone who crossed her – in the family and outside it. She liked Kitty to style her now greying hair, but nothing too modern. Kitty was happy to oblige – she hated seeing her in that old, hand-made floral apron and she wished her mother's life could be a little easier – she always looked so tired. 'I see in one of your women's books that this is all the rage now, Kitty; do mine like that – not too young-looking mind, I don't want to look like mutton done up as lamb'. She wore small, round horn glasses when she wanted to read a library book or the *Falmouth Packet* to catch up with the local news. Whenever she went out she would dab on a little powder and the minutest amount of colour on her lips. Although there wasn't much money, being a skilful needlewoman meant that the family always looked well dressed whenever they went out.

As Rose, Jack, and Kitty sat at the table, and Bill shovelled some more coal on the fire, the door from the hallway opened and the youngest Pengelly girl, Ruby, stood, dressed to go out.

'Where d'you think you're goin'?' Rose enquired of the girl.

'I told you, Ma,' replied Ruby, 'I'm meetin' Frank, we're goin' dancin' tonight.'

'Ooh, I say, I'm meeting Frank,' Kitty mimicked her sister then let out her familiar and uncontrollable peal of laughter. 'When're we goin' to meet this Frank of yours then, Ruby?'

''E's shy, I told you before.'

Rose grabbed the girl's coat; she looked at her daughter, just nineteen, she didn't seem old enough to be out dancing with a man the family didn't even know, although she looked so grown-up, always in the latest fashions and her face made-up; most of her wages went on clothes, make-up, and going out. Rose thought it seemed like yesterday that she had held her as a newborn baby.

'You're not goin' – take your coat off and sit down. You've only just eaten.'

'No, Ma, I promised 'im and I want to go.'

Ruby sat at the table and, taking a small mirror from her handbag, propped it up against the milk jug which stood on the table and began to put on even more make-up.

'You're flogging a dead 'orse,' quipped Jack and winced when a long hatpin appeared as if from nowhere and pierced his buttock.

'Ma, Da, did you see that? Tell 'er, Da, Miss 'Igh-and-Mighty. Anyway, Ruby, no woman should wear more make-up than clothes.'

Bill's eyes twinkled. 'I've told you before, boy, when you insult your sister, make sure you're not standing next to 'er.' Everyone laughed, except Jack.

Rose looked at her beautiful daughter and knew she couldn't stop her going out – she had been just as headstrong at Ruby's age and she could see herself in the girl. She tried a last resort, half-knowing she was wasting her time. 'You tell 'er, Bill. Look 'ow much of that stuff she's got on 'er face – an' what's that smell?'

Jack intervened. 'Someone let that old tom cat in 'ere again?'

'The perfume you are enjoying at the moment is best quality cologne, called Nights of Passion, an' for your information, Lillian Gish wears this shade on 'er lips – and that is called Sweetest Ruby – I 'ad to 'ave it cos that's me name and it's a nice red,' came the reply from the lips pursed in mid-application. 'Frank's taking me to the cinema tomorrow night – we're seein' Lillian in *Broken Blossoms*.'

Rose looked at her husband for support.

Bill sighed and tapped his pipe on the fire-place.

'Nights of Passion – do you think she's old enough for that, Mrs Pengelly?' Bill was smiling, he didn't want to spoil his daughter's fun; equally, he didn't want to upset her mother.

The pipe pointed in the girl's direction. 'Ruby, I want you back in this 'ouse by 'alf past eleven, on the dot.' Rose sighed heavily; she'd thought he'd side with Ruby, that girl could get away with anything where her father was concerned. She was the apple of his eye and didn't she know it!

'But, Da,' Ruby protested, 'that's early, nobody comes 'ome that early...'

'Don't push your luck,' came the reply. Ruby scowled, picked up her handbag and left quickly before he changed his mind, her heels clattering on the slate floor of the hall-way to the front door.

'Don't be too 'ard on 'er, Ma', said Kitty, sensing her mother's anxiety, 'she'll be all right.'

There was no reply from Rose, who sat cutting irregular slices of bread from a home-made loaf of gigantic proportions, which was precariously balanced on her lap. As she spread the cold butter thickly and holes appeared in the bread she hoped Kitty was right.

At a quarter past eleven Bill stood in the doorway looking out into the yard and enjoying his last pipe of the evening before turning in. This was a ritual he had observed since he had sat outside with his father at night as a young man in the old house. There wasn't much to see now; the fog was much thicker and he could hear the muffled sounds of people walking home from the pubs and dances. He decided that he was too tired to wait up for Ruby as he normally did and, thinking that she'd probably be late as usual, he turned to go back in the house. Suddenly, he stopped, listening. He heard a noise, a faint sobbing. He listened again; it was definitely a woman crying.

'Ruby, Ruby love, is that you?' he called out softly.

A sound came from the corner of the yard and his daughter stepped into the small patch of light thrown out through the doorway.

'Da, Da.' The girl's sobbing was uncontrollable now.

'What's the matter, my 'ansum, what're 'e doin' out 'ere in the dark and the cold?'

He put his arm around her and took her inside and they sat down in the parlour. Ruby composed herself and stared into her lap.

'What's so bad, girl?' Bill asked, taking her two small, pale hands into one of his large old brown ones. 'Shall I fetch yer mother?'

'No thanks, Da, don't wake 'er, she's tired tonight.' Her lip trembled. 'Oh, Da, 'e didn't come, 'e stood me up. I waited outside the library till 'alf past ten, then I came back 'oping you'd all be in bed. I knew Jack would laugh if 'e knew, I knew Ma would say that's what men are like and I knew Kitty would say I was wasting me time with 'im, so that's why I was waiting outside.'

'You don't know what they'd say,' said her father reassuringly. 'There must be a reason, anyway, for the chap not turning up.'

'There is, Da,' Ruby began sobbing again. 'I was waiting on the Moor and about five and twenty past ten I saw Pearl Bray and Betty Trevaskis walking past to go 'ome, and they said they'd seen Frank at about ten o'clock with Ivy Williams. 'E 'ad 'is arm round 'er, Da and they was laughin'. Pearl and Betty said 'e only 'ad eyes for 'er.' She cried again.

'You waited for 'im 'til half past ten?'

Ruby dabbed her eyes with the large white handkerchief Bill offered her.

'There, there, it must be a mistake, you know what they two girls are like, they was 'aving a bit of fun. That Ivy Williams, anyway, you know what sort of a girl she is; it's a good job 'er poor mother can't see what's become of 'er, God rest 'er soul – and 'er such a clean, respectable woman too. No, there must be a mistake. You'll see 'im tomorrow and 'e'll explain ev'rything, I'm certain.'

Bill made her a cup of cocoa and went to bed. Ruby sat, holding the cup, and staring into the ashes forming in the fireplace. Eventually, at about half past one, feeling very tired she went to bed but the events of the evening had taken over and she lay awake nearly all night.

How could he go with a woman like that, she thought to herself, an awful, awful woman who had no respect for anyone, not even herself. And Frank? Hadn't he promised that they'd have fun together? When he sold his boating business he'd have plenty of money and they would be able to do anything. Just words now, they didn't mean anything. He was just like all the rest; why didn't she listen to her family? But Frank was so lovely and so kind to her. He really seemed sincere. The night passed slowly and Ruby was exhausted by the time the early morning light filtered through the gap in the bedroom curtains. She looked across at Kitty in the next bed; she was still asleep. In two months time, the older girl would be married and leaving home. Ruby wished she had a lovely man like her sister did. Soon Kitty and Eddy would be settled into a beautiful home that Eddy's parents were going to let them rent in Trelawney Road. Ruby was happy for her sister, she deserved all the happiness in the world. She still felt envious though. She sat up in bed and thought about the night before. How could he?

Ruby was glad she didn't have to work today. The shipping office she worked in was only open until midday on Saturdays and, being the senior assistant, she was allowed to choose her half day. She liked a nice long weekend. All the other assistants had to work today so she considered herself to be very lucky. She slid back under the covers and tried to sleep but she was too upset. She got up and dressed at about nine o'clock and went into the kitchen. Rose was sitting at the table drinking tea. Bill and Jack had gone to work and Kitty was still asleep.

'Come in love, 'ave a cup of tea.' Rose went to the kettle on the range. 'Yer Da told me what 'appened last night. Didn't I tell you, I knew 'e wasn't right for you – and I 'aven't even met 'im yet.'

'Please don't, Ma, I know I've probably been stupid, let's just leave it, eh?' The two women were joined by Kitty shortly after and, as they all sat and talked, there was a knock at the door. Rose opened it to find a policeman standing on the doorstep.

'Good morning, Madam, Constable Hawkins, Falmouth Police Station, may I please speak to Miss Ruby Pengelly?'

'Oh, my God, what's 'appened?' Rose went white and felt sick.

'May I please come in, madam?'

'Do.' Rose led the officer into the kitchen where the girls, having overheard the conversation, sat clutching each other's hands.

'What's 'appened, Ma?' asked Ruby.

'This policeman wants to speak to you, love – what's it about, Constable?'

The constable addressed Ruby, 'Are you acquainted with Mr Francis Arthur Wilson, miss?' He stared at Ruby and she felt uncomfortable.

'Frank? I know 'im, yes, why what's 'appened to 'im? Is 'e all right?'

'We're not sure, miss. You see, he seems to have disappeared and I was hoping you might be able to tell me where he is. I heard you were a friend of his?'

'What's 'e done, Officer? Is 'e in trouble?' asked Kitty.

'We want to speak to him in connection with a lady by the name of, er ... let me see, um ... oh yes, here it is, Ivy Williams. They were seen together last night in Falmouth.' Ruby felt sick. What now?

The constable continued, looking at Ruby as he spoke.

'I'm afraid I can't tell you anything else – I was told that you were a close friend of his. Do you know where I can find 'im, miss?'

'I've got no idea, Constable. I was supposed to meet 'im last night and 'e didn't turn up so I came 'ome.' Ruby's voice was shaky.

'Well, if 'e does show up, would you be

kind enough to let us know at the station, as soon as possible please, miss?'

'Yes, yes, of course I shall.'

Rose showed the policeman to the front door. She let him out and closed it behind him. She stood in the hallway, her head spinning. She slowly made her way back into the kitchen where her two daughters were crying.

'What's goin' on, Ruby?' she asked the girl. Her voice was stern now.

'I really don't know, Ma, honest I don't. I can't believe it. I don't know why the police are looking for 'im.'

''Ow could you get mixed up with a man that the police are lookin' for? And, another thing, 'ow do the police know that you've bin goin' round with this 'ere Francis Arthur Wilson? People must be talkin' about you. I don't want any scandal in this family, Ruby, and I don't want you getting involved with the police or anyone who's in trouble with 'em. This family is a good family with a decent reputation an' I don't want any Pengelly bringing shame upon us – are you listenin' to me, my girl?'

Rose took off her slippers and put on shoes. She stood in front of the mirror, combing her hair. She didn't speak. Ruby didn't say anything; she knew she had upset her mother and she didn't like it. At last, reaching for her coat, Rose looked at the girls. 'I'm off to meet

Mrs Tregido to 'elp 'er with the church jumble sale and then I'll be goin' down the street to get something for tea tonight. I don't know what all this is about, but I do know that I don't want you getting involved any further with that man; do you 'ear me, Ruby? That's final.'

'All right, Ma, I 'ear you.'

While Rose was helping Elsie Tregido, a childhood friend and widowed for about thirty years, a small group of people had begun to congregate at Swanpool Beach. Several police officers were trying to move everyone away but gossip was spreading fast. News that a terrible crime had been committed had soon seeped through the local community. By about eleven o'clock almost a hundred onlookers had turned up at Swanpool to feed their desire for witnessing a gruesome event. Men, women and children, ignoring the police and their cordons, stood up on the cliff tops and even scrambled across the rocks to get a better look. Falmouth was normally such a quiet yet industrious town, with hard-working people making up its population. There wasn't really much crime, maybe one or two burglaries or late-night fighting when the pubs closed, but nothing like this today.

On the sand, in a heap of clothing soaked by the salty tide, lay the body of a woman, only recognisable as such by her female curves and her feminine garments. She wore a bottle green satin skirt which was at least one size too small, even for her slim frame, a pale green blouse with short, puffed sleeves, strangely inappropriate for the time of year, no stockings, and black shoes, made of cheap leather with a strap across. On one foot, the strap had come undone and a mark showed where the leather had cut into her skin over some time. Her facial features had been mutilated beyond any possible identification, and what remained of her hair was bound to her head with dark red blood. The waves were gently lapping around her lifeless body, each time receding and taking more of her blood out into the English Channel. The onlookers waited. Nothing was going to deny them their story in the pub tonight, nothing was going to rob them of their chance of being one of the first to see the battered body – they might even get themselves in the newspapers. In next to no time, news of the murder was spreading throughout the town. Who was the dead woman? Who killed her? Was any woman safe in Falmouth?

At the police station in Berkeley Vale, the atmosphere was tense. Inspector George Bartlett was assigned to the case and had already tried in vain to keep the news of the murder as quiet as possible. After returning from the beach, he sat looking out of his

30

office window, watching the traffic in the street below and wondering how he was going to keep all this from the public – he didn't feel hopeful in the least; so many people had gathered at the beach within what seemed like minutes of the discovery, it'd probably be halfway round Falmouth by now. He was well-liked locally, and wouldn't do anything to upset the good people of the town who had made him feel so welcome, but he really could do without the inevitable gossip. He knew that at any second the reporters from the *Falmouth Packet* would be on his doorstep hounding him for details for a good story. He despised the press and knew how much trouble they were capable of causing; the less he had to do with them the better, as far as he was concerned.

George Bartlett was happily married to Caroline who was, sadly, weak and never in good health, and he adored her. Caroline wasn't happy that her husband had taken a reduced rank to bring her to the coast – it made her feel such a burden. She could not deny that she had felt better since they came here though. And George, dear George, he seemed much more relaxed than he was in their London days. She loved to see him in the garden tending his beloved roses, his pipe seemingly always in his mouth. She liked sitting next to him when he was concentrating on his crossword – how he hated it

31

when she pointed a finger at the paper and told him the answer. Caroline had given Bartlett his beautiful daughter, Irene, and the girl's good looks now reminded him of his wife when they had first met. His great sadness was the loss of his son, John, mortally wounded in France in 1916. Caroline had taken their loss very badly and Bartlett felt she had never truly recovered from this devastation. He worried about her and he worried about Irene. He idolised his daughter and didn't think it was right for such a young girl to live at home looking after her sick mother; how many times had he told her they were fairly comfortable now and they could get a woman in to do for them? Irene should be looking for a husband to take care of her. Then again, one of his favourite qualities he found to admire in the girl was her single-mindedness and stubbornness – just like her father. Hadn't he always taught her to be herself and to have her own mind? Well, it was probably too late to complain about it now. Anyway, secretly, he loved having her at home, his only remaining child.

As Bartlett sat looking from his window, his assistant Archie Boase, a keen young constable and well-liked by Bartlett, stuck his head round the door.

'I've done what you asked, sir. I've questioned some of the people that said they thought they saw something, or heard something, but, you know how it is – absolutely nothing. Fancy a cuppa?'

'I wouldn't say no – and thanks, Boase. We'll get the formal inquiry underway and just hope it all comes together nice and quickly. I don't like it, Boase, I don't mind telling you, especially with Norma Berryman missing – where is she?'

Missing persons and murders were so rare in the town that Bartlett couldn't help the nagging feeling in the back of his mind – did the disappearance of Norma Berryman have something to do with this? The fact was that, at present, he knew very little about either of the cases. But, there was Boase – and Bartlett knew he was going to be thankful for his sharp wits. The two men got on so well that Bartlett was glad the young constable had been brought to him. Superintendent Bertram Greet had been in charge of the station since Bartlett had first arrived in the town. Bartlett couldn't bear the man and the two agreed on nothing. Greet wanted everything immediately, while Bartlett took time and care and valued precision. But the two men tolerated each other – Greet knew he had a good man and Bartlett didn't expect to be working under him for much longer. For the time being it would do – one good thing to come of it was that Archie Boase had been assigned to work as Bartlett's right-hand man and that was definitely working well for everyone.

They weren't alike, not in the least, Bartlett and Boase; the younger man had been born and brought up in Redruth, he was an only child and had had quite a good education. Bartlett's family had been very poor and large; growing up in the East End of London had not been easy in the last quarter of the nineteenth century, and while some meagre elements of an education had been taken up, Bartlett had no qualifications and had never had any intention of becoming a police officer. When little else presented itself and money was short his parents thought it would be a very good career for their son, and so they pushed him into it. Bartlett had only just begun to find real satisfaction and happiness in his work since moving to Cornwall. He regularly pointed out the opportunities that could become available to Boase, and how lucky he should feel living in such a wonderful place as Falmouth, with all that refreshing sea air. Boase had never been to London. He had never even had a proper girlfriend. He liked Irene Bartlett, though, and he knew that her father wanted him to like her. Living alone in rooms in Melvill Road, Boase welcomed the frequent invitations to tea and dinner at the Bartletts' – partly because the food was so much better than his landlady's (although she did her best, it was pasty, stew or roast most days of the week, with the occasional saffron cake), but mainly he liked seeing Irene. He liked the way Bartlett asked him to help her with the washing-up after their food. Probably the best part was being alone with Irene in the scullery. He was very nervous of her and awkward and as much as he wanted to please her, he never attempted to change his appearance or try to impress her. Irene was glad – she liked him just as he was.

Boase brought Bartlett a strong cup of tea, the way he always took it, with two large sugars and just a splash of milk. He stooped and put the cups on the desk. His height always made Bartlett laugh and his first comment to the younger man when they met had been 'How tall are you?' Boase, at six feet one, was almost six inches taller than his superior. His slim frame, contrasting with Bartlett's larger build, blond, wavy hair and green eyes reminded Bartlett of his son – at twenty-five, Boase was the same age now as John had been when he was killed. The older man, strangely, didn't resent the other; in fact, he felt rather paternal and wanted Boase to succeed. Unlike Boase, though, John was never much of an artist, or a birdwatcher, though he had always enjoyed woodwork and showed promise as a cabinet maker. Bartlett didn't really understand why Boase was embarrassed about his hobbies, but he respected the boy's privacy and left him to it.

'I should think this is as bad as trying to catch Jack the Ripper, isn't it, sir?'

Boase grinned and sipped his tea.

'Yes, well, you may mock, but I tell you, I almost had him ... I was so close.'

'Of course you were, sir.'

As Bartlett finished his tea, the door to his office burst open and the desk sergeant, flushed with excitement, stood on the threshold.

'Pardon me, sir, we've just had a positive identification of the dead woman. An officer found her handbag amongst the rocks about a hundred yards away from the body. Constable Hawkins was right, it's Ivy Williams.'

'That's good news,' replied Bartlett, rising to his feet, 'are we sure it's her handbag?'

'Seems fairly certain, sir – there was an address and note book with her name in it too. It's all just being sent to you now, sir.'

'Right, Boase, Hawkins thought he knew her, he recognised her clothes. Apparently, he saw her in the town last night; he was having a drink with his wife and this woman was there in the pub – making a spectacle of herself, in drink. Hawkins asked his wife who she was. It seems Mrs Hawkins had a run-in with her a couple of months ago. Still, she didn't deserve this.'

Bartlett gathered some papers together on his desk and told the younger man to put his overcoat on.

'We've got a start, Boase. Get together everyone we can spare for making enquiries – I want this maniac caught as soon as we possibly can and before anyone else comes to harm.'

Boase had already left the office, a surge of anticipation welling up inside him. This could mean better things for him if he played his cards right – and who knows – maybe for him and Irene?

Chapter Two

Almost the full complement of Falmouth police officers gathered together at the station to hear Bartlett's instructions.

'Gentlemen, your efficiency this morning has started to pay off. We have a positive identification of the dead woman, a Miss Ivy Williams, of 42, Kimberley Park Road. She was temporarily renting a room there, the owner being a William John Gibbons. She was paying rent, as far as I know, from her earnings as a barmaid in the Grapes public house, supplemented by prostitution. She had been known to offer her services in Falmouth and Penryn so we must keep an open mind; she must have known plenty of men, and, possibly, their wives. We need to think of anyone with an axe to grind. We also need to speak to Gibbons at length – get on to it will you Boase? And take Penhaligon with you – his questioning techniques are severely lacking – show him how it's done. Oh ... and, Boase – let's speed this up a bit shall we? I know I'm normally a patient man but I really can't tolerate Greet breathing down my neck much longer ... he's threatening to call in the Met. if we don't wrap this up quickly. And, another thing, he's said he wants us to ditch the uniform – apparently it's upsetting people and he thinks we'd be more successful in mufti.'

Boase and Penhaligon took the short walk from the station to Gibbons's house. They walked up the gravelled path to the front door. Boase knocked and waited then knocked again. Upstairs a window opened and a dishevelled figure peered out.

'Mr Gibbons – Mr William Gibbons?' Boase looked up, craning his neck.

'Yes, I know why you're here; wait, I'll come down.'

The two policemen stood on the doorstep and presently, after much turning of keys in locks and withdrawing of bolts, the man opened the front door.

'You'd better come in,' said Gibbons.

He led the way into the front parlour. Boase noticed he walked with the aid of a stick, his right leg slightly bent. He was about thirty-six years old, short, with thick brown hair and a thick moustache neatly trimmed. The parlour was generously furnished, with about two dozen photographs in gilt frames displayed on the walls giving the room a distinctly cluttered, Victorian feel. Penhaligon wandered across the room looking at each of the pictures.

'It's about that Williams girl, isn't it?' Gibbons invited them both to sit down.

'Yes, sir, no doubt you've heard the news then?'

'I have.' Gibbons looked uncomfortable. 'Can I give you some tea?'

'That would be very nice.' Penhaligon rushed back across the room, never one to miss an opportunity.

'No thank you, sir, we won't.' Boase wasn't there to pass the time of day. He continued his questions – he was here for information, not to take tea. Penhaligon would do well to learn a lesson or two from Boase – he had been taught by Bartlett, after all, and that was about as good as you could get.

'Miss Williams was found murdered this morning and we're making enquiries. You were obviously one of our first ports of call, being her landlord, and all that.'

'What do you mean, "and all that"?'

'Nothing at all, sir, just a figure of speech.' Boase couldn't work this character out.

'You think I'm involved?' Gibbons lit a pipe.

'No, sir, we just want to ask you a few questions.'

'Well I'm afraid I can't really tell you anything, she kept herself to herself – out most of the time, too.'

'You a military man, sir?' interrupted Penhaligon, completing his examination of the photographic collection'

'Yes, yes I was. Durham Light Infantry –

invalided out though; my legs – don't like to talk about it.'

Boase, ex-military himself, could sympathise with that philosophy and motioned to Penhaligon to let it drop. He reverted to questions about Ivy and Gibbons began to look uncomfortable again.

'When did you last see Miss Williams, sir?'

'Oh, must have been about three o'clock in the afternoon, on Friday – yesterday.'

'Did she say or do anything unusual, have any visitors, say where she was going?'

'No, no she didn't.'

'Well, was she behind with her rent at all?'

'No. As I said, she kept herself to herself, she was a quiet person while she was in the house and she always paid her rent – on time. Always on a Friday evening.'

Boase couldn't help thinking that something wasn't right. 'So, did she pay you yesterday?'

'No.'

'How did you feel about that?'

'I didn't feel anything, I knew I'd get it.' Gibbons fidgeted in his chair. Boase stood up.

'But you didn't, did you? Mind if I take a look at her room, sir?'

Gibbons, walking with difficulty, led the two men up one flight of stairs, across a small landing and up a second, smaller staircase which reached a door. Gibbons pointed

41

to it.

'That's her room, there.'

Boase entered the room, almost surprised to find it unlocked. He wondered why Gibbons hadn't offered him a key – had he known it wasn't locked? It seemed strange that a tenant would do such a thing. Walking across the room, Boase soon realised that there was little in the way of possessions there. A bed stood on one side of the room, a chest of drawers under a small recessed window, and a rag rug on the floor. An old gilt-edged mirror hung on the wall next to the bed.

Boase turned to Gibbons who was waiting on the landing.

'Did she ever bring anyone back here, sir – any men?'

'This is a respectable house, not a knocking shop. No she didn't. I'll leave you to it.'

The landlord negotiated the descent to the ground floor and left Boase and Penhaligon checking the room for any clues to Ivy's murder, or even anything at all about the woman herself. After several minutes of searching the small bedroom, the men had found nothing. A few clothes in the drawers, a bit of make-up and scent on the dressing table; just the usual things any woman might have but much less of it.

'Didn't have much, did she?' remarked Penhaligon, looking out of the window down on to the well-kept gardens.

'Doesn't make much sense', replied Boase, 'it's almost as if she wasn't planning on staying here much longer.' He sat on the bed and rose again immediately.

'Look at this, Penhaligon.' He had drawn back the pink satin eiderdown. Underneath lay a woman's sequinned evening bag. Boase opened the clasp and emptied the contents onto the bed; a pair of nail scissors, a comb, about five shillings in loose change, and a powder compact. Boase turned the compact over and over in his hand. It was enamel, quite cheaply made. He opened the lid. Strangely, there was no trace of powder inside and where the mirror should be was a photograph, carefully cut out into a little circle and pressed inside. Boase stared at the photograph, while staring back at him were about twelve servants in Victorian dress. There they all were – butler, footmen, parlour maids, scullery maid, cook. Through necessity, on account of the size of the compact, some of the servants were missing, but this didn't look like a small household. Boase wondered what a woman of Ivy's lowly status could want with a photograph of what looked like a country house and its staff. He muttered to himself, 'We identified this woman from her handbag ... now here's another.'

He quickly stuffed the small bag and its contents into his pocket; he'd show it to

Bartlett when he got back to the station.

The two policemen thanked Gibbons, who watched them walk down the front garden path, and made their short trip back to the station. Within ten minutes Boase was standing in Bartlett's office showing him the handbag. On the other side of the door the whole building was buzzing with activity. Reporters from the *Falmouth Packet* were beginning to irritate the desk sergeant who had been given strict instructions to say nothing. The streets had become quieter now and an atmosphere of shock seemed to hang over the town.

Ruby had had no word from Frank.

The first day of December brought wind and rain and a thick mist hung down like a grey blanket over the bay. On the water little boats bobbed up and down; they wouldn't be going out today, the weather was far too dangerous and uninviting. Fishermen sat on the quays repairing nets, however desperate for work and food they were, they couldn't afford to take too many risks when their families depended so much on them. They'd seen too many tragedies over the years and didn't have any desire to add to the number. Around the bay and docks, small, plucky tugs continued about their work, hauling their large sea mates in and out of the harbour.

It was now ten days since the mutilated body of Ivy Williams had been discovered, and there was much disquiet in the town. The police were the main target – they should be doing something; they should have caught the killer by now. Ordinarily, most of the locals couldn't have cared less about a cheap prostitute and barmaid, but this was an opportunity to cause some trouble and make life difficult for the local constabulary. Some real troublemakers had even smashed the windows of the station late one night – they probably didn't care about Ivy Williams either, but it was an excuse to cause a scene.

At a quarter past eight in the morning, a well-dressed woman stepped from the London train at Falmouth Station. She looked anxiously around her as she walked along the platform and as she came through the station doors she quickened her step, pausing once or twice to look over her shoulder. Although she appeared by her manner not to want any attention, she must have attracted plenty, simply by her clothes. Hers was not the usual attire for most local women, and anyone watching would have surmised that she was not returning to Falmouth but coming from London or some other large town or city. About five feet five inches, with wavy auburn hair straight from a Paris fashion magazine, her face was immaculately made-up.

She wore a small hat, which made no

attempt to cover her forehead, and a long, camel-coloured coat with a very expensive fur collar. The ensemble was finished with cream silk stockings, and beige shoes with quite high heels and straps fixed with two mother of pearl buttons. She carried a beige handbag which hung down by her left side and, on the other side, a small grip which, presumably on account of its limited capacity, looked ready to burst.

The woman made her way towards the dockyard entrance and proceeded to walk past the elegant sweep of houses known as Bar Terrace and on towards the town. As she continued through the streets, people stared, they stared hard. They nudged each other and came out of shops to look at her. She was aware of this and felt uncomfortable. Looking at them and their clothes, she couldn't help feeling a little over-dressed. Reaching Church Street and seeing a sign which advertised 'Rooms to Let', she entered the building over which it hung and went up the stairs. Thirty minutes later, she re-emerged to be met by a group of boys, mostly school-children, but some errand boys also. They stood, again staring at her. As she moved forward, they parted either side of her and let her through. How strange these people were, she thought to herself as she quickened her step and returned back the way she had come earlier. After about a fifteen minute walk, the woman stopped outside a large house in Avenue Road. Again, she looked nervously over her shoulder, opened the gate and walked up to the front door. Pausing for a second, she looked on the ground then quickly bent to lift a large stone from under which she pulled a key. She went up two steps, turned the key in the lock and let herself in.

George Bartlett sat in his office at the police station looking exasperated. He unlocked the top drawer in his desk where the compact with the photograph from the dead woman's second handbag lay. He wished he knew what connected Ivy Williams to the servants in the photograph. She certainly wasn't old enough to be one of them. Boase had called on her father soon after the murder but, because of her recently discovered occupation, he didn't want anything to do with the investigation. He couldn't even help the police with information. Perhaps Bartlett would pay a visit himself – Boase was very good with a brilliant and analytical mind but Bartlett had more experience with people. Yes, perhaps he'd see Williams himself. There was always the possibility he'd forgotten something or withheld it, thinking it unimportant. Bartlett wasn't convincing himself much – he was really clutching at straws, but at the moment there wasn't much else. He finished his cup of tea and looked at the clock. Ten to nine. There was a knock at the door and Boase came in, grinning.

'Morning, sir, not so nice today – might brighten up later though, eh?'

'Shut up, Boase,' barked his superior.

'What's up, sir? Bit under the weather?' risked Boase handing over Bartlett's newspaper.

'I am not under the weather, over the weather, or in any other meteorological position,' came the sharp reply. 'I'm fed up, man – almost a fortnight now and not a single clue to the Williams murder, not one lead. The whole thing is preposterous and I'm fed up, fed up and I don't mind who knows. It's preposterous.'

'Something'll turn up, sir – it always does.' Boase didn't like seeing Bartlett feeling so dejected. If anything, it made the younger man feel insecure.

'No, Boase, you're wrong; it doesn't always turn up, and well you know it.'

'It's quite cold in here this morning, sir, shall I ask Penhaligon to light a fire?'

'If you like.'

The older man put down his newspaper and tried to ignore his assistant. Boase sent for Penhaligon to light the fire and within minutes the young constable entered the room armed with a stack of newspapers and kindling. He knelt on the floor and began his work.

Boase thought it best to keep quiet when his boss was like this, although it didn't happen very often. Bartlett was usually so easygoing. A real family man, he liked nothing better than tending his garden, particularly his roses – Boase thought he treated them almost like children, such was the attention he lavished on them. When he wasn't gardening, he was walking across the cliff tops and the beaches with his dog. Topper was an Airedale terrier and a very good friend to Bartlett. When his master wasn't working, Topper was always beside him, walking at his heel or lying next to him in the garden. Bartlett was, for the most part, even-tempered at work too, but today that was different. Boase hoped it would be short-lived and carried on with some paperwork.

Bartlett had stood up and wandered over to where Penhaligon had prostrated himself, and was now blowing gently into the fireplace. Bartlett tutted and bent down to pick from the top of the pile of newspapers where he had spotted an unfinished crossword. He shook the paper open and returned to the chair behind his desk. His brow furrowed as he looked over the puzzle; within a minute he had thrown the paper down on the desk. He stared at it. Then he stared closer.

'Good God!' Bartlett jumped to his feet, knocking over his empty teacup.

Boase was glad of some reaction.

'Calm down, sir, now look, you've broken your favourite cup.'

'Good God, man, never mind that, take a look at this.' Bartlett was frantically folding the paper to present to the younger man.

Boase took the newspaper and read the page that had been held in front of him.

'Would Miss Ivy Williams, daughter of the late Maude Mockett, and last known to be living in Falmouth, Cornwall, on reading this, please contact the following firm regarding a matter of the utmost importance.'

Bennett, Bennett, Thornton & Bennett
127, Oxford Street
London

Boase frowned. 'What does this mean, sir?'

'I've no idea, Boase,' replied Bartlett, 'but I intend to find out – come with me.'

Leaving Bartlett's office and pausing only at Superintendent Greet's open door to leave a hasty message, the two men crossed the lobby. As they reached the main door, a short man entered from the other side. Round in the face with a hat at least two sizes too small perched on his head, and wearing a grey raincoat with a tartan scarf around his neck, he held the door open for his wife who was slowly making her way to the entrance. She was small and thin with grey hair and wearing a brown felt hat and brown overcoat. Her face looked almost blue. She paused at the door and seemed to have difficulty breathing.

'Come on, love,' the man beckoned his wife. 'You can sit down for a minute now.'

Bartlett and Boase immediately recognised the couple as Mr and Mrs Berryman, the parents of Norma.

Bartlett looked at his assistant. 'Oh no, I want to get to the railway station, quickly' he muttered, half under his breath, knowing he was now likely to be delayed. He had a great deal of respect for the Berryman couple and felt, at least, he should listen to what they had to say.

Mr Berryman approached them.

'Officer, Mr Bartlett, sir.'

'Good morning, Mr Berryman, Mrs Berryman. What can I do for you?'

'You can find out what's 'appened to my daughter, that's what.' Mrs Berryman, having regained her breath, seemed suddenly rejuvenated and lunged forward at the senior officer. Her husband put his arm around her, half heartedly trying to restrain her.

'Don't, Peggy. It's not Mr Bartlett's fault.'

'It bloody is. All of you in this police station, doin' nothin'. You should 'ave found my baby by now. Call yerselves policemen?'

Her husband kept his arm round her, trying all the while to reassure her.

'Is there no word at all, Mr Bartlett, sir?'

Bartlett put his hand on the man's shoulder.

'I'm so sorry, Mr Berryman, there's still no news of your daughter, if we learn anything, anything at all, you have my word I'll let you know immediately. I admit I was confident to begin with, I really thought we'd have news by now but please don't give up hope.'

Bartlett led the way into his office and Mr Berryman, leaving his wife in the lobby, followed. He lowered his voice. He looked pale and drawn and it was obvious that he had had very little sleep.

'It's Peggy,' the man removed his small hat and was turning it over and over in his hands, 'she ... she says she's sure our Norma's ... our Norma's ... *dead.*' As he spoke the final word he clutched his chest and sighed as if a pain had struck right through his heart. He was grimacing now as he fought back the tears.

'Please, Mr Berryman, you mustn't think like that, you must have hope.'

This was one of the rare occasions that George Bartlett didn't know how to reassure and wasn't comfortable trying. His own daughter was the same age as Norma Berryman and he knew how it would affect both his wife and himself if they were ever so unfortunate as to be in this terrible position. He remembered how he had felt waiting to hear of his son John during the war. Months and months had gone by until he had received such devastating news. Caroline Bartlett had never got over the death of her beloved son, and never would.

The Berrymans left the station and Bartlett called Archie Boase into his office.

'I don't like it, Boase, none of it.' He sat with his head in his hands and looked desperate.

Boase sat on the corner of the desk.

'What now, sir?' he asked, sensing the other man's frustration.

'We're off to London, Greet's given us permission to go – we might just be in time for the train.' Bartlett grabbed his hat and coat and stuffed a brand new pair of reading spectacles into his top pocket – he didn't like them but needed them. When he grew tired of squinting he put them on.

The two men made their way to the railway station. They entered and approached the ticket office. Bartlett pulled some money from his pocket and addressed the clerk through the small arched window.

'I'd like two return tickets to London Paddington, please.'

The official was a thin man of about sixty years with a long, pointed nose, and what thinning grey hair remained was swept over the top of his head in an attempt to make him look younger. It didn't work. He peered over his half-moon glasses and smiled.

'I'm sorry, sir, that train left just ten minutes ago, there's repairs going on this week – there's only one train today,' the smile turned to a smirk as the clerk's lips curled up at the sides, 'and that was it. You can go tomorrow, if you like.' The smirk broadened.

Bartlett flushed and held identification up to the glass. 'Look here my man, you are impeding official police business; I wish to travel to London, by train *today*.'

'Well I'm very sorry to 'ear that, sir, very sorry I am, but, as I said, no trains today.' With that the window closed sharply almost shattering the glass.

'Damned impertinence,' muttered Bartlett. 'We can't wait 'till tomorrow, Boase, we'll have to see what we can find out by telephone first. I know a couple of chaps in the Met. who could help me out if necessary – you know, make enquiries for me.'

The two men made their way back to the police station, Bartlett more than a little agitated. 'Get on the telephone to that firm of solicitors, Boase. Tell them we're investigating the girl's murder and we'll be up tomorrow to discuss any information they may have to help with our enquiries. We've missed the blasted train now but we've got other things we can be doing today. How

54

did I miss that notice in the paper?'

'Right you are, sir, I'll get on to it now.' Boase left the room and closed the door quietly behind him, leaving Bartlett feeling angry with himself.

There must be something I've got wrong, he thought to himself. He drew a sheet of paper from his desk and wrote in large letters at the top:

MURDER OF IVY WILLIAMS/DIS-APPEARANCE OF NORMA BERRY-MAN

He began to sketch out the events of the past few weeks; the disappearance of the girl, the murder of Ivy Williams, the disappearance of Francis Wilson, the strange photograph in the powder compact. It just didn't add up. The sun had burst through the clouds about half an hour previously and Bartlett felt the heat on his face through the window; he felt uncomfortable and sweaty. The fire lit earlier by Penhaligon was ablaze and the room was now far too hot. Bartlett loosened his collar and mopped his face and neck with his voluminous handkerchief. He got up from his chair and walked to the door to go out into the street for some fresh air. He didn't feel too well. As he reached for the door knob he jumped back quickly as the door burst open and Boase rushed through into the office. His face was flushed red and his eyes glowed with excitement.

'Sir, sir, you'll never believe this one...' he stopped, savouring his moment.

'Well, come on man – surprise me.' Bartlett rubbed his chin in exasperation and went back to his chair to await his assistant's news.

'I've just spoken to the solicitors in London; I told them what was happening and that we'd be coming up to London tomorrow, just as you said, and then...' he paused again, enjoying the delicious feeling of triumph, 'and then...'

'Then what?' Bartlett was becoming more irritated.

'Then, they told me that Ivy Williams had been to their offices *last week!*' Boase stood tall and proud at the effect his findings were having on his superior.

'Are you quite sure about this, Boase? There must be some mistake, must be some mistake.'

'No mistake, sir. She turned up last Thursday with the copy of the newspaper and they said to me that they had been satisfied with her means of identification. They wouldn't discuss it further on the telephone but they'd be glad to see us tomorrow if we'd like to go up.'

'If we'd like? We'll be there. But...' Bartlett paused, frowning, 'but what do they mean, she went there last week – the girl's been dead almost a fortnight.'

Bartlett had a headache.

The day dragged on slowly and mundane enquiries continued. Bartlett called Boase into his office.

'Doing anything tonight, lad?'

'No, sir, nothing.'

'Mrs Bartlett asked if you'd like to have supper with us tonight – I forgot to ask you what with everything going on today. Not too short notice is it?'

'Not at all, sir. I'd love to come.' Boase's thoughts turned to Irene.

'Well, good. Come over about eight then?'

'Thank you, sir, I'll look forward to it.' He walked on air from the office. He knew he'd be doing the washing-up with Irene, alone in the scullery.

Bartlett looked at the handbag which had been found on the beach. It was old and cheap. The leather was cracked and it had definitely seen better days. He thumbed through the address book. It was almost empty, save for a couple of grocery items where the book had been converted for use as a shopping list. The few names therein had already been eliminated. He turned to the notes section at the back, nothing there either. What was the point of an address book with no addresses? Mind you, how sad if the dead woman really had had no friends, he thought.

At about seven thirty Boase, dressed in his decent suit and carrying a bunch of flowers for Mrs Bartlett (although they could never compete with George Bartlett's home-grown blooms), left his lodgings, walked up Melvill Road and headed for Penmere Hill. Arriving at the house he knocked at the front door and waited, straightening his collar and smoothing his hair. A figure was visible through the glass, walking slowly to the door. Caroline Bartlett appeared, smiling. A slim woman in her late forties, she was always well dressed although not particularly fashion-conscious. Her long, mousy-coloured hair was always in a loose but tidy bun. She wore ankle-length skirts with high-necked blouses and always a gold pin at the centre of the collar. She was quite a contented woman now but things were very different and her life had changed so much, especially since the death of John. Secretly, Bartlett was very, very proud of his wife – she had her own opinions and ideas and that was one of the things that had made her attractive to him in the early days. Not so many years ago she had been such a lively young girl and in the peak of health. Nowadays, she had difficulty getting about but he still often caught that old spark of determination in her eyes. Outwardly, she was quiet, respectable and demure.

Today Caroline was wearing her gold pin as usual. Irene had told Boase that her father had given it to her mother when they were young sweethearts; it was in the shape of a small crown with a diamond in the centre to remind her that she was George Bartlett's princess, a name he always called her by – never 'Caroline', unless her was speaking about her to someone else.

'Archie, oh how lovely to see you again, do come in, how are you?' Boase handed her the flowers and she leaned forward and kissed him on the cheek. He blushed.

'George, Irene, he's here.' Caroline led the way into a very neat parlour, still Victorian in style but comfortable. There were house-plants everywhere. Caroline had very green fingers but, often finding the garden diffi-cult, she had turned her attentions to greenery and flowers in her home. Bartlett stood up from his favourite armchair.

'Hello, my boy, come in, sit down.' The older man looked more relaxed now in the comfort of his own home as he drew on his pipe and supped a pint of London Ale. Beside the chair lay Topper, asleep. He had stood up when Boase's knock at the door came but Bartlett said reassuringly, 'All right, boy, it's only Boase,' and Topper took up his place again. Now he managed to open one eye and raise an eyebrow, but there was no threat to his master and he remained still.

Topper was Bartlett's constant companion, never judging him like almost every human did.

Bartlett spoke, still with his pipe between his teeth;

'Princess, where's Irene, what's that girl doing? She's been upstairs for ages.'

Caroline, standing behind Boase, glared at her husband. Her daughter would not want anyone to think she had gone to any trouble – women were like that. Just as Boase sat down, the door opened and there stood Irene. She wore a simple dark grey dress in a woollen fabric with a silver grey collar and silver grey shoes. Around her neck was a simple pearl choker. Boase immediately got up from his seat. He thought she looked beautiful. Irene came into the centre of the room.

'Hello, Archie, how are you?'

'I'm very well thanks, Irene; here, have my seat.'

The girl sat down on the arm of the chair and patted the cushion beside her.

'You sit here, then we can talk.' Boase nervously took his place in the armchair next to her. He could smell her perfume – it was just like lilacs. He quite liked it. Even if he hadn't liked it, it didn't matter because he was close to Irene. Caroline walked to the door. 'George, could you help me with the plates?' Bartlett sank into his chair.

'I'll be there in a minute, Princess.'

'George, I need help, now.' Caroline could see the couple wanted to be alone and she didn't want anyone to spoil it for them. She liked Archie Boase. Irene could do a lot worse. Bartlett rose from his seat and, closely followed by Topper, went into the kitchen.

The four were presently seated in the dining room which looked out over the back garden. It was dark now but the moonlight shone down and was reflected in the small pond in the centre of the lawn. The four ate a meal of beef stew with potatoes and dumplings, followed by a treacle pudding with custard, while Topper lay under the table at Bartlett's feet hoping his master would let something slip from his plate.

'I hear you and Dad are off to London tomorrow, Archie.' Irene had always been interested in her father's work from when she was a small child and now, having a good knowledge of the town and its people, she had even more reason to follow his activities.

'Yes, that's right.' Boase hastened to finish his mouthful of food; he felt self-conscious when he was eating with other people. 'Yes, we're going up in the morning. Long day ahead.'

Irene continued, 'I hardly remember London now – I said the same to you, didn't I Dad?'

'Yes, you did,' Bartlett nodded in agreement, 'but you should always remember where you were born even if you can't remember what the exact house or street looked like, because it's your heritage – never forget that, you youngsters.' The pair considered themselves told and giggled. Bartlett was very proud to be a Londoner and hadn't lost his East End accent at all. He missed the old place although he had suffered many hardships there over the years, especially as a boy. Cornwall was better for a man of his age; it was quieter, the air was fresher and, above all, Caroline liked it here. She had never really settled in London, although she always maintained that her home was wherever her beloved husband was. Yes, Falmouth was definitely the nicest place they could ever imagine living in.

Caroline got up from the table and began stacking the plates. 'Leave that, Mrs Bartlett, I'll do it,' Boase volunteered, his motive not being entirely for the benefit of the older woman.

'Well, all right, but come and have a sit down by the fire first and finish your drink.' All four moved towards the fireplace where Topper, knowing the nightly ritual, was already on the rug warming himself. Bartlett patted the dog's head. 'You're a good'un, Topper, mate, come and sit by your old man.' The dog obliged.

'George, you treat that animal better than your family sometimes,' grumbled Caroline.

'That, Princess, is because he is my family, and well you know it.' Topper let out an approving sigh.

'Dad, Mum, tell Archie how you met, it's so romantic,' Irene sat on the floor at her father's feet.

'I'm sure Boase isn't interested in that old nonsense,' said Bartlett, semi-embarrassed.

Caroline snorted. 'You never *used* to think it was nonsense.' Bartlett looked more embarrassed still.

His wife continued. 'I had gone to London with my mother because she had a consultation there at the Eye Infirmary with a very good and highly recommended doctor. She'd been troubled with eye problems since a child. Anyway, while I was waiting for her, someone stole my bag with our return train tickets in and all my money. While I was frantically trying to sort it out, George turned up with something in his eye. He'd been outside when something flew up off the road and hit him – a stone or something. He was, fortunately, soon sorted out and he waited with me. My mother came out in the middle of it all and George made himself known to her and gave us the money to return home. He said if I gave him my address, he would see that my bag was returned if anyone handed it in – it never was and he knew it wouldn't be, but I received a very nice letter from him, we met again and my mother allowed us to marry on my eighteenth birthday, just four months later.

Bartlett grunted from the depths of his armchair, 'Hmm, you never did repay that money.'

'George!' A slap on the arm was forthcoming, whereupon Topper crawled forward a little nearer to his master.

'Isn't that just too romantic, Archie? And so Bohemian.' Irene thought this was the stuff of fairy tales.

'I ought to get on with the plates.' Archie stood up. 'The supper was lovely, Mrs Bartlett, thank you.'

'I'll help you, Archie.' Irene was by his side in an instant and the two carried the crockery into the scullery. 'Dad, remember next time, you promised to tell us about your Jack the Ripper days again. There's so much we haven't heard yet.'

'All right, next time. It's getting late now, I'm almost ready for my bed.'

At about eleven o'clock Boase left for home, having arranged to be in bright and early next morning for the journey to London.

Chapter Three

The morning soon came and it was a sunny and cold one. There was a strange atmosphere in the town. As usual at this time, people were beginning to think about Christmas and to make plans, but something was different this time – people appeared more subdued than they might otherwise be. But then, they knew that a killer might still be in their midst.

Bartlett and Boase met up at the police station, and made their way from there to the railway just in time to catch the London train. They settled into their seats and prepared for the journey; both looked and felt a bit bleary-eyed on account of a later than usual night the previous evening, and an early morning – it was still only a quarter to seven. Boase's landlady had been up even earlier and packed some food for him, as she had felt sure he didn't want to be 'buying eatables from any Tom, Dick, or Harry'. After three or four minutes, as the train pulled out of the station, he opened up a small brown paper bag which he had pulled from his pocket and leaned forward to his superior who was sitting opposite.

'Hard-boiled egg, sir?'

'No thank you. Haven't you had any break-fast?'

'Didn't have time this morning, sir, over-slept a bit.'

Bartlett sighed. 'You need a woman to do for you, that's what you need, good cook, good company. It's time you thought about settling down.' The older man suddenly felt paternal.

'Maybe you're right, sir – pork pie?'

The train pulled into Truro station, where there was to be a fifteen-minute wait and a change. This change being quickly effected by the pair, Bartlett jumped quickly out again on to the platform and ran to buy a news-paper. Boase watched him from the com-partment window and yawned. The sunshine was bright and the carriage was warm. The station was busy already and people rushed here and there, some getting on the train, some getting off. Others stood on the plat-form waiting. A train on the other line was being unloaded – there was milk and news-papers and, out from the guard's van jumped a dog exactly like Topper. People at this end of the country often bought dogs after seeing advertisements in the papers for them and, having sent their money, their chosen animal would travel from up-country by train.

As Boase continued watching the activities, half asleep, he was startled to see William

Gibbons running for all he was worth along the platform. He stood up looking through the cloudy glass, not believing his eyes as the man ran to the station exit and disappeared. Why, he'd recently interviewed the same man about the murder of Ivy Williams, a man who could barely walk without the aid of a stick due to his war injuries. What was going on?

As Boase sat back down, completely puzzled, the guard began to close the doors, and seeing him about to put his whistle to his already pursed lips, he panicked. Where was Bartlett? Boase didn't want to end up in London on his own; he hadn't even been there before. At that, the object of his worry bounded into view and the guard opened the door and pushed him in. Bartlett was panting as he readjusted his attire.

'Damned cheek, pulling my coat like that I had plenty of time.'

'I don't think so, sir.' The younger man grinned at the sight of his superior looking so unusually dishevelled. 'Where were you?'

'Damned ridiculous. I ran after a girl, could have sworn it was Norma Berryman. This case is taking it out of me, I don't mind admitting it, Boase. We're going round in circles and we're running out of time – let's hope today comes up trumps.'

'Running out of time, sir? Why?'

'Think about it; we've got one girl dead, another one missing, possibly dead – God forbid. We can't afford another casualty. And, according to Greet, we'll be the next casualties if we don't sort this mess out sharpish. We need to see if these two girls are linked in any way or if it's all just a horrible coincidence. We don't need another murder.'

The two men sat back in their seats and Boase proceeded to tell Bartlett about his strange sighting of William Gibbons.

Some hours later the train pulled into Paddington Station and the two men quickly set off for Oxford Street and to the offices of Bennett, Bennett, Thornton & Bennett. Boase was absolutely amazed at the sights he saw. The shops were enormous, there was so much traffic, and so many people – he liked it in a strange sort of way but he didn't think he could ever live there; there was no sea for a start and, apparently, nowhere to go to be alone. Bartlett, however, was back on old ground and expertly led the way to the solicitors' offices without putting a foot wrong. It was like he had never been away – he still thought it had changed over the last ten years though.

On reaching the very modern building, they entered through two huge glass doors. The decor and furnishings were also very stylish and modern ... Bartlett didn't like it one bit.

'Look at this rubbish, Boase. All glass – it's like being in a goldfish bowl. When I'm on official police business, I don't want people out in the street staring at me.'

A gold sign with an arrow pointing upstairs indicated that the offices they were looking for were on the first floor. The two men went up the stairs and, as they reached the top, a huge reception area lay in front of them. Approaching the main desk, they were greeted by a tall, slender middle-aged woman with thin black hair scraped into a bun that sat neatly on top of her head. She wore a black two-piece suit, black stockings and shoes, and heavy black eye make-up. Boase didn't know whether she was young and looked old or was old and looked young. Around her fairly scrawny neck a rather large diamond was suspended from a black velvet ribbon.

'Good morning, madam,' Bartlett approached the woman's desk and introduced himself and Boase, 'we are here on police business and I believe we are expected.' The woman stood and gestured to two modern red seats underneath a large window.

'Wait, please.' The woman sat down again, lifted a telephone receiver and spoke into it.

After two or three minutes a large door opened slowly behind the woman's desk and a grey-haired man, slightly bent with a small, neat, grey moustache and wearing a tail-coated suit appeared and came towards them. The distance across the room, to him, must have seemed interminable and the further he walked the more he seemed to stoop. Boase couldn't help thinking that this man must be at least ninety. He wore half-moon glasses from behind which, two blue, watery eyes strained to see what was going on around him.

'Er ... good morning, gentlemen, and what a pleasant one. Do come into the office. I'm Bennett Senior – very senior, I'm afraid.'

Shrinking more, the man led the way back across the room to the office from which he had just emerged.

'We had expected to meet with Mr Thornton,' interrupted Bartlett.

'Yes, I'm sorry. My nephew was unable to come in, at the last minute, to see you. He telephoned a little while ago to ask me to step in for him as it were. He's told me what you wish to know. I'm the head of this firm now. I started working for my grandfather in ... in, let me see now...' Bartlett sighed and drew up a chair to the old man's desk, '...in 1872, I do believe. I don't do too much these days – getting a bit long in the tooth. I leave it to my son, nephew and grandson.'

'Do you have some information for us, sir?' Bartlett leaned forward impatiently on the desk.

'What? Oh yes, do forgive an old man going on. Yes, about the Williams girl. Well, you see, she replied to our notice in the

70

newspaper and fortunately came up straight away to see us.'

'And why did you want to see her?'

'Well, this becomes a little ... shall we say, delicate,' the old man replied.

Bartlett drew in his breath sharply – he hadn't come all this way to learn nothing.

'Please, sir, it's very important that you tell us as much as you can, our enquiry is in connection with a murder investigation.'

The solicitor sat back, with difficulty, in an enormous burgundy leather armchair from which his feet, which must have been no more than a size four or five, dangled a few inches above the floor.

'This firm had a client, who sadly is now deceased, but we had the pleasure to represent him for many, many years. He was the natural grandfather of Ivy Williams.'

The two men looked at each other, startled. Percy Williams, Ivy's father, hadn't mentioned anything about this when Boase had interviewed him. He had been reluctant to get involved at all.

'Go on, sir.'

'It seems that you don't know much about Miss Williams, gentlemen, and, if it wasn't police business I wouldn't be at liberty to tell you this. Ivy Williams was illegitimate, and she was adopted a couple of weeks after she was born. Her poor mother gave birth to her in the Falmouth Union Workhouse, dying the very next day of post-partum fever. It seems that she had been working – following her own parents' and younger brother's death in a house fire – for Lord and Lady Hatton of, um ... er ... Budock, is it? Yes, that's right. Lord Hatton had two fairly indiscreet sons, Rupert and Algernon, and when he found out that one of them had fathered this child, he felt he had to make sure that no one ever found out that a member of the Hatton family, of some standing, too, had liaised in that way with a mere servant girl. They had a reputation to keep and the boys were always under pressure to uphold the family's good name. The girl was very young, about fifteen or sixteen, but nevertheless Lord Hatton had her taken to the workhouse. Some years later, he visited me and told me he had some instructions for me that were never to be made known to his wife, Lady Cordelia. He explained that he had felt dreadfully guilty about his actions and often wondered how his grandchild was – she would have been about nine or ten at the time, I suppose. He wanted to make provision for her -it was too late for her poor mother, but he could help the child. He wanted me to provide, from his estate, on his death, the sum of one thousand pounds for every year the girl had lived to the time of his passing – which finally amounted to twenty-four thousand pounds. We were satisfied with her documentation yesterday and she took the money.'

Bartlett couldn't believe how complicated this was becoming. He thought back to the photograph in his desk drawer – now that part, at least, was clearer; those servants must have been the Hatton household's staff.

'How did she take the money – cheque?'

'Oh, no, sir, we offered a cheque but she asked for cash. We had a right old time of it, trying to get that much at short notice, but she absolutely insisted and, I'm afraid, we complied.'

'So that woman walked out of here yesterday with twenty-four thousand pounds in cash?'

Bartlett could hardly believe it.

'Yes, sir, she did.'

Bartlett and Boase thanked Mr Claude Bennett and made their way out into the street. Bartlett paused to light his pipe. As he squinted through the pipe smoke he looked at Boase.

'Well, what do you make of that?'

'I don't understand, sir, how could that have been Ivy Williams, here yesterday, when she's already dead?' The older man drew long and hard on his pipe. He looked around the old, familiar streets and buildings and paused for a moment while he tried to think of a sensible response.

'The answer must be one of two things – either the dead woman has been wrongly identified by us, or,' he paused, '...or the woman here yesterday is an impostor and if that's the case, I honestly don't know what to do next. Is it possible that someone could have masqueraded as Ivy Williams just to get the money? If that's so, it must be someone with inside knowledge and someone who could either get hold of the right document-ation, or forge it well. We're talking about an awful lot of money – a fortune, in fact.'

Bartlett and Boase began their journey back to Cornwall, arriving home in the very early hours. They both slept fitfully until morning, the mysterious events of the day playing on their minds.

In the basement flat in Killigrew Street, the Pengellys had spent the previous evening decorating the parlour and Jack had brought home a very fine Christmas tree, which was soon potted up and taking pride of place in front of the window.

The next morning, as the smell of the day's bread pervaded each room and weak sunlight filtered through the curtains, Kitty and Ruby got up and dressed and went into the kitchen for some breakfast, where Rose was just taking some loaves out of the oven.

'Morning, you two. Ruby, move that stuff over, love, let me get the bread onto the table. There's a pot of tea ready and I've done you some bread and dripping; there's no butter or jam 'til I go down the street this morning. Make sure you're back nice and early tonight, Ruby – you know you said you'd 'elp me write the Christmas cards. The arthritis is worse today, there's no way I can do all that. You don't mind?'

''Course I don't, Ma, I'll make sure I'm back by five, then I can 'elp you with the tea as well.'

'Thanks, love.' Rose looked exhausted already and the girls knew she was suffering so much with her arthritis; she worked too hard and had done all her life. Years spent working in the laundry, standing on a stone floor washing other people's clothes, had taken its toll on her. Her daughters admired her so much and wished they could be as strong in character as she was. They helped themselves to the food and a couple of cups of tea each before grabbing their coats, kissing their mother goodbye and leaving for work. Outside, Ruby ran to catch up with Kitty.

'Don't walk so fast, Kit ... wait.'

Kitty slowed down and waited for her sister.

'You 'eard from Frank yet, Ruby?'

'No, I already told you, I 'aven't. I just want to try an' forget the whole thing – I don't know what's 'appenin'.'

'If you believe the *Packet*, neither do the police,' came the reply.

The two girls went their separate ways on the Moor – Ruby to the shipping office in Church Street and Kitty to Mrs Williams's tobacco and sweet shop in High Street.

As Kitty let herself into the still-dark shop, a noise stopped her in her tracks. She stood still and listened. 'Pssst, PSSSSSST!' The sound grew more intense.

'Who's there?' She called out again. 'Who is it?'

She knew Mrs Williams wouldn't be down from the upstairs flat for about twenty minutes yet and she felt nervous. There was never anyone around when she got to the shop in the mornings.

She couldn't see much in the gloomy interior; she asked again, 'Who's there?'

Kitty stepped forward, closing the door behind her. Her heart began to race. A loud thump came from behind the counter and she let out a scream.

'I know you're there – I 'eard you ... who is it?'

Another loud thump came this time with some scrambling of feet.

'It's me. It's me – Norman.' From behind the counter appeared the head and shoulders of Norman Richards, one of the shop assistants who worked with Kitty. She rushed across to the back of the shop to put a light on.

'NO! Don't put the light on, she'll see me.'

'Norman, what on earth are you talking about? Who'll see you? Why are you here, you're not due in for almost another hour?'

'Mrs Williams don't know I'm 'ere, Kitty. I've been 'ere all night.'

'Now you're being ridiculous – all night? Why?'

Kitty was beginning to wonder what Norman was talking about when he emerged fully from under the brown wooden counter. His hair was sticking up all over the place, his braces hung loosely down by his sides, and he clutched his Fair Isle jumper and jacket in front of him in an attempt to cover up the worst bits, which, at that moment, were probably all of him. He spoke in a low voice, urgently.

'Last night, when we'd all gone 'ome, I was taking a walk into town and that's when it 'appened.' Kitty listened, bemused. She knew Norman liked to walk – everyone in Falmouth must have known it. A lot of people liked him, others were really irritated by him. He had a habit of following people around, trying to be one of their group or gang. Whenever they turned round, there was Norman. He would spend his money on them – buying flowers or small items of jewellery for the girls and penknives or beer for the boys. As a child, the other boys had used him terribly – in fact, they still did. When he was younger they would get him to steal things from shops: sweets, cigarettes, money. When he came out, and was a safe distance from the shop, they would be waiting to take everything from him. He put up with it because he was anxious to have them for friends and to have their approval; of course they never did make him a friend or one of their gang, they just carried on using him. Occasionally they'd accepted him, but usually they'd ridiculed him.

Norman was slightly backward from complications arising at his birth, but he got on all right – although Kitty hated to see him being taken advantage of. He often did stupid or childish things in an attempt to make people laugh so that they might like him. He was so kind-hearted and he and Kitty liked each other a lot. Sometimes Rose Pengelly would invite him round for tea – how he could eat! Eighteen years old, he was always well dressed, clean, and tidy with jet black hair which had a centre parting that looked like he had cut it with a razor blade. Cheap hairdressing preparations made it gleam blue-black. He always wore a tie and a Fair Isle sleeveless jumper. He lightened Kitty's day with far-fetched stories of boy heroes and high seas adventures. He lived mostly in a fantasy world of film stars and their characters – cowboys, gangsters, pirates. Now, though, he looked awful, and Kitty waited for what he could possibly say next.

'I was walking past the shop when I saw someone inside – 'ere beside the counter – they must have been tryin' to pinch fags or something. I knew Mrs Williams would be in danger if she disturbed 'em so I went round the side and slid open the little window – look, I'll show you.'

Norman pointed to the small window and Kitty felt herself wondering how anyone over about five years old could ever get through this window. Norman went on with his story.

'I got in but there was no one 'ere – they must have just escaped. Anyway, I 'eard a noise and the window slammed shut – that could have been them – and I couldn't open it and I knew I was trapped. So, I just had to stay 'ere all night. Mrs Williams don't know. You won't tell, Kitty, promise you won't tell.'

Kitty had to try hard not to laugh – poor Norman.

'Of course I won't tell – you'd better get 'ome and make yerself presentable, you're due to start work in less than an hour. My, you almost gave me a heart attack.'

'I'm really sorry, Kit – I didn't mean to scare you.'

Norman gathered his things and ran out of the front door at top speed. He knew he could count on Kitty.

'Thanks, Kit – I won't forget this,' he called

behind him. Kitty smiled and prepared the shop for opening.

At the police station, Bartlett and Boase were worn out. Their trip up to London the previous day had been a complete disaster and neither of them could think what to do next. It seemed that every time they felt they were getting somewhere, things became more involved or more difficult. Bartlett lit his pipe.

'Let's go round to see Percy Williams again – there's something he's not telling us, Boase. He never mentioned that Ivy was adopted; could be a clue.'

'But why wouldn't he tell me about her, sir?'

'Let's go and find out.'

The two men walked across the Moor, along Market Street, Church Street and Arwenack Street and made their way to the Falmouth Dockyard. Stopped at the gates by the duty policeman, who didn't recognise them due to their plain clothes, they were soon admitted and they asked for directions to Percy Williams's workplace. The yard was busy this year with plenty of repair work, and, happily, overtime. Bill Pengelly, coming out of one of the dockyard buildings, saw the two men and touched his cap in acknowledgement. Presently they arrived at the right shed and went inside. Percy Williams was teaching some apprentices the finer points of his trade but left them when he saw the two police-men. He walked across to them.

'What is it now? I told you I don't know any more about Ivy.'

Bartlett reassured him. 'You may not know anything about your daughter's tragic death, Mr Williams, sir, but we feel you haven't told us enough about her background, which might be vitally important.'

'What else do you want to know?'

'Ivy was adopted, wasn't she?'

Shocked that they knew this much, the man sat down on a bench and rested one elbow on the table next to it. Approaching sixty, Percy Williams didn't know how he was going to make it until his retirement at sixty-five. He was tired of work, he'd been in ship repair man and boy – he was tired of life. He hadn't had much luck over the years, all in all. His hands, old and brown, were the hands of a grafter. All he'd ever wanted was a quiet life and a nice family; he'd had that once, now it had all been taken away from him. He looked up at Bartlett and Boase.

'Yes, yes, Ivy was adopted. How did you know?'

'We found out during our enquiries.' Bartlett wasn't going to let on about the money and the solicitor. 'Please tell us as much as you can now, it may be important. We really want to catch whoever did this to your daughter.'

Percy walked over to the apprentices. 'I'm goin' to be busy for a bit – you go an' 'ave yer croust.' The boys, who were starving by now and happy to oblige, left the shed and Percy returned to the bench.

'In 1896, my dear wife, Mary and me were expecting our first child. We were so happy. We loved each other so much and really wanted a family. I thought the world of 'er. Well, to cut a long story short, the baby was born, a beautiful little boy, we called 'im Nathaniel. Mary suffered during the birth. The midwife was with 'er an' I was sent for from work. I could 'ear 'er screamin' 'alfway down our street – she was in so much pain. I felt so useless, waiting downstairs. What use are men at a time like that? Anyway after about ten 'ours the midwife bid me come up and there was my beautiful wife and our baby. We couldn't 'ave been 'appier. I 'ad a lovely son.

'All of a sudden, the baby went stiff in 'er arms and then 'e went blue. I called the midwife over but it was too late – our little Nathaniel was gone, 'is short little life snuffed out like a candle after only about an 'our. We were distraught. The doctor who came said it was just one of those things that 'appens – but Mary never believed that; she blamed 'erself. The little boy 'ad come early like. The pains came while Mary was lifting a huge pan full of water for the laundry. We didn't 'ave much money at that time and she used to take in washing – I didn't like it, mind, I said we'd manage, but she was very strong-minded was Mary and always said a few shillings extra would come in 'andy, 'specially what with the new baby on the way. She had such 'igh 'opes for our baby, Mr Bartlett. Boy or girl, she said, they'd be successful, get on and make a name for theirselves, you know, do better and 'ave more than we. She thought she brought the little boy into the world too early because she 'adn't been sensible and that 'e didn't 'ave a fair chance because 'e was so small. I tried to 'elp 'er through it, but 'ow can you? We got through the funeral, it broke my 'eart to see 'is little coffin lowering down into that grave; 'e's buried in the cemetery at Swanpool – with 'is mother now, God rest their dear little souls, an' I go there every week, regular, to see 'em both.'

Bartlett felt for the man – he knew how he himself felt when he found out that John had been killed. He touched the rough, clenched fist which lay on the table;

'Please go on, Percy.'

'Well, after that, I still wanted children – so did Mary really, but she was too afraid that it would 'appen all over again.' He looked up at Boase, 'I'm sorry to say this in front of you, young man, but, after that, she wouldn't let me go near 'er, you understand these things, Mr Bartlett, sir, she was that afraid. I knew she was desperate to have a child but she was just too scared. Anyway, after about a year, someone we knew who worked at the Union told us there was a little baby girl who 'ad been born there and, poor little thing, 'er mother 'ad died giving birth to 'er. Well, we was lucky enough to be offered the child and we adopted 'er. It made both of us so 'appy – she brought joy to our lives like I can't tell you. Mary even seemed to be getting over Nathaniel a bit. Ivy was such a lovely girl growing up and then, suddenly, she changed. She must 'ave been about eighteen or nineteen. She would stay out all night, always out with soldiers that was 'ere durin' the war; she was rude to 'er mother and me – in short she was uncontrollable. Then, about three years ago, we found out 'ow she was makin' 'er money. Well, I think that's what finished Mary off. She was such a respectable woman and we brought Ivy up to be the same. In the end, Mary's 'eart got so bad, she was taking pills for everything and she couldn't carry on no more. I lost 'er two years ago next April.'

Bartlett stood up.

'Did the workhouse indicate to you who Ivy's natural parents were, sir?'

'No, Mr Bartlett, they didn't – we didn't want to know really, we were just glad to 'ave the little girl.'

Bartlett apologised.

'I'm sorry we had to pry. I know that was hard for you. We'll leave you alone now.'

The two men left the shed and, walking back through the dockyard, returned to the station. Bartlett sat at his desk while Boase went to find some tea. They sat down together to have their drink and the younger man produced a brown paper bag from his pocket.

'Fancy a sausage roll, sir?' he asked, offering the bag.

'No, I told you before, you need a woman – you can't carry on eating like that; don't you ever sit down to a meal apart from when you're at our house?'

'I get a meal at my digs in the evening – not as nice as Mrs Bartlett's and Irene's cooking though.'

'I'm sure you're right, Boase.' Bartlett was looking at the small photograph of the servants he had pulled from his drawer. He leaned across his desk and picked up a large magnifying glass to examine the photo more carefully. He concentrated for several minutes while Boase finished his sausage rolls.

'Boase, do you remember a man by the name of Samuel Hoskins?'

'Should I, sir?'

'He used to work for my father-in-law in his saddlery business – 'course, that was before your time wasn't it? Sometimes it feels like

85

we've been together for years, you and me.'

Boase wondered if this was a compliment or not.

'I remember him visiting my mother-in-law some years back when she was ill. He was a nice chap, if I recall, brought Caroline's mother some flowers from the garden. He was very fond of my wife's parents.'

'What about him, sir?'

'Well, I only saw him a couple of times when we were visiting but, one thing I always remember was what a ridiculous moustache he had, it was enormous, really thick and bushy.'

'So?'

'So, I think he's in this photograph – in fact I'm sure of it. If that's so, it means I can identify this picture. Samuel Hoskins left the saddlery business and became a blacksmith. Later on he got a job at a big country house – he came back to tell us all about it. He worked at Penvale Manor, the Hattons' place out at Budock – we know now that old man Hatton was Ivy's grandfather. If this is Hoskins, then this would have been taken in about 1895 or 1896, so maybe Ivy Williams's real mother is in this photograph and that's why she had it. If so, she must have known that she was adopted. If this fits, Boase, we might be nearer to a motive and a suspect.'

'What do you mean, sir? That perhaps the Hattons murdered Ivy Williams? But even so, what has all this got to do with Norma Berryman?'

'I don't know yet. I need to think. I'm going to knock off now, it's been a long couple of days – I suggest you do the same, and get your thinking cap on tonight, we'll be looking for some answers in the morning.'

Bartlett arrived home at about six, much to Irene's horror.

'Oh, Dad, you're early – I was going to do the cooking tonight and I've barely started.'

'Is your mother all right, Irene? Where is she?'

'She's upstairs, Dad, having a lie down, she had a bit of a headache. I was just about to start peeling the vegetables – I didn't expect you for ages yet.'

'That's all right. I'll just go up and see her, don't worry about dinner – I'm not hungry yet, anyway, I'll look forward to it whenever it's ready.'

Bartlett climbed the stairs and crossed the landing to his and Caroline's bedroom. He tapped lightly on the door – he always did; he respected his wife's privacy. Caroline laughed whenever he did it and she'd say: 'I'm your wife, you don't need to knock,' but he always did. He peered round the door; she was lying with her back to him. Quietly he crossed the room and went around the other side of the bed. She was sound asleep. He thought how beautiful she always looked and how much he loved her. He wanted to wake her up to let her know that he was back, but it seemed such a shame, especially if she wasn't feeling well. He almost hated her being asleep because he wanted to spend every moment possible in her company; it was such a waste when they weren't together. He leaned forward and kissed her forehead, then went back out on to the landing. He looked at his pocket watch – it was ten past six. He went downstairs into the kitchen where Irene was chopping some onions.

'Your mother's still asleep, I think I'll take a little walk if you don't mind – about an hour or so.'

'That's all right, Dad, dinner should be about ready when you get back. Perhaps Mum'll be feeling better then too.'

Bartlett put on his old raincoat and as soon as Topper heard the rattle of the coat stand he appeared. He came to the door when Bartlett had arrived home and then went back to sleep. Now he was ready; if his master was going out in his old coat that meant he could come too.

'All right, lad, go and fetch your lead.'

The dog obliged, running into the kitchen where a little hook, just at his height, held a tartan lead. He brought it back at top speed, sliding along the runner laid over the wooden floor in the hall. 'All right, steady, now let's straighten this mat before your mother sees it. Right, come on, we're off.'

Topper ran back to his basket in the kitchen and appeared with a red rubber ball in his mouth, his head cocked enquiringly on one side.

Bartlett looked at him. 'If you take that, you carry it all the way.' Topper, who had an uncanny knack of locating the ball even yards and yards away in the dark, followed his master out of the house and down the path. Man and dog walked up Penmere Hill and headed for the sea front. It was dark by now, but there was no rain at the moment and the two walked briskly enjoying the fresh breeze that was coming in off the sea. Arriving at Gyllyngvase Beach, Bartlett released Topper from his lead and watched while the dog paddled at the water's edge. It was so dark he could barely see him but a few well-lit ships in the bay turned Topper into a shadowy silhouette as he trotted back and forth across the sand. Bartlett stood, enjoying the air and wondering about his suspects. Did he have any? He felt that tomorrow would bring better things. He sincerely hoped so.

'Topper, come on, mate, time to go, boy.' The dog ambled up the beach and sat at his master's side. Bartlett attached the lead to the collar and the pair walked off towards Pendennis Castle to continue their round trip of the bay and the docks.

Chapter Four

The next day saw a turn for the worse in the weather with heavy snow having fallen in the night and strong winds bringing blizzard conditions. Bartlett left his house later than usual; Caroline had been quite unwell with a headache all through the night and, although she tried not to wake her husband, he stayed up with her all night to take care of her. The couple were absolutely devoted to one another. Bartlett didn't want to disturb Irene and to worry her so, when she came down to breakfast, he told her that her mother had been unwell. Naturally, as he had expected, she was angry that he hadn't called her in the night but she had promised to take care of her during the day. He checked on Caroline who had managed to fall asleep by the time he was ready to leave for work. He hoped it was nothing serious; she was his life, she meant everything to him.

Bartlett struggled to walk up Penmere Hill, holding on to his hat, head down with his coat flapping madly in the wind. He felt almost frozen and hoped Boase would make him a decent hot cup of tea when he arrived.

Walking down Killigrew Street the pavement felt slippery under his feet and he trod carefully for fear of falling. He soon arrived at the police station, bade good morning to the desk sergeant and walked into his office. Boase was already there.

'Morning, sir. Cuppa? You must be frozen.'

'Morning, Boase, yes, thank you, I'm ready for one. It's cold enough for a top hat! Talking of which, I think we should take a car over to Penvale Manor today, see if we can talk to the Hatton twins – perhaps they can shed some light on things. I know there was some connection between one of them and Francis Wilson during the war – perhaps they know where he is. We need to find him. Whatever he's been up to, I'm sure he can tell us something.'

Within half an hour Bartlett and Boase were driving through the narrow lanes that led to the village of Budock. The snow had fallen heavily and covered the hedgerows and fields. The short trip to Budock from Falmouth was a pleasant one with fine views of the countryside. They passed a group of schoolboys running a paperchase, the cold air highlighting their warm breath as it left their mouths. They turned into a road fronted by two enormous wrought iron gates, which were open, and a long drive led the way to the house. As they rounded a bend,

they saw their first glimpse of Penvale Manor
– a splendid Georgian building standing
boldly in defiance of the, by now, howling
blizzards.

'How the other half live, eh, Boase?'

Bartlett looked out of the car window,
almost incredulous at the size of the house
and its grounds. They stopped outside the
front of the building and got out. Having
made their way up the stone steps to the
front door, Bartlett rang the bell. Almost
immediately a young woman in maid's uniform opened the heavy door. She looked at
the two policemen enquiringly.

'Yes?'

'Are the Hatton twins at home, miss?' asked
Bartlett politely, offering his identification.

'One of them is,' came the reply.

'Good.' Bartlett was feeling the cold and
wanted to get inside.

'I'll see if he's available.' With that the
front door closed abruptly.

'Would you believe it?' remarked the older
man to the younger, 'no manners these
days, none of them.'

He stamped his feet impatiently while
Boase surveyed the parkland in the distance
and the landscaped gardens which surrounded the house. The house was in the
centre of a vast deer park and the estate
supplied venison to several parts of the
country, particularly some high-class Lon-

don butchers. In fact Penvale Venison was a thriving business with a very good reputation. The grounds immediately surrounding the house were extensive, and looked like something from a fairytale now with the thick snow still falling heavily. As the two men waited the door reopened and the maid stood there.

'Come in, please, follow me.'

She led the way into an imposing but impressive hall where, as if from nowhere, a butler emerged and requested to take their hats and coats. Relieved of their cold and damp outerwear, the two followed the maid up a central staircase, Boase marvelling quietly at the paintings which lined the walls. Many portraits hung there and the younger man was impressed at the colours and the skill of the artists. Bartlett meanwhile thought he had never seen so many pale and foolish beings depicted over the centuries. No constitution. Never done a day's work, he thought, and yet they had all this. Having negotiated three long corridors, they arrived at a large oak door. The maid knocked and was bidden enter by a voice on the other side of it. The young girl announced the visitors and left.

A big burgundy leather armchair faced towards the window, the back of it to Bartlett and Boase. From where they stood, it looked empty. As they waited, a man rose from the chair and walked towards them. He was in his forties, Boase thought. He had thin grey hair which had receded and glistened with hair preparation. Standing at about five feet six inches, and stout, he wore a navy silk smoking jacket with what looked like cream silk pyjamas underneath. Bartlett wondered how anyone could still be in bedclothes at this hour, let alone could receive guests in this state of attire. The man slid towards them almost cat-like, with a cigarette in a long holder between his pale and dispro-portionately slender fingers.

'You are?'

Bartlett, already disliking this person, as he suspected he would, moved forward.

'I am Inspector Bartlett, this is Constable Boase.'

'Oh,' came the reply.

Bartlett felt as though he were keeping this fellow from his bed, so difficult did it appear for him to hold a conversation.

'I am conducting a murder enquiry and would like some information regarding the victim's background. Did you hear there was a murder in Falmouth recently?'

'No, I didn't. And how do you suppose I can help?' came the reply, followed by a long draw on the cigarette, it in turn followed by the resulting smoke being blown in Bartlett's direction.

'I understand, sir, that the victim may have

had a relative who worked for your family some time ago...'

'And who is this, ummm ... victim?'

'Is your brother here today, sir?' enquired Bartlett wondering if he would get either more sense or at least some respect from the sibling.

'No, he's gone to London for a few days, visiting a friend. This victim, who was she?'

'*She*, sir?'

'What?'

'You said 'she'. I didn't say if the victim was a man or a woman. What made you say she?'

The man looked flustered.

'I don't know, aren't nearly all murder victims women?'

'No, sir, they're not.'

Bartlett couldn't fathom this particular Hatton.

'Would you mind telling me which twin you are, sir?'

'I'm sorry,' came the reply, 'I thought you knew. Rupert Hatton, that's me. I'm always taken for my brother and vice versa. What japes we've had in the past, being identical, that is.'

'I'm sure,' grunted Bartlett under his breath. He'd heard about, and even wit-nessed the kind of japes these types got up to – he didn't want to hear any more.

'The dead woman was Miss Ivy Williams. Does that name ring any bells?'

Hatton stared intently at his cigarette holder for some time before replying with a firm 'No.'

Bartlett continued. This character was becoming tedious and very hard work.

'The dead woman's mother worked here over twenty years ago, as a maid, her name was Maude Mockett – do you remember her, sir?'

'I don't believe I do,' replied Hatton, sliding across to a tray of drinks, which stood on a small mahogany table, and pouring himself a large gin. Bartlett looked at the mantel clock. Half past ten in the morning. What sort of people were these, he thought to himself.

Hatton continued. 'We have so many servants coming and going, it's impossible to remember and, to be perfectly honest with you, I don't really mix with those types.'

'Would your mother, Lady Hatton, remember?'

'It's possible, but she's away. She's gone to Switzerland for some air. She hasn't been well, poor dear.'

Bartlett fiddled with the powder compact which he had brought along in his pocket. He wasn't going to bother showing it to Hatton now.

'So are you absolutely sure you don't know anything about Ivy Williams, or that you couldn't put me in touch with someone who might have some information?'

'Sure.'

'Well, I'm very sorry to have troubled you at this early hour, sir,' remarked Bartlett sarcastically.

As Bartlett reached for the door knob, he paused and, looking back at Rupert Hatton, asked, 'Do you know a man called Francis Wilson, sir?'

'Wilson? No, I don't believe I've ever heard of anyone by that name.'

'Well, thank you anyway, sir. Goodbye.'

The two men left Rupert Hatton and, collecting their hats and coats, made their way back to the waiting car and headed for the police station.

Back at the station Boase picked up a small pale purple envelope which had been placed on his desk during his absence. As he began to open it there was a distinct odour of lilac in his hands. He withdrew a matching sheet of paper from inside and began to read.

Dear Archie
I would very much like to see you over Christmas – that is, if you haven't already made plans to do something else. Mum and Dad would like to see you too and have asked me to invite you to stay here with us for a couple of days. Please come if you can – it'll be such fun, I know.
Hope you say yes.
Sincerely yours
Irene

Bartlett looked across at Boase who was looking slightly worried, but in the best sort of way one can took worried. 'Billet-doux?' he enquired, smiling.

'Did you know about this, sir?'

'About what? I must say that looks remarkably like my daughter's writing paper and envelope.

'Irene says she'd like me to visit you at Christmas...'

Bartlett rose from his chair and patted the younger man on the back. 'And Mrs Bartlett and I would be very pleased if you would stay a couple of days.'

'I don't know what to say, sir.' Boase looked confused and was thinking of Irene – he'd have to buy her a very nice present; what would she like?

'Just say you'll come to us on Christmas Eve and stay till Boxing Day.'

'Well, then, I accept – that's very generous of you, sir, very generous indeed.'

Boase arrived at the Bartletts' at about four o'clock on Christmas Eve carrying a small suitcase in one hand and with a large box under his arm. Irene, sitting in the window, had seen him struggling up the path and was waiting on the doorstep for him. It had been snowing ever since he left Melvill Road and his coat was white and damp. Irene giggled.

'Come in, Archie, you must be frozen, you look just like a snowman – I'm so pleased you came.'

She pulled him in through the front door and he dropped his case and the box on the hall floor.

'Do take your coat and hat off,' said Irene, helping him shake the snow from his clothes. As she pulled his scarf from around his neck she looked at him and winked. He knew this was going to be the best Christmas ever.

Caroline called to him from upstairs, 'Hello, Archie, nice to see you again; come on up, I'll show you your room.'

Patting Topper, who had appeared as soon as Irene had opened the front door, Boase carried his things upstairs. He entered a small bedroom at the back of the house.

'I hope you'll be comfortable here, Archie,' said Caroline drawing the curtains as it was by this time quite dark.

'I know I shall,' replied Boase who would have been quite happy sleeping on the floor just to be under the same roof as Irene. As it was, it was probably the nicest room he had ever stayed in. A single brass bed stood under the window; it had a cream eiderdown with three matching pillows, all delicately embroidered. There was a chest of drawers and a small wardrobe on the other side of the room and a bookcase full of several interesting books: from cookery to crime.

Caroline walked over to the door.

'The bathroom's just next to the kitchen. Come down when you're ready and we'll have some tea.'

Within fifteen minutes, Archie Boase was sitting at the tea table with the three Bartletts. The dining room looked lovely, he thought, with a big Christmas tree in one corner and several presents underneath. Boase stood up.

'Would you all excuse me please, I've left some things in my room.'

Moments later he returned with four neatly wrapped presents. He placed them under the tree. Topper stood up, stretched, and walked over to the tree to investigate what was going on.

'It's all right, boy – there's one here for you too; look.' Topper sniffed his present and, with a snort of what Boase hoped would be approval, returned to his master's side.

'You didn't need to bring anything, Boase,' said Bartlett, tapping his pipe on the fireplace.

'It was the least I could do, sir,' came the reply.

Caroline looked at the two men in turn;

'Do you think we could dispense with the formalities of the station, just for the holiday? How about Archie and George?'

'That sounds fine to me, Princess.' Bartlett

looked at Boase.

'If you're sure that's all right – I suppose it all sounds a bit formal, doesn't it? Archie and George it is, then,' replied Boase.

Christmas Day brought still more snow and Boase was awake early. He opened his curtains and looked out at the snow falling onto the back garden. He'd had the best night's sleep. He wondered what the day would bring, wondered how the Bartletts celebrated Christmas. It had been a long time since Archie Boase had enjoyed a family Christmas. He hadn't seen his mother for almost four years. She had gone to live with her sister in Doncaster. When Boase's father died, she had spent a year on her own while Boase was in France during the war. She had not managed at all well and they both agreed that she would be better off with her sister, who was also widowed. He would love to see her again soon. They wrote many letters, telling each other their news. He hadn't told her about Irene yet – perhaps that would be his next letter.

As he lay in bed looking out, he heard footsteps on the stairs and presently a door opened and closed. Seconds later Topper appeared in the garden with his red rubber ball. Boase watched as he threw the ball in the air over and over again, pawprints appearing on the fresh snow. One more throw into the air and the ball landed in the middle of the pond. Topper stood watching it, his head on one side and ears cocked. The sound of the door opening again and there stood Irene with Bartlett's old coat over her dressing gown. Boase watched as she and Topper mulled over how to retrieve the ball. Presently Irene found a long stick and proceeded to tap the ball until it reached the edge of the pond, whereupon she pulled it out and handed it to Topper who had been waiting patiently. He barked his gratitude and the two returned inside. Boase lay back on his pillows. Irene was so beautiful – he could watch her all day.

When Boase came downstairs it was about half past eight, and the smell of food was all through the hall leading to the kitchen. The Bartletts were up and dressed and Caroline called him into the dining room.

'Merry Christmas. Are you hungry, Archie? Did you sleep well?

'Yes, I am rather, and yes I did sleep very well, thank you. Merry Christmas to you too.'

'Good morning, Archie, come and have some breakfast, my boy.' Bartlett was already at his place drinking a cup of tea. As Boase sat down, Irene came into the dining room carrying a tray of food.

'Good morning, Archie, Merry Christmas, I hope you're hungry.' She pecked him on the cheek and his heart fluttered.

'Merry Christmas to you too, Irene,' he almost stuttered. Irene put a large plate in front of her father and the same for Boase ... bacon, eggs, sausages, fried potatoes, tomatoes, and mushrooms, with lots of fried bread. Caroline and Irene sat down but ate only toast, butter and home-made jam with several cups of tea.

'We normally open our presents at lunchtime, Archie,' said Caroline pouring four more cups of tea. 'Is that all right with you?'

'Of course, that would be lovely,' replied Boase.

Bartlett stood up, wiping his mouth with his napkin.

'Me and Topper are off for our constitutional, Princess – we won't be long in this snow.'

His wife kissed his cheek.

'I'm going to keep an eye on the lunch and the youngsters can have some fun together – Irene, I've brought out some gramophone records. If you and Archie roll back the rug, you can dance.'

Boase looked mortified – he had never danced.

Irene sensed his anxiety.

'It's all right, Archie – I know all the latest steps; I'll teach you.'

Boase felt relieved. He'd seen these 'modern' dances where you got to hold your girl really close; he'd learn to dance all right.

At Killigrew Street, the Pengellys were making the most of the festive season and the two days they all had off work – the only time of the year that ever happened. Rose had been up early as usual to prepare the food, but the girls had sent her back to bed with a hot cup of tea and one of their magazines.

'We're doing everything for you today, Ma,' Kitty had told her, 'you just relax and enjoy Christmas Day with Dad.' Even Jack was up early, lighting the fire and helping to prepare the vegetables. Kitty and Ruby shared the kitchen chores and cooked a very large Christmas meal. Bill had managed to get hold of an enormous turkey and this was prepared with roast potatoes, parsnips, Brussels sprouts, carrots, gravy and stuffing. A foreign ship had docked at Falmouth the previous week and, as a thank you for her speedy repair, the captain had given tins of fruit from his cargo to the men who had done the work. Bill wasn't even sure where the ship was from, but it didn't matter – the captain had generously given him four tins of pineapple, four tins of peaches, and two tins of pears. The family had never seen so much fruit all at once.

'I wonder what 'appened to Frank,' Kitty asked her sister.

'Don't know, don't care,' came the reply – 'I don't want my Christmas ruined thinking about 'im now, do I?'

'Course not, Rube – I'm sorry I mentioned 'im.'

Ruby was still upset; she had liked Frank a lot – what had he been up to since she last saw him? Definitely not murder; she didn't believe that, not for a minute.

Jack had set a very nice table with the best cutlery, dinner service, and even Christmas crackers, and the whole family sat down to eat at about two o'clock. After their meal, Bill and Jack washed up, Rose went to have a lie down, and the two girls sat by the fire eating oranges and looking at the presents they had opened that morning. Ruby pulled on a woollen hat with matching scarf and mittens.

'It was so nice of Ma to knit these, don't you think, Kit? 'Specially with her bad fingers an' all. Funny, I never saw 'er doin' 'em, did you?'

'No, no I didn't – p'raps she did 'em when we was at work. Look at all this sewing she did for me, four tray cloths and two embroidered pillowslips – definitely for my bottom drawer. D'you think she liked the things we got 'er?'

'I know she did,' the other sister replied – 'just wish it could've been more.'

Jack appeared in the doorway of the kitchen. 'I got washday 'ands,' he laughed. 'Who's for a cuppa?'

Kitty stood up, folding her tray cloths. 'All round, please, Jack – don't forget one for Ma if she's awake.'

Bill came in from the kitchen and lit the new pipe he had received from the girls.

'Is it all right, Dad?' asked Kitty anxiously. Bill puffed on the pipe for a moment and looked at the two girls through the smoke.

'I'd say that that woman you work for, Kitty, does a very good line in pipes – and this must be the finest. All in all, I think this has been a very happy Christmas Day.'

At Penvale Manor the grounds of the house looked like a picture from a Christmas card with much snow and high winds causing drifting. It was unusual for this part of Cornwall to experience such weather and the local people were unused to it. Inside the manor house, the Hattons were at home. Lady Hatton had returned from Switzerland and Algernon from London. An enormous Christmas tree had been cut which measured about twelve feet in height and it stood in the hall reaching almost to the ceiling. The Hattons were in the dining room enjoying their customary fine food and drink and the servants were in the kitchen preparing for the evening house party.

Outside, a large figure, struggling to progress through the howling wind and driving snow, and clutching fruitlessly on to a wide-brimmed hat, stopped on turning a bend in the road and surveyed the front of Penvale Manor. The figure, hurrying as quickly as was possible in the appalling conditions, crossed the large lawn and, hesitating only to look behind, ascended the front steps and made its way around the terrace, pausing at each and every window and peering inside. Finally the stranger reached the invitingly lit dining room. Yes, there they all were, eating, drinking, enjoying themselves – not a care in the world. The door leading from this room to the terrace was, conveniently, unlocked and so the stranger entered. As the door opened, the wind howled through and extinguished the eighteen candles which had been merrily burning in two silver candelabra. The twins looked up, Lady Hatton looked up and the four stared at each other in silence.

Rupert Hatton sprang up from his chair.

'What are YOU doing here? Get out or I'll call the police.'

Frank Wilson smiled as he pulled a revolver from his pocket.

'Call them – I'm sure they'd like to hear all about you, about both of you. Now get your mother out of here; we need to talk.'

Lady Hatton, dabbing her eyes with her handkerchief and sobbing, walked to the door helped by Algernon.

'Oh, by the way, don't try to call the police

– for your sons' sakes.'

Algernon returned to the centre of the room.

'Look here, Wilson, what are you playing at?'

'It's easy – Ivy Williams is dead; I didn't kill her, but you got your way and, to keep me quiet, I want paying.'

'Well even if I was going to pay you, I can't get money on Christmas Day,' Rupert looked indignant. 'Anyway, who did kill her?'

'Thought you might know the answer to that one, Duke,' replied Frank insultingly.

'I want you out of here, and not a word to anyone – we know plenty about you, don't forget.' Algernon looked at the gun still in Frank's hand. 'Planning to use that, were you? Well, just you remember that I saved you from that court martial back in '17 – I'm beginning to wish I hadn't bothered.'

Frank put the gun back into his pocket.

'I never killed Private Tremayne and everyone knew it.'

'You're a liar – we know that – and the worst batman I could have had.' Algernon pointed to the doors through which Frank had entered the room.

'Go on, get out.'

'Okay, but I'll be sending you instructions about my payment – look out for them.'

Frank disappeared through the terrace doors and Algernon closed and locked them behind him.

Back at the Bartletts', Christmas had turned out to be the best Archie Boase had ever spent. He and Irene had spent the morning together and he had learned the latest dances. Irene was thrilled when she opened his present to her – it was a beautiful golden bracelet with a tiger's head in the centre and two sparkling green eyes. Boase told her it had reminded him of her green eyes. She, in return, had given him a pocket knife which had everything a man could possibly want, including a bottle-opener, comb, and a small fork. Boase thought it was the best and most useful thing he had ever seen. On the outside of the knife she had had engraved: A.B. 1921.

The Bartletts, with Boase, continued to enjoy their Christmas break and by the 27th of December, everything was back to normal; all except one thing, that is. Everyone had returned to work, most of the shops had reopened, the dockyard was again buzzing with activity, but, as for Boase, well – he had realised that he was in love with Irene Bartlett and nothing would ever be quite the same again. This was something he would have to get used to, but he knew he was going to enjoy it.

Chapter Five

Bartlett's first day back at the station was a disjointed one. He couldn't seem to settle into anything. He thought over and over about Ivy Williams, Norma Berryman, everything surrounding them and whether there was a link that he had overlooked.

Boase came into the office, whistling and looking very happy.

'Good morning, sir, thank you for a lovely Christmas holiday. Cuppa?'

'Thank you, Boase, I haven't had one since I got here. We were very pleased to have you staying – it was nice for all of us. Listen, I think there's something more to those Hattons than meets the eye. One of them is the father of that dead girl and they say they know nothing – they must be able to tell us something. Mind you, do they know who she really was? I don't think I want to bring that up just yet – even so, I vote we go back again. Rupert Hatton lied when we spoke to him; they both know Francis Wilson all right and I mean to get to the bottom of it.'

'Good idea, sir. Are you hungry, only I've got an extra pork pie here if you'd like it?'

Bartlett shook his head. 'You're going to

end up in hospital the way you're carrying on. There isn't a scrap of meat on you and you never stop eating – you need a woman to look after you.'

Before long the two detectives arrived at Penvale Manor. Bartlett rang the bell and almost instantly, the maid they had met before appeared in the doorway. Before Bartlett had a chance to speak, he heard loud voices from inside the hall. He peered over the maid's shoulder and saw the Hatton twins both standing on the staircase. They were shouting and gesticulating and, as Bartlett watched, one took the other by the lapels and shook him vigorously. The older detective barged past the maid and stood at the bottom of the staircase. The argument continued with Bartlett still unseen. The underdog in the pair was leaning back precariously against the banister and yelling loudly and hysterically.

'I told you this would happen; I said don't get involved. You're always the same, you think you know everything. Well – do you know what? You know nothing.'

The other twin, who had been holding on to his brother's lapels, suddenly released his grip. 'Maybe I do know everything, maybe I'm sick of you telling me what to do all the time...'

Seeing Bartlett and, by now, Boase, observing them, the twins stopped, straightened

111

their attire and descended the staircase.

Bartlett removed his hat.

'Good morning, gentlemen, I'm sorry to disturb you, but I really needed to speak to you again.'

Rupert Hatton walked across the hall.

'Algie, I'd like to introduce you to these two policemen, Bartlett and er ... Boast.'

Bartlett hurriedly put them straight on his assistant's surname.

'Gentlemen, we'd like to speak to you about the death of Ivy Williams–'

'Dear Lord, not this again,' interrupted Rupert Hatton.

Algernon indicated towards the back of the hall. 'Please come into the drawing room – would you like some tea?'

'No, thank you.' Bartlett beckoned to Boase to follow.

The drawing room looked very welcoming with a huge log fire and comfortable leather armchairs and sofas. Bartlett thought that each chair would probably cost him a year's wages.

'Gentlemen, it is becoming more urgent that we find out about the events surrounding Ivy Williams's murder and I implore you to think of anything that you can – however trivial or irrelevant it might seem.'

Rupert stood up and moved towards the fireplace. From a tortoiseshell box on the mantelpiece he took a long cigarette and from a small table next to him he picked up a slender cigarette holder. As he pushed the cigarette home, Bartlett couldn't help thinking what a feminine holder this was for a man to be using, and what small, pale hands Rupert Hatton had. He looked across at the other twin who was fiddling with a silver cigarette case, apparently undecided whether to light a cigarette or not. By comparison, his hands looked almost normal. Bartlett collected his thoughts.

'Is there anything at all, gentlemen, that you could tell us?'

'Looks to me like you're getting pretty desperate,' volunteered Algernon, 'from what my brother tells me.'

'I say, I'm in a blasted rush, Bartlett,' ventured Rupert. 'If I hear anything that might help you, I'll contact you immediately, how's that?'

'Off somewhere nice, sir?' enquired Boase.

Algernon finally lit his cigarette and drew long and hard on it.

'Off to meet your gentlemen friends at your club, no doubt? Give my regards to Harry, old sport, won't you?'

Rupert extracted his cigarette from its holder and, throwing it on the fire, marched towards the door.

'I'm sorry, but I really do have to go. Goodbye.'

Bartlett turned to Algernon Hatton.

'When I recently came to see your brother, I asked him if he knew anyone by the name of Francis Wilson – he said he didn't. Do you, sir?'

'No, the name doesn't ring any bells with me either. Sorry.'

Bartlett persisted.

'Oh, I think it must – he was your batman, wasn't he? Why are you denying all knowledge of him?'

Hatton looked flustered.

'All right then, have it your way – yes, yes, I knew him – unfortunately for me. He got into some very serious scrapes, not least being charged with murder. I got him out of it, back in '17 and I haven't seen him since, that's all there is to it.'

'Well, thank you for being so honest with us, sir – eventually. Good day.'

Bartlett and Boase returned to Berkeley Vale and walked into the police station. As the younger of the two opened the door, Peggy Berryman crossed the lobby towards them. This time she was alone.

'Good morning, Mrs Berryman, how are you?' Bartlett enquired politely.

''Ow d'you think I am?' the thin, ill-looking woman answered. 'What do you think it's been like all over Christmas without my daughter, not knowing where she is, whether she's...' at this she paused, 'dead or alive. I'm begging you Mr Bartlett, sir, please do something to bring 'er back to me. It's the not knowing that's so 'ard.'

'I'm really doing everything that I can, I assure you, Mrs Berryman. Boase, fetch Mrs Berryman a strong cup of tea. Have a seat, won't you? Stay as long as you like; you're all out of breath. Would you like me to get a car home for you?'

The tired old woman sat on a long leather bench seat. 'I'll take the tea, thank you, but I'm quite capable of getting 'ome.' She coughed vigorously into a handkerchief.

Bartlett followed Boase into their office.

'That woman's not well. I wish I could find the girl for her, Boase.'

'Maybe we're barking up the wrong tree, sir,' said Boase.

'What do you mean?' Bartlett was removing his hat and coat.

'Well, think about it. That day we went up to London, you said you followed a girl because you thought it was Norma Berryman.'

'I was having a bad day – and it was very early in the morning.'

'Right, but why did you decide it wasn't her after all?' Boase persisted.

'Because I lost her in the crowd and I suddenly realized how stupid I was being – wishful thinking and all that.'

Boase took Peggy Berryman her tea and returned immediately.

'Listen,' he went on. 'We're assuming that something terrible has happened to her, if we're honest, right?'

'Go on.' Bartlett was listening.

'What if nothing terrible has happened? What if she's just run away from home?'

Bartlett sat down behind his desk.

'That's not likely – she was a very nice young woman; she wouldn't do something like that to her parents, she was devoted to them.'

Boase perched on the end of Bartlett's desk. 'You're doing it again, sir.'

'Doing what?'

'Was, was, was. You keep referring to Norma Berryman in the past tense – haven't you thought that she might just not want to be found?'

Bartlett puffed out his cheeks with a long sigh. 'So, you think we're on the wrong track?'

'I think we're looking too hard. Let's go back to the beginning, stop looking for a dead body and start thinking that she might still be around. This may seem a bit radical for around here but what about a campaign?'

'What do you mean, a campaign?'

'Let's distribute pictures of her all around, let's say, the major county towns, Truro, St Austell, Bodmin – to begin with. Maybe someone's seen her in another town.'

'You just might have an idea there, Boase

116

my boy.'

Bartlett was looking out of his window, watching Mrs Berryman struggling down the road, pausing frequently to catch a breath.

'I'll go round to the Berrymans' later and suggest it to them. Well done, Boase.'

For Boase, the rest of the day passed by slowly; he didn't know when he was going to see Irene again and he was beginning to miss her. He wondered how this could be – he had never felt like this before. Archie Boase, always independent, happy in his own company, now craving being with a woman. He used to like Amber Cosgrove when they were at school but that wasn't like this; he was fifteen and Amber Cosgrove fourteen. He liked her for almost a year then she left school and got married. Amber Cosgrove – whatever happened to her? He wondered where he would be ten years from now. Would he still be friendly with Irene? He hoped so – he couldn't imagine being with anyone else. Irene was lovely.

At five o'clock George Bartlett knocked on the door of Number 7, Railway Cottages and waited, admiring the neat front garden. Presently the door was unlocked and opened and Arnold Berryman appeared.

'Mr Bartlett, sir. How nice to see you – have you some news for us?'

Before Bartlett could reply, Peggy Berryman appeared in the hall, patting her wispy hair into place and smoothing her apron.

'Come in, Mr Bartlett – I didn't expect to see you this evening.' She beckoned him into the warm kitchen where they had obviously just begun their meal.

'Sit yourself down – would you like a cup of tea?'

'Well, thank you, that would be most acceptable, that is, if I'm not interrupting, you appear to be about to eat.'

'Don't you worry about that, Mr Bartlett.' Peggy Berryman was rushing around making an enormous pot of tea – Bartlett, a great tea drinker, approved. 'I've got a couple of extra chops in the oven, Mr Bartlett – would you like to join us?'

'That's very kind of you, Mrs Berryman, but my wife'll have my dinner ready and I'm going straight home from here. She wouldn't be too pleased if I didn't have room for her meal. It does smell rather nice though.'

Bartlett installed himself in a very large armchair by the range whereupon an enormous black-and-white cat crossed the kitchen and jumped into his lap. Mr Berryman smiled – 'That's Sydney's chair, as a rule; but don't you mind 'im, Mr Bartlett, push 'im off. Go on Sydney – shoo.'

Bartlett stroked the cat, who obviously had no intention of vacating his position,

118

and man and feline decided to share the armchair.

Mrs Berryman patted Sydney's head as she handed Bartlett a cup of tea.

''E's fourteen now – we got 'im as a kitten for Norma, when she was a little girl; 'e still waits at the top of the road for 'er, ev'ry night, waiting for 'er to come 'ome from work. She was five when we got 'im. She said to the farmer out at Maenporth who we got 'im from, "What's his name?"'

'"Sydney – with a Y," 'e replied. "Then I shall call 'im Sydney with a Y too," she said.'

Mrs Berryman looked upset, thinking of better times.

Bartlett put down his cup and saucer.

'I've had an idea, well, my assistant has – it's something new; Boase has got lots of fresh, young ideas – some good, some not so good; you know what youngsters are like, think they know the secrets of the universe. This idea, though, might just help our enquiries.'

Bartlett put forward the plan he and Boase had talked about and the Berrymans, glad of another avenue to explore, agreed. Bartlett left the Berryman house and walked home to Penmere Hill. He arrived just as Irene was taking a very large casserole from the oven.

'Hello, Princess, I'm back. Hello, Irene.'

'Your dinner's just going on the table, George,' Caroline called back from the

119

kitchen, 'come and wash your hands, please.'

Bartlett smiled. He loved the way Caroline treated him like a child sometimes – she was the same with Irene who, now a young woman, hated it.

New Year's Eve 1921 came with an unexpected thaw giving a break in the harsh weather over Christmas. Revellers planned to dance and drink like never before – especially the younger members of the community. That night saw all the dance halls full – Kitty, Ruby, and Jack Pengelly were at the Magnolia Club in Arwenack Street where a new dance band were being introduced: Harry's Havana Orchestra led by Harry Watson-Booth, a twenty-two-year-old musician from Oxford. A talented concert pianist, he had now diverted his attention to setting up his own orchestra which had successfully travelled up and down the country for over a year. Now, however, something was keeping the players in Cornwall where they were experiencing more popularity than ever; they were quite happy to follow their leader and, as far as they were concerned, Harry Watson-Booth was in charge.

At around eleven o'clock, while the band were being inundated with requests, a very drunk Rupert Hatton fell up the front steps of the Magnolia Club and, in a bid to negotiate the revolving glass door, managed to almost encapsulate himself permanently therein. As he continued rotating, a doorman, who had been seeing someone into a taxi cab, saw Hatton's plight, stopped the revolving door, and pulled the drunk out by his coat tails.

'I say, old man, no need for that, what! Blast you, mind the suit – can't a fellow get a drink here?' Rupert Hatton was indignant. The doorman pulled him further towards the club entrance.

'I'm sorry, sir, I think it's time you went home, don't you? Shall I call a taxi cab for you, sir?'

Rupert attempted to straighten his collar and tie.

'Unhand me, my good man. I do not want a car – look, I have my own, see? There's my driver waiting for me.' He pointed to the road where a very large chauffeur-driven motor car had been parked.

'I've come here to meet a friend, so please be good enough to permit me to enter.'

'I'm sorry, sir. You've had too much to drink to come in here tonight. Goodnight, sir.' The doorman, extremely familiar with such scenes, firmly installed Rupert Hatton into the one quarter compartment of the revolving door with 'Remember to get out on the other side,' and then returned to his duty.

Oblivious to Hatton's plight – not that anyone would have cared anyway – the revellers continued their party. 1922 was close and hopes of happy times ahead were high. The Great War was beginning to recede further into the past and the future was eagerly anticipated. Times had been hard for many, and few had escaped with their families intact after the horror of war. Now the time had come to look forward. Tonight was no exception and the party was in full swing. The old-fashioned dances, as well as the latest crazes, could all be witnessed at the Magnolia Club tonight – as the band continued playing, a young man stepped on to the dance floor with his partner and, as they danced, the others on the floor stepped back and formed a circle around them. No one had ever seen anything like this before. Before long the word had got round that these were two American students staying in Falmouth and they could really dance; within minutes everyone was copying them and the clock struck midnight. Nineteen twenty-two was here.

New Year's Day passed quietly in Falmouth, much the same as it usually did. It was dry and sunny and most people either did some gardening or walked across the cliffs and beaches with their friends or families. A couple of braver souls took a dip in the sea at Gyllyngvase but they were very much in the minority.

The evening saw Ruby Pengelly sitting on the floor with her sewing box and mounds of material for dressmaking.

'Kit, are you going to 'elp me with this or what?'

Kitty entered the room with a cup of tea and a plate of beef sandwiches. She sat on the floor next to her sister.

'What are you trying to do, exactly?' she asked the younger girl.

'Well, you know the frock that American girl 'ad on last night? I want to make one like that. Look, I've spent all day making this pattern.'

She held up a few irregular shapes cut from newspaper. Kitty laughed. 'This is going to be the queerest frock I ever saw. Come on, let's see what we can do.'

As the two girls sat cutting and pinning, arguing over just exactly what the American visitor had been wearing there was a loud knock at the door. Kitty got up.

'I'll go. Who can that be at this time of night? – It's almost nine o'clock.'

As she drew back the large bolt and opened the front door, there stood Norman Richards in a great state of excitement. 'What're you doin' 'ere so late, Norman?'

'Kitty, Kitty, you'll never believe this...'

'...No, I don't suppose I shall. You'd better come in.'

Kitty led the way in to the parlour. She liked Norman, very much, although sometimes he could drive a person up the wall.

Ruby looked at him. He was looking rather dishevelled. His hair was a mess, his shoes were covered in mud, and his tie was undone.

'What's goin' on, Norman?' she asked.

'I've just come down 'Igh Street an' someone's breaking into the shop.'

Kitty laughed out loud.

'Not that again, Norman.'

'It's true. I promise – I 'eard glass breaking an' all. D'you think Mrs Williams is all right?'

Kitty patted his hand – it was only recently Norman had done this same thing and ended up in the shop all night.

'I'm perfectly sure she's all right, now, you go on 'ome – we've got work in the morning.'

'All right, Kitty – if you're sure ev'rything'll be OK?'

'I'm sure. Goodnight, Norman – see you tomorrow.'

Kitty locked up behind Norman, suggested to Ruby that she had done more than enough dressmaking for one day, and the girls went to bed.

Early the next morning, on unlocking Mrs Williams' tobacconist's shop, Kitty could hardly believe her eyes. On the floor as she opened the door lay a large quantity of broken glass. As it chinked under her feet, she walked further into the shop and switched on the lights. There must have been two dozen packets of cigarettes missing, plus several large bars of chocolate, and the money drawer lay open, completely empty. Kitty could hardly believe her eyes; so Norman must have been telling the truth. She went to get a sweeping brush then stopped in her tracks – what about Mrs Williams? What if she'd been hurt? Dropping the brush on the floor of the stockroom, Kitty ran up the two flights of stairs that rose from the back of the shop. When she reached the living accommodation, she paused – she could be in danger. She could hear no sound. Thinking only of Mrs Williams, she continued on until she reached the bedroom door. She knocked softly. No reply. She knocked again, this time louder.

'Mrs Williams, Mrs Williams.' She waited. Slowly she opened the bedroom door and peered inside. The room was sparsely furnished with a wooden bed in one corner. A bundle on the bed was visible. Kitty, worried as Mrs Williams was usually moving about by this time, gingerly moved towards the bed. The old woman lay with her face to the wall. Kitty put her hand out and touched the figure. With the loudest scream, Mrs Williams leapt into the air, simultaneously drawing a very large bread knife from under her pillows. Kitty screamed nearly as loudly and the two women looked at each other in shock. Mrs Williams spoke first.

'What on earth...?'

'I'm sorry, I'm really sorry.' Kitty was half frightened to death by the experience. 'I ... I came up to see if you were all right. I'm afraid we've been burgled. I was worried that you might have been hurt.'

'What do you mean, we've been burgled?' Mrs Williams was scrambling out of bed.

'Didn't you 'ear anything in the night then?' Kitty asked her.

'No, I never. I took an extra large drop of me sleeping medicine – I 'aven't been 'aving very good nights lately – and I used these.' She produced two small soft pads from her bedside table which Kitty had just seen her removing from her ears.

'Wait for me downstairs.'

Kitty did as she was asked and returned to the shop. Norman was just arriving. He stepped onto the broken glass.

'Mornin', Kit. What on earth has 'appened here?'

'Looks like you were right, Norman. We've been broken into. Mrs Williams'll want to call the police, I'm sure – you'll have to tell 'em what you saw.'

Norman all at once felt very excited and very important. Yes, oh yes, he'd tell the police all right. He'd heard about people being questioned by the police They'd need his evidence. He'd tell them everything. They'd soon catch the man that did this – or wait, maybe it was a woman. How exciting would that be? The evidence of Norman Richards, tobacconist's assistant from Falmouth, catches the town's first woman cat burglar. He could already see the headlines in the papers. What if she had an accomplice? She might be doing this all over the country – he'd be in the national news then. He'd be a hero. He'd be in newsreels all over England. Yes, he'd help the police with their enquiries. While Norman was lost in thought and away on his very own adventure, Mrs Williams emerged from the stockroom. She took one look at the damage and asked Kitty, 'How much did they take?'

'I'm just making a list now,' Kitty replied.

'Better let the police know, I suppose – Norman, telephone them, will you?'

Kitty and Norman thought Mrs Williams seemed not particularly upset about this incident – perhaps she was mellowing with age. Perhaps she was still under the influence of her sleeping draught. Norman, highly delighted at his new found responsibility, went to put through the telephone call.

The police arrived and had a thorough look around the shop. Constable Penhaligon, himself a very young-looking policeman, was accompanied by an even younger-looking, acne-ridden youth in a smart uniform. Penhaligon asked Norman to sit down.

'Now, Norman, exactly what did you see last night?'

'Well, I was walking past the shop, when I 'eard glass breaking and I crossed over the street to 'ave a look, but I couldn't see anything inside.'

'So, you didn't actually see anything?'

'Well, no.' Norman sprang to his feet. 'But I bet I know what 'appened. 'E, well, or she, cos it could 'ave bin a lady, right, smashed the window, then climbed in and then crawled round be'ind the counter, see? Like this.' Before anyone could say anything, Norman was on his hands and knees, scampering like a rabbit around the shop. Constable Penhaligon stifled a snort and asked Norman to stand up. 'Thank you very much, Norman. I think I get the picture. You may have heard there have been a few break-ins in the town over the last week or so.' He turned to Mrs Williams.

'You'll have to try to be vigilant, Mrs Williams. Make sure you lock up securely, and especially your living quarters.'

'Yes, thank you, Constable, I will.' Mrs Williams looked uneasy.

The two police officers departed and Kitty and Norman continued with the clearing up. As they swept and cleaned, there was a knock on the still-locked shop door. A small round face peered through the small round hole where the glass had been.

'Cooeee, Kit, it's me.'

Kitty looked up to see Mabel Roberts, the

128

woman who worked a few hours a week in Mrs Williams's shop. Kitty unlocked the door and Mabel entered.

'I say, Kit, what's going on here? This looks exciting, 'ave I missed anything?'

Kitty explained while Mabel listened intently. Looking older than her forty-eight years and excessively overweight, Mabel lived alone in a flat on Greenbank. She was about five feet two inches and weighed about fourteen stone. She had red, curly hair and rosy cheeks – Bill Pengelly said that the latter was on account of the quantities of alcohol she regularly consumed. She had never married, but there was talk that she had suffered a broken engagement at the age of eighteen and that she had never wanted another man. Alone and miserable, she found comfort in food and alcohol. She had moved from her home town of Cardiff following the break-up of her relationship and had lived in Falmouth ever since, although never losing her Welsh accent. She was always so very kind and Kitty liked her a lot – she also felt sorry for her. Mabel had been very happy to receive an invitation to Kitty's wedding and was looking forward to seeing the bride on her big day. She was always to be seen outside a church whenever there was a wedding – she almost made a hobby of turning up just to see the bride. Kitty had always thought how sad this was.

Chapter Six

The fourteenth day of January 1922, long awaited by many, soon arrived. Today Kitty Pengelly would be marrying Eddy Rashleigh at the Parish Church in Falmouth. There was much panic in the basement flat as the family prepared for Kitty's big day. The bride had saved for so long to have the wedding she wanted. She had made her own dress, copied from a magazine – the latest look for 1922. Made of ivory silk, the dress was delicately embroidered with 'E' and 'K' on each sleeve. A beautiful lace veil and ivory satin shoes completed the outfit. Jack knocked on Kitty's bedroom door.

'Kitty, Ruby, the florist has brought the bouquets and the buttonholes. Come an' see 'em – they're some posh!'

Kitty and Ruby came out of the bedroom, both sporting hair nets with all manner of pins and clips protruding from their heads. The girls unwrapped the boxes which revealed a large tied bouquet of lilies for Kitty and a smaller one for Ruby, her bridesmaid. There were also enough buttonholes for all the guests.

Rose came into the kitchen and looked at

the flowers.

'They're absolutely lovely – did they bring mine?'

Kitty opened a third box and pulled out a lily corsage.

'This is yours, Ma,' she said, handing it to her mother.

Rose took the lily and quickly dabbed her eye with her handkerchief.

'I've never 'ad anything as nice as this – won't it look lovely on me new outfit?'

'You always look lovely, Ma,' said Ruby giving her mother a hug.

Rose composed herself.

'Come on now, you two, time's marching on – I want one of you to do a nice hairstyle for me – nothing too modern, mind, just really nice for the bride's mother.'

Another hour passed and soon everyone was ready. Bill and Jack looked very smart in dark suits, Rose in a blue woollen dress with blue hat and shoes, Ruby in a cream silk and lace dress, and Kitty in her wedding gown. Bill nudged Rose.

'Go on – give it to 'er now.'

Rose pulled an envelope from her handbag and gave it to Kitty.

'We want you to 'ave this and we 'ope it 'elps you set up yer new 'ome.'

Kitty opened the envelope and pulled out some notes. She looked at her parents.

'Twenty pounds,' Bill said, 'and we 'ope

you'll put it to good use – pr'aps buy something nice for your new place.'

Kitty burst into tears.

'I can't let you do this, it's too much.'

'Just put it in yer bag and enjoy spending
it,' Rose replied. 'We saved it for this day
and we'll do the same for Ruby.'

'Whenever that might be,' Jack replied,
'we'll all be dead by then.' He ducked as
Ruby's handbag came flying across the
room in his direction.

The sound of cars outside caused the
Pengellys to run to the window.

'The cars are 'ere – they're 'ere,' screamed
Ruby. 'Come on, come on, they're waiting.'

Jack ran out into the courtyard and stared
at the two cars.

'They're Armstrong Siddeleys, Da,' he
shouted in to his father. 'They're really
swanky.'

Rose, Jack, and Ruby left in the first car
followed shortly by Bill and Kitty. Bill
squeezed his daughter's arm.

'You all right, love?'

'I'm just fine, Da – not long now, eh?'

Anyone watching outside an hour later
would have seen a very happy couple indeed
emerging from the parish church. There was
much laughter and cheering, and Mabel
Roberts was cheering the loudest. She ran
up to Kitty outside the church, where she
stood arm-in-arm with her new husband.

'Kit, can I give you this – I'd really like you to have it. I had it for when I got married but you're the nicest person I know, so please take it.' She handed Kitty a small coin which looked like a sixpence but was a token. On one side read:

Now you are married

On the reverse:

Love, Good Luck and Happiness Always.

Kitty hugged Mabel, knowing how the older woman must be feeling right now and what a selfless gesture this was. Mabel kissed her on the cheek and, blushing, kissed Eddy too.

'I hope you'll both be so happy – I know you will.' She retreated into the crowd.

Kitty, Eddy, and their guests enjoyed a wonderful reception at the Bank House Hotel and the couple left for a three-day honeymoon in Porthcurno. The Pengelly house would seem strange without Kitty.

At the police station in Berkeley Vale, Bartlett was exasperated. Boase brought him a cup of tea and perched himself on the edge of his superior's desk while he drank it.

'I've been thinking, sir,' Boase began, 'do you think Lady Hatton might know anything about the murder? Do you think she knew about Maude Mockett? Claude Bennett told us that Lord Hatton said his wife must never know about anything, but maybe she did know something – maybe she knows something now. Frank Wilson has mysteriously disappeared, but I can't believe those Hatton twins are so innocent – can you, sir?'

'I don't like them or trust them one bit, Boase. You know that. That Rupert – he can barely stand up and breathe at the same time. I suppose it wouldn't hurt to see Lady Cordelia Hatton – just to get a bit of background. Come on – no time like the present, and I've got no better suggestions. I'm getting too old for this game, Boase.'

The two men called at Penvale Manor and were shown into Lady Hatton's drawing room. She was alone.

'Good morning, gentlemen – can I offer you a drink? Tea, perhaps?'

'No thank you, Lady Hatton, we won't stay long.'

Lady Cordelia Hatton was a tall and slender woman, approaching eighty years old, with silver-grey hair and protruding teeth. She wore very expensive clothes and jewellery, including a gold watch which was suspended from her neck by a gold chain.

Bartlett sat in the armchair motioned to by the hostess, Boase in another.

'Could you tell me, Lady Hatton, what happened to Maude Mockett?'

'Who is Maude Mockett?' she replied.

'She was a servant working for you some

twenty-five years ago, surely you remember her?' Bartlett didn't believe that Lady Hatton had forgotten.

'Well, the name sounds familiar, I admit. Yes, yes – do you know, I think she went away.'

'Yes, she certainly went away all right,' muttered Boase under his breath.

Bartlett turned to face the woman.

'Lady Hatton, have you heard about the murder which occurred at the end of last year in Falmouth?'

'Yes, I did hear something about it. Terrible business. You just can't believe that people could be so vicious, can you?'

'Indeed not, Lady Hatton.' Bartlett continued. 'It is vitally important that you tell us anything you can about Maude Mockett and her time here – a young girl's life could depend on us solving this murder.'

Lady Hatton looked pale.

'Oh dear, oh dear me. I do have something to tell you, Mr Bartlett. I feel I shouldn't, but if another murder happens because of me I could never forgive myself. There are two things you must know, actually. In the late spring of 1897, and shortly after Maude Mockett quickly disappeared from my employ, I was doing some charity work for the Union Workhouse. I was paying a visit to the unmarried mothers there and who should I see but Maude Mockett. Well, I was shocked, I can tell you. She was on her hands and knees scrubbing floors and, as she sat up to allow me to pass, she quickly looked at the floor again in the hope that I wouldn't see her. Of course, I already had – I'd have recognised her anywhere. I had had no idea that she was there. I asked the matron's permission to take her into the grounds, saying that I knew her, and permission was granted. The second thing you need to know is what Maude Mockett had to say to me next – it absolutely astounded me. She proceeded to tell me that she had been very happy working at Penvale Manor – she had come to us when her parents were killed in a house fire, shocking business – but she had got into trouble with one of my sons; she said that he had made her pregnant. I could hardly believe my ears. My boys were always so good, so honourable. She wouldn't say which one had done this terrible deed – I'm not even sure I believed her, but she was definitely with child. I was horrified. She said that my husband had arranged for her to be put in the workhouse – well, he had never said anything to me, and when I returned home, I never said anything to him; I couldn't. As far as I was concerned, it was never mentioned again and that was a quarter of a century ago. My husband died very recently, as you may know. Actually, now I come to think of it,

I've got a photograph which you may be interested to see.'

Lady Hatton walked across to a large oak bookcase and withdrew a leather photograph album. She laid the album on a table next to the window and began turning the pages.

'Yes, here you are, look. This is a photograph of my staff the Christmas before Maude Mockett left; she must have been with child then.'

Bartlett looked at the picture – it was the same as he already had, the one from the compact, only this one was much larger. He could see the wretched girl more clearly now – what a bad end she had come to, and all because of these over-privileged buffoons. He didn't tell his hostess that he'd already seen this photograph.

Lady Hatton closed the album.

'But why are you asking about Maude Mockett – I don't know where she is now.'

Bartlett felt uncomfortable but there was no going back now.

'Maude Mockett died a few weeks after you met her that day.'

'No!' Lady Hatton looked aghast.

'I'm afraid so. She died in childbirth and, this may be hard for you, Lady Hatton, but we have fairly strong evidence to suggest that her child was the murdered woman – your grandchild.'

Lady Hatton shook and looked on the

verge of fainting. Boase ran quickly to the sideboard and poured a brandy for her. She sipped it slowly and her colour gradually returned.

'Oh no, I can't believe what you're telling me, Mr Bartlett. Oh! Say it's not true. My only grandchild, oh no.'

The old woman regained her composure.

'Do you think my sons are involved with this murder? Is that why you're here?'

Bartlett sat next to her.

'We're not saying that – we came to see you for information.'

Lady Hatton stood up.

'There is something else too. At Christmas, while we were in the dining room, a horrible man, like a vagrant, burst into the room with a gun. My sons took me out of the room so I never found out what happened. I thought he would kill us all. I don't know if he was after money – they told me not to speak about it; I shall be in terrible trouble when they find out I've told you. Do you think they knew him, Mr Bartlett? Do you think that he had something to do with the poor girl's murder?'

'I couldn't say at the moment, Lady Hatton. You did the right thing in telling us all this. Could you describe this man any better or tell us anything he said?'

'Well, no, I couldn't. As I said, he made me leave the room, and he had a scarf wrapped tightly across most of his face and a hat with the brim pulled down – I suppose he was quite tall, and very, very scruffy, very unkempt.'

Bartlett and Boase stood up to leave.

'Well thank you, Lady Hatton, for being so helpful, and so truthful,' said Bartlett. 'I'm sure you have nothing to worry about. Please tell us if there's anything else we need to know, won't you?'

'Yes, yes, of course. Are my sons in danger from this man? Did he kill the girl? Will he come back here?'

'We really don't know enough yet, I'm afraid, but please don't worry. I'm fairly sure you won't see him again. Goodbye, Lady Hatton – and thank you.'

As Bartlett and Boase walked across the driveway in silence, they suddenly looked at each other.

'Frank Wilson,' they uttered together.

The January weather worsened again and by the end of the month heavy snow had fallen once more. Many were struggling to keep their homes warm and the police station was absolutely freezing with ice forming on the insides of the windows.

Bartlett walked into his office where Boase was already writing a report.

'Boase, please get a fire lit in this room – ask Penhaligon to organise it.'

Bartlett stamped his feet a few times, paced the room for a minute or two, then sat in his chair clad in hat and overcoat.

Boase fetched Penhaligon and the constable returned with the necessary items for preparing a fire. As he began laying the fire he paused to pull a gold watch from his pocket, checked the time, and replaced it.

'That looks like a very fine watch there, Penhaligon,' observed Bartlett, hands deep in pockets.

'Thank you, sir, it's a birthday present from my parents.'

'Important birthday?' Boase enquired.

'Yes, sir, I'm twenty-one today, actually.'

Bartlett walked over to the young constable and shook his hand.

'Congratulations, my boy – and here's me making you lay a fire on your twenty-first birthday – Boase, go and buy some buns, we'll have a twenty-first birthday celebration!'

Boase dutifully obeyed. Bartlett laid and lit the fire himself and within fifteen minutes flames were blazing in the fireplace and tea and buns were being served to mark the occasion of Penhaligon's twenty-first birthday.

As the celebrations continued, the desk sergeant knocked on the door and announced that a man, a farmer rather the worse for drink, was in the lobby asking to see Bartlett or Boase.

'I'll go, sir,' said Boase rising to his feet, 'you finish your tea.'

Boase went out to meet the man. The visitor's odour went before him. An old man, clearly under the influence of alcohol, sat on the bench in the lobby. Boase went over to him.

'Good morning, sir, I'm Constable Boase, what can I do for you?'

The man stood up unsteadily.

'My name is Petroc Tregenza and I'm from Truro. I've come to Falmouth to buy an 'orse and, since I was passing by your station, I thought you'd like to see me.'

'Oh? And why would I want to do that?' Boase looked surprised.

'I was in the market in Truro last week and I 'appened to see your 'andbill about that missing girl – wass 'er name?'

'Norma Berryman,' Boase ventured.

'Norma Berryman, exactly her.'

The old farmer sank back down on the bench unable to stay up any longer.

'I'm sorry, sir – I've 'ad a couple of drinks while I was waitin' to pick up me 'orse...'

'Don't worry about that at all – tell me about Norma Berryman – why are you here? Have you got information?'

'Yes, sir, I 'ave. That girl, well, I seen her photograph didn't I, and I says to myself, Petroc, I says, that'll be the exact same girl as

141

you see every week in Truro market, in the office. There – what do 'e make of that?'

Boase was stunned.

'Are you absolutely sure about this?'

'Yes. It's 'er.'

'Well thank you very much – you've been a great help.' Boase proceeded to show the man to the door. As they stood in the doorway the man turned back to Boase.

'I don't suppose there's likely to be a reward for this information?'

'Not as far as I know, no,' replied Boase firmly. He rushed back to the party in Bartlett's office to relay his news. He stuffed the last remaining bun into Penhaligon's hand and showed him to the door. Bartlett listened as Boase told him about the conversation he had just had.

'Do you believe him?' asked Bartlett, 'this drunken farmer?'

'Well, I didn't at first, but then I remembered when we were on the train to London and you said you thought you saw Norma Berryman at Truro station.'

Bartlett was deep in thought.

'It did look remarkably like her, I admit. I'd do anything to find that girl and return her to her parents. Look, the next market is this Saturday – why don't we go over and see if there's anything in this information; I'm not getting my hopes up, mind you.'

Saturday brought still more snow, and

Bartlett and Boase decided to take an early train to Truro to see if they could spot Norma Berryman. Boase was, as usual, well-prepared, with two pork pies, a hard-boiled egg, and two jam tarts. As the train steamed out of Falmouth station and headed towards Penryn, the extent of the previous night's snowfall became apparent. The fields and barns and small cottages were thick with white, and occasionally the fields were dotted with prints where the farm animals or the farmers had spoilt the clean white ground.

Before long the train pulled into Truro station and Bartlett and Boase headed towards the market. Bartlett stopped Boase just before they entered the market.

'Now, if she's here, and I'm not convinced myself, don't alarm her – if she's here, presumably she has her reasons so tread very carefully.'

'Right you are, sir,' replied Boase.

The two made their way through hundreds of chattering farmers, some buying cattle or sheep, others selling them. The smell was unwelcoming and Boase pulled his scarf tightly around his mouth and nose. At one end of the market was the market house and office, ugly tin and wooden buildings which looked as though they had seen better days. They were raised up and looked down on the activities, and were reached by an iron staircase.

Bartlett and Boase made their way up the staircase and reached a door with frosted glass and bearing the words *Trevanion and Sons.*

Bartlett grabbed Boase's sleeve.

'Remember what I said, now.'

Boase nodded and knocked on the door. It was opened immediately by a tall, thin middle-aged man in a grey tweed suit. Almost bald, he had a long, thin nose which curved at the tip, almost like a beak. He was almost unbelievably red in the face and wore extremely thick round glasses – Boase looked at him and thought the man must have needed very good eyesight to see through those. He invited the two men to step into his office. 'Good morning, gentlemen. I am Thomas Trevanion, livestock auctioneer – how can I help you?'

Bartlett introduced himself and Boase to Thomas Trevanion and thought returning his handshake was rather like trying to hold a lump of blancmange.

'I was wondering, sir, if we might speak to Norma Berryman; I have been informed that she works here in this office.'

The auctioneer looked puzzled.

'I'm sorry, officer, we have no one of that name working here – I think you have been misinformed.'

Bartlett wasn't too surprised; he hadn't held out much hope on this. 'Well, if you're quite sure, I'm sorry to have troubled you, sir – you're obviously correct and we are misinformed. I bid you good day.'

As Bartlett and Boase began to descend the staircase back down to the market, the office door reopened and Thomas Trevanion called them back up.

'Come in, gentlemen, please – I've just had a thought. I don't suppose you have a photograph of this girl?'

Bartlett hurriedly pulled a photograph from his pocket and showed it to the man. He hadn't really thought it worthwhile previously.

'I thought so – I just saw a bill this morning with her on it; I thought it didn't all add up.'

'What didn't, sir?'

Boase was confused now.

'Well, this isn't Norma Berryman...'

'I'm sorry, it is, sir.'

'No, this is Jane Perkins, and, yes, she did work here.'

'Is she here today?' Bartlett was hopeful now.

'I'm sorry, no – she left on Wednesday. All rather strange really.'

'How long had she been working here?' Boase could barely hide his disappointment.

'Oh, about three months I suppose.'

'Do you know where she is now?' Bartlett was pressing him now – they'd come so far and Peggy Berryman was uppermost in his thoughts.

'I'm very sorry – no I don't, I have absolutely no idea.'

Bartlett and Boase said goodbye to Thomas Trevanion and asked him to make contact with them immediately if Jane Perkins should reappear.

Chapter Seven

The first day of February arrived and the weather was quite cold but the weak sun shone through the clouds. The snows of January were gone now and Falmouth was looking forward to spring. The daffodils and crocuses came early to this corner of England and would soon be emerging from the ground.

Kitty and Eddy had returned from their short honeymoon in Porthcurno and were busy making plans in their new home in Trelawney Road. At six o'clock in the evening, Kitty, already settled and very happy in her new role as Mrs Rashleigh, took a large casserole from the oven and placed it on the kitchen table; it was Eddy's favourite. She had so much more time on her hands now as she was only working part-time at Mrs Williams's tobacconist shop – Eddy said that they could afford it and, besides that, Mabel Roberts was a bit short of cash and wanted to do some extra work at the shop. Kitty had laid the kitchen table and ran into the front room to peep through the net curtains to watch Eddy coming up the road. As he came past the window he saw her and winked. She ran to the front door and greeted him with a hug.

'Come in, take your 'at and coat off – your food's ready now.'

'I could get used to all this attention, Mrs Rashleigh,' he said, patting his new wife's arm.

As the newly-weds sat eating, Eddy took Kitty's hand.

'Guess what, Kit? It looks like in a couple of months' time we might be getting a motor car – what d'you think of that?'

'A car – what, you mean for us? I can't believe it; can we afford it though?'

'Yes. It won't be new of course, but we'll get a nice one from work – just think, we'll be able to go anywhere we like: picnics, shopping, anything you want really.'

Kitty leapt from her chair and planted a huge kiss on her husband's lips – a car of their own, how wonderful.

Eddy finished his meal.

'Something strange happened at work today. A man came into the workshop, all wrapped up in a hat and with a scarf almost covering his face – I know it's been cold but this was overdoing it a bit. He wanted to know if he could hire a car next week at short notice. I told him it would be possible but he wouldn't leave any particulars – he just said he'd be back next week. Strange, eh? We don't get many people asking to hire a car.'

Kitty took the plates over to the sink.

'Well, there are some strange people about – look at what 'appened to that poor woman at Swanpool last year. I mean, you'd 'ave to be a bit strange to do something like that to someone.'

The next day, at Penvale Manor, the postman came early as usual. Annie Bolitho, one of the maids, saw him pass the kitchen window and ran through the back entrance to meet him. He was quite sweet, she thought. Patrick McGinn was nineteen with carrotty hair and freckles, and his broad Irish accent made her melt. They always found time to stand talking and teasing each other until Cook sent another maid out to fetch her back.

'There's a letter from London today, Annie – not for you though. It's for the twins, addressed to both of them – look.'

Annie took this letter along with the others.

'There's never any letters for me, Patrick McGinn, and well you know it – who's going to write to me, I ask you?'

'I might,' came the reply followed by a wink as the young postman remounted his bicycle and made off at top speed, whistling as usual.

Annie Bolitho sorted all the post and put those letters for 'upstairs' on a silver tray as she always did. It was only half past seven –

no one upstairs would even be awake yet. She placed the tray on a small table at the foot of the big staircase and returned to the kitchen.

At about eleven o'clock the Hatton twins sent to the kitchen for their breakfast. It was brought into the dining room – eggs, bacon, sausages, haddock, mushrooms, and fried potatoes – and laid out on a large mahogany sideboard which stood under a monstrous portrait bearing the title: Woodford Membury, Earl of Stokedene. Woodford Membury was Lady Cordelia Hatton's great-grandfather and she insisted that the portrait remain on the wall even though, not having being blessed with good looks, the subject had been known to frighten small children, not least Rupert and Algernon many years ago. The twins very much resembled him, being portly with protruding teeth and hooked noses. The look was finished by greasy grey hair above a very high, pale forehead.

Rupert paused to open the post he had collected from the hall. He looked at the 'London' envelope.

'I say, old man – this one's for both of us. Shall I open it?'

Receiving a nod from Algernon, he pulled open the envelope and read the contents.

'What a blasted cheek! I don't believe this – take a look.'

His brother walked around to Rupert's side

150

of the table and read the letter. It had been badly typed on tatty, buff-coloured paper:

I told you I'd be asking for my money and I meant it.

I didn't do it but someone did.

You wanted the job done and you got your way. It time to pay up.

If you don't pay, I will tell the police that you asked me to kill her.

You won't want that much trouble and shame on your good name, will you?

Put £500 in a bag and take it to Swanpool cemetery. Near the hedge by the hill there's a big memorial – a foreign one – you can't miss it.

LEAVE THE BAG THERE AT MIDNIGHT ON THE 8TH.

If you don't, I'm telling them.

Regards,

Your old chum.

The twins looked at each other and Algernon began to panic.

'I didn't think he'd be this stupid. What shall we do?'

Rupert returned to his breakfast.

'Do nothing. He won't say anything, it's too risky for him.'

'But he will. I know him better than you do. He'll go through with it, I know.'

Rupert sighed and wiped his mouth with his napkin.

'Then, if you really believe that, we must give him the money.'

'That's madness. We can't give him all that money. Besides, even if we do, he might keep coming back for more, then what do we do?'

'Have you got any better suggestions, Algie?'

Algernon paced the room, clutching his head.

'Yes, I have actually.' He lowered his voice. 'Simple – we kill him.'

Rupert was on his feet immediately.

'Algie – are you absolutely mad? What are you thinking of, man?'

'I'm thinking of us, Rupert – and mother, of course. If all this got out it would be too much for her to endure, poor dear. We've got no choice.'

Rupert didn't like this side of his brother – he'd never seen him like this before, so determined to do wrong. He'd got Algie out of many scrapes in the past and talked him out of lots of mad ideas, but this – this was serious.

'Algie, look, you're not thinking rationally. He won't do or say anything. He's just seen a chance to make some money out of us – if we don't go along with it, there's nothing he can do, really, you've got to trust me on this – you'll just end up in worse trouble.'

'No, I know exactly what I'm doing and you've got to help me.'

'Nothing doing, old man. You know I'd do anything for you, but this is going too far, Algie.'

Algernon wouldn't be dissuaded.

'I know how we can do it and no one will ever know and we won't have to worry about him any more. He's got to go – I knew he was trouble right from the start.'

'Algie, listen. He says he didn't have anything to do with the murder – but he would say that, wouldn't he? It probably was him, and, if so, just look at what he's capable of. You read the reports about the dead woman and the state she was in when they found her, and you've heard the servants gossiping about her. Only a madman could do something like that. You know the police are already looking for him – why would he want to draw attention to himself in that way – by raking us for money? The man's extremely dangerous. Listen to me and do as I say – I don't want to get involved with that man and end up as another of his victims – are you listening to me, Algie? He's bluffing.'

'No, Rupert – I've made up my mind and I'm counting on your help.'

Ruby Pengelly applied more red lipstick and dabbed her nose with powder. Closing her compact, she turned to her brother.

'Jack, do I need more rouge, would you say?'

'I shouldn't think so, Rube – you look like a clown already; wait 'til Ma sees you.'

'You just don't understand the modern look – you wouldn't, you're a man.'

'Thanks for the compliment, I'm sure,' came the reply, 'nice to know my sister's so observant.'

'Oh, shut up, Jack, you've been a pain in the pinny ever since Kitty left, you really 'ave.'

'Where are 'e goin' tonight then?'

'I'm meetin' a friend, we're entering the marathon dance competition at the Magnolia Club – and before you say anything, I've got time off work and Ma knows about it. The first prize is five pounds, split between the winning couple; that'd be 'andy, wouldn't it?'

Ruby finished getting ready, said goodbye to her parents and Jack and made her way to the Magnolia Club. What a lot she could do with fifty shillings.

As Ruby arrived outside the club, there was her dance partner waiting on the steps for her as promised. It was Ernie Penhaligon, the police constable. Ruby patted her hair, had a quick check in her compact mirror and ran up the steps towards him.

'Hello, Ernie – ready to win some money?'

Ernie Penhaligon smiled at her.

'You bet!'

The dance hall was full of hopeful couples, all certain that the five pounds would be theirs. As they collected their numbers and read the set of rules laid out for the competition, Harry's Havana Orchestra began to play. They would be taking the opening shift, followed in turn by several other smaller groups of players.

Rupert Hatton arrived at the club at about ten o'clock. Instructing his chauffeur to go home, he went up the steps, passed through the revolving door and made his way to the bar. He sat watching the competition, looking at the posters advertising the prize and thinking it was amazing what some people would put themselves through for a paltry five pounds. He smiled to himself, pushed another cigarette into its holder and turned his attention to the orchestra.

At about four o'clock in the morning, a small group of musicians known as the Park Players arrived to take over from Harry Watson-Booth and his troupe. Two or three couples had dropped out already but Ruby and Ernie still had lots of energy. Rupert Hatton had stretched himself out on a chaise longue. He sat up when Harry Watson-Booth came over to him.

'I say, you must be sick of all that playing, Harry.'

'I'm a bit tired, yes.'

'Look, what say you come back to the house and we'll have a few drinks?'

Harry yawned.

'It's four o'clock in the morning and I'm exhausted, Rupert.'

The older man was persistent.

'Come on, it'll be fun – we haven't seen each other for ages. Please say yes.'

'No, Rupert, really – the chaps and I might get called to the club again later on today, depending on how long the dance lasts; I really need to get some shut-eye.'

The two men left the Magnolia Club together and walked in opposite directions along Arwenack Street. As Rupert reached the bend in the road known as Church Corner, between the Parish Church and the King's Head, he heard someone behind him. He stopped walking but didn't turn around. The street was very dark.

'Who's there?'

A hand moved swiftly around his neck, the other across his mouth.

'Shut up and listen. You've been a very naughty boy, haven't you? You and that brother of yours don't want to pay me. But I've been very patient – yes, very patient, see? That was a bad move, Duke, not paying up. But I'm a nice sort of person and I'm prepared to give you another chance – okay? You got my letter?'

Rupert attempted, with difficulty, to nod.

'No one messes around with Frank Wilson – you should know that.'

The grip relaxed slightly.

'Oh, and one other thing – don't think I don't know what you get up to with that pretty bandleader. Bit young for you, I'd say. Can't you get someone your own age? It'd be a shame for 'im to lose 'is looks now, wouldn't it – or for something to 'appen to Rupert or Algie; how would Mummy feel about that? Now you be a good boy and get my money. Put it where I told you at midnight – don't try to cheat me again now, will you?'

Rupert was released and he ran along Church Street, not looking behind once.

Rupert Hatton didn't go to bed when he eventually arrived home at about half past five in the morning. He poured himself some more drinks, smoked some more cigarettes, and sat in the study thinking about the earlier events. He was still sitting there when Algernon came downstairs, earlier than usual at nine o'clock.

'I say, old man – have you been here all night? This room stinks – mind if I open the windows?'

Rupert shrugged.

'I had a run-in with a mutual acquaintance at about four this morning.'

'Oh?'

Rupert told his brother what had happened.

'I told you, Rupert, there's only one thing to do – but you wouldn't listen. Well, believe

157

me, it's still on the cards.'

'Count me in, Algie, you were right. We've got no choice now. We can't put Mother at risk. He even threatened to harm Harry.'

Algernon sighed very audibly.

'How on earth did you get mixed up with him? If Mother ever found out what you do, it would break her heart. How can you be so vile?'

'Well, Algie, you might think I'm vile but I'm not hurting anyone and Harry and I are becoming very close; actually, I'm thinking of asking him to move in here with us; he's got nowhere else to go, the lease on his flat runs out next week.'

'Are you totally mad?' Algernon couldn't believe what he was hearing.

'Mother would never hear of it – and then she'd find out about you; what then?'

Rupert began to get irritated by his brother's attitude.

'Look, Algie, this morning we've had what amounts to death threats by a man who we know is extremely capable of carrying them out and you're worrying about my social life. Forget it!'

'All right, it's your business, but I won't have Mother upset – do you hear me, Rupert?'

Rupert nodded.

At the Magnolia Club, Ruby and Ernie were still in the running for the five pounds.

There were still eleven other couples, all with plenty of stamina, and the competition wasn't going to be easy. Ernie was glad he was having a week off work. Ruby's feet were beginning to ache but she wasn't going to miss the chance of that money. At about midday, Kitty and Eddy arrived at the club. Rose Pengelly had sent them to see how the dancers were getting on. She was worried about Ruby. Personally she thought it was a daft idea – dancing to win money; wearing yourself out like that, but that was youngsters today. She asked Kitty and Eddy to give her a full report when they returned. The Rashleighs stayed and watched the competition for about half an hour and, reassured that Ruby was, indeed, perfectly well, returned home, via the Pengellys' flat to relay the news.

George Bartlett sat at his desk playing with a pencil. Boase looked at him.

'Everything all right, sir?'

'Not really, Boase. I've been thinking about that William Gibbons. You said that you saw him running along the platform at Truro station, didn't you?'

'Yes, I did. And to be truthful, I couldn't believe my eyes. He was in a right state when Penhaligon and I went round to see him at his house – limping all over the place, with a stick he was.'

'I think we'll pay him another visit. He knew Ivy Williams pretty well, wouldn't you say?'

'Well she *was* living in his house, sir.'

'Exactly. He must know something and this business with his legs is all a bit strange. Add to that the frustration of missing Norma Berryman so narrowly and I'm beginning to wonder which way to turn next. I'll have to see the Berrymans later too – it's only fair to tell them what we know – do you think?'

Boase agreed and the two men set off to Kimberley Park Road to see William Gibbons.

Arriving at the house, Bartlett knocked and waited. After what seemed like a very long time, Gibbons opened the front door and stood there leaning on a stick. Bartlett introduced himself – Boase needed no introduction, as Gibbons recognised him immediately. He led the way into the front parlour.

'I've already told you everything I know,' he volunteered.

'I'm sure that's true,' replied Bartlett, 'but there's something else I want to clear up with you, sir. A while ago my assistant and I were travelling by train to London on police business and while we were waiting at Truro station, Boase here saw you from the window of the train; you appeared to be running at top speed along the platform, carrying your stick. Could you explain to us, sir, why a war invalid would be able to do such a thing?'

Gibbons knew he was in a hole now. He had no choice but to come clean. 'All right, I've been rumbled. Look.'

Gibbons walked across the room unaided, and swiftly back again.

'I'll tell you everything but I still don't know any more about the murder. I was injured quite badly in the war – 1917 – and spent eight months in hospital; first in France then here. Before that I'd been in and out of trenches for twelve months, almost without a break, apart from one or two trips home. By the time the war ended I was still in hospital. I saw an opportunity to make some money out of my injuries so I took it. I fooled all the doctors that I couldn't walk properly and couldn't return to my old job – gamekeeper, that was – and so, because of the extent of my injuries, I was allowed to claim a small pension. It really isn't much, but it helps me to get by – when you saw me I was about to miss my train; I was going to visit my mother in Sunderland. So I suppose now you're going to report me to the authorities?'

Bartlett patted the man on the shoulder.

'No, Mr Gibbons, I'm going to do no such thing.'

George Bartlett realised how hard life in the trenches must have been; Gibbons was lucky to have come back at all, unlike his son, John. No, he wasn't going to take anything away from a man who had fought for his country in such a terrible and unnecessary war. Gibbons was grateful.

'Well, thank you, sir. That's very decent of you – I don't know what to say; I felt sure you would intervene to stop my pension.'

'No, you're wrong – I think you've been through enough. Just make sure no one sees you running for a train again; the next person might not be so sympathetic. Now, are you sure you can't tell us anything else about Ivy Williams or anything surrounding her murder? Any callers to the house, any mention of boyfriends or meetings?'

'I'm sorry, sir, no, nothing. She kept herself to herself, paid her rent on time just like I told your assistant here, and seemed generally well-behaved. I really can't tell you anything more. I'm sorry.'

'Well, thank you, Mr Gibbons, for your help.'

'And thank *you*, sir, thank you very much indeed.'

Gibbons held out his hand to both men then saw them both to the door and watched as they walked down the front path and left through the gate.

Bartlett lit his pipe.

'Well, Boase. Next stop the Berrymans, I think.'

Bartlett and Boase walked up the Berrymans' neat front path and Bartlett knocked on the door. As the two men waited, Sydney the black-and-white cat wound his rather large body around Bartlett's legs then jumped up on a nearby wall and attempted to drape himself around the back of the older man's neck, much like a scarf. The door opened and Peggy Berryman stood there.

'Hello, Mr Bartlett, sir, Mr Boase – Sydney, you naughty boy, get down. Give 'im to me, Mr Bartlett; there now, look at Mr Bartlett's collar, all covered in your 'airs, that's a nice thing, I must say. Come in, Mr Bartlett, I'll fetch a clothes brush.'

Bartlett and Boase entered, both smiling, Boase because he had never thought to see his superior got the better of by a cat, Bartlett because he felt that he had such hopeful news for the Berrymans. Peggy Berryman began brushing Bartlett's collar using a large brush from a hat stand in the hall, and her husband, hearing the sound of visitors' voices, quickly dropped his newspaper and stood to put on his jacket.

'Well, gentlemen, what can we do for you?' Mr Berryman offered the pair a seat.

Bartlett unbuttoned his overcoat.

'We think we may have some good news for you – we've still got some further enquiries, but I wanted you to know it looks promising.'

'What is it, Mr Bartlett?' Peggy Berryman sank down into an armchair.

'We think someone has seen your daughter.'

'Is she all right?' Mr Berryman sat on the arm of his wife's chair and took her hand.

'It seems so. She's been working in Truro – someone told us they had seen her working in an office there. Unfortunately, when we got there she had just left the employment but we've got new hope now and, believe me, we're more determined than ever to bring her back to you.'

Peggy Berryman was sobbing quietly. Her husband put his arm round her shoulders.

'Come on now, Peg. That's such good news. 'Ere now, 'ave a nice 'ot cuppa.' The old man poured a cup of tea and handed it to her. The cup rattled in its saucer as she took it from him. She took a sip and handed it back.

'Why did she run away, Arnie?' She looked up at her husband.

'I've no idea, but that doesn't matter at the moment – if Mr Bartlett can bring 'er back to us then that's all we could wish for.'

Bartlett and Boase felt they should leave the couple alone and, promising to keep them informed, they left the small cottage and returned to the police station.

Rose and Bill Pengelly sat in their kitchen talking. They had just received some wedding photographs from Kitty and Eddy and were choosing one to frame.

'What a lovely day that was, Bill.' Rose looked at the pictures over and over again.

'I'm sure I don't know which one to choose – what do you think, Jack?' Jack was sitting at the kitchen table making a model aeroplane.

'Boy Jack, I'm talking to you, an' I 'ope you've got plenty of newspaper on my table with all that mess you're makin' – come an' look at these photographs.'

Jack put down his model and walked over to his mother's chair. He looked through the pictures.

'Well, I dunno – what're 'e askin' me for – what do I know about stupid weddings?'

His father, standing up and reaching for his pipe, clipped his son's ear.

'Don't talk to yer mother like that – at least try and look interested; it's yer sister after all.'

Bill walked out into the yard for some fresh air and to smoke his pipe, hopefully uninterrupted. If he was honest, he didn't like weddings either but, this one had been special; his first daughter getting married – to a nice boy too. He secretly didn't hold the same hopes for Ruby. What a fly-by-night she was turning out to be, but what a lovely daughter too. He idolised his baby girl – whatever she did. As he sat thinking about his beloved girls he heard voices in the street above.

'Hold on now, nearly there – you'll 'ave to walk down the steps yourself.'

Bill stood up and walked across the yard. He couldn't believe his eyes. There at the top of the steps was Ruby, being carried by a man. He ran up to them.

'What's going on 'ere?' he asked. 'Ruby, are you all right?' The young man dropped his precious cargo to the floor and held out his hand.

'Mr Pengelly? Ernie Penhaligon, sir. I've been partnering your daughter in the dance marathon.'

Bill was astounded by the state of the couple.

'Well you don't look very well on it – you'd better come inside.'

Having reached the bottom of the steps, Ernie Penhaligon carried Ruby into the house – she was half asleep. Her mother came out into the hall.

'Oh, my God – what's 'appened to 'er?'

Ruby opened her eyes.

'We won, Ma – we won.'

Rose plumped up the cushions on the couch.

'Lay 'er on 'ere. I told you my girl – what

a stupid idea. What a way to spend a few days off work. Look at the state of you.'

She turned to Ernie. 'I think you 'ad better go 'ome, young man – you don't look too good yourself'

Jack came into the parlour.

''Ello, Ernie – you all right?'

Ruby opened her eyes.

'You two know each other?'

'Jack and I use to sail our model boats at Swanpool when we was kids,' replied Ernie.

Bill stood up.

'Well, in that case, you'd better stay and 'ave a cup of tea – you look all-in, young man. And thanks for getting 'er 'ome safely.'

Bill, Jack, and Ernie went into the kitchen to have a drink and a sandwich. Rose looked at Ruby lying on the couch.

'Well. I 'ope you enjoyed it – you're both mad.'

'We won five pounds, Ma – to share, of course.'

'Well I 'ope the first thing you do with it is buy a new pair of stockings – look at the state of these. You better take 'em off an' let's 'ave a look at yer feet.'

Ruby sat up and peeled the stockings off – there was barely anything left of the heels and toes and her feet were red, with the skin broken and sore. Rose rolled the stockings up into a ball.

'Not even I can darn those – they're only

fit for the rubbish. When the men are out of the kitchen you should go and soak yer feet in a bowl of 'ot water – you must be mad, my girl. You better get a good night's sleep tonight and rest tomorrow.'

The three men sat around the kitchen table. Jack showed Ernie his half-finished model.

'Hey, Ern, do you remember when we 'ad that lovely big yacht out on the pool and it went out of control?'

Ernie laughed. 'Yeah, it went shooting off into the water so fast it capsized David Treloar's punt. What a laugh that was.'

'You should 'ave bin there, Da. That David Treloar always thought 'e was better than anyone else and thought 'e could make the best boats too. 'E told ev'ryone that 'is punt was so good that he could sail 'is chicken sandwiches away in it and they would come back dry. You should 'ave seen the look on 'is face when the punt capsized and an enormous swan came over and ate the bread. I've never laughed so much in all my life. David Treloar's working down the docks now, Ernie – did you know?'

'No, I don't care if I never see 'im again – what a half-wit! Anyway, I must be going. Thanks very much for the tea and the sandwich, Mr Pengelly.'

Ernie Penhaligon said his goodbyes and Bill and Jack came into the parlour. Bill sat

168

in his armchair.

'Very nice boy, that Ernie. You didn't say you were courtin' a policeman.'

'Yes, 'e is nice, Dad – 'e's takin' me to the fair on the Moor tomorrow.'

Rose looked disapproving.

'Nice or not, I told you to rest tomorrow – look at the state of yer feet; go an' soak 'em now – there'll be no fair for you.'

The following morning found George Bartlett at his desk earlier than usual. By the time Boase arrived the older man had already been working for two hours. He looked up as his assistant walked into the office.

'Morning, Boase – put the kettle on will you, here's my cup.'

'Morning, sir, you're in early today. Would you like a piece of saffron cake with that?' he added pulling a paper bag from his coat pocket.

'No thanks, just the tea. I've been trying to figure out how to trace Norma Berryman – the look on her mother's face yesterday when we told her the news; I can't let her down now, Boase – we've got to find that girl. I thought today we could go over to Truro again, we've got a few hours to spare. If you get a couple of men to come with us we can spread out a bit; I don't think now that this business has anything to do with Ivy Williams but it'll be one less thing on our books to worry about.'

'Have you thought any more about Ivy Williams's murder, sir?'

'I think of nothing else my boy – I still don't trust those Hattons and I bet any money that Frank Wilson was their visitor.'

'Why didn't we question the Hattons about that visit after we spoke to their mother, sir?'

'Mainly because I don't want them to know that their mother let us in on what happened – I'm not sure yet that I even trust them to take care of her and, also, I'm not so convinced that Frank Wilson is a danger – if he's got something to hide, why was he still in the area at Christmas?'

Boase thought that this made perfect sense. He made himself and Bartlett a cup of tea and sat at his desk proceeding to unwrap a large piece of saffron cake. Boase shared his superior's office as there was limited space in this part of the station and also because Bartlett wanted to keep Boase under his watchful eye – this young man had great potential he had thought to himself, much like himself in his younger days, although, alarmingly, Boase was the quicker-witted of the two. The younger man's part of the office was small and occupied the back wall in the corner; the two desks faced each other although Bartlett, naturally, was nearer the fire in winter and, the window in summer. The two men got on remarkably well together –

complemented one another and made a very strong team.

As Boase reached the end of his saffron cake he looked across at Bartlett.

'I was wondering, sir...'

'Yes, Boase, what is it?'

'Well ... well ... nothing really.'

'You know I hate it when you do that, man – what do you want to say?'

Boase wished he had never started this conversation.

'Well, sir, I was wondering... I was wondering, well, if you thought that Irene might like to come to the fair with me tonight?'

Bartlett smiled.

'Well, you should really ask her, not me. Why don't you come round later – what time does this fair start?'

As Bartlett spoke he looked out of his window – the fair was outside on the Moor and was preparing to open for the afternoon. He watched the fairground workers going about their business; it reminded him of the fairs in London – they were different years ago, mind. The rides were cheaper, the food was better, how things had changed since his younger days.

'Well, about seven o'clock is a good time to go, sir.'

'Well then, why don't you come to the house and I will tell Irene to be ready?'

'What if she doesn't want to, sir?'

Bartlett raised his eyebrows.

'I really don't think there's any danger of that happening, my boy. Now, get these men together and prepare for a trip to Truro.'

As Bartlett and Boase collected their coats, the desk sergeant knocked on the door and entered with a letter, announcing it had just come as a special delivery. Bartlett opened the envelope and read:

Dear Sir
I have some information which may help you with your enquiries following your visit to my office. Jane Perkins (or Norma Berryman) I have discovered is living at 17, Lemon Street in Truro. She has a room there. I wish you well.
Yours faithfully
Thomas Trevanion, Livestock Auctioneer

Bartlett couldn't believe his luck.

'Boase, we'll have our first stop at 17 Lemon Street today – here, read this.'

The two men, together with two constables, arrived in Truro at eleven o'clock. Boase was keen to find Norma Berryman but his mind wasn't on the job. He couldn't wait to see Irene – what if she said she would come to the fair with him? They could get into a swingboat together and he would be close to her again; how could he live without her? He looked at his pocket watch – less than eight hours, but what a long day this was going to be; every minute seemed like an eternity, why couldn't they be together all the time, never have to go home, never have to write to each other – just to look up and there they'd be, always?

While Boase had been thinking of Irene, Bartlett had sent the constables off – he didn't want to frighten the girl – and so he and Boase had arrived outside 17 Lemon Street. It was a smart house with a flight of steps up to the front door. The two men went up and rang the bell. A young woman opened the door. Bartlett and Boase identified themselves. 'Could you tell me if a young lady is living here in a room at the moment, please Miss?' Bartlett enquired of the girl. It then became apparent that the girl was French and spoke barely any English. Bartlett tried again, to no avail. Boase, looking somewhat embarrassed, addressed the girl:

'*Pardonnez moi, mademoiselle, nous cherchons cette fille. Elle s'appelle Norma Berryman ou, peut-être, Jane Perkins. On m'a dit que nous pouvons trouver cette fille ici.*'

Bartlett pushed his hat back above his forehead in amazement – a man of many talents was his assistant; what else was he hiding? The girl was so relieved that she began to speak at high speed, enthusiastically gesticulating as she did so and smiling broadly at

Boase whom she had obviously taken a shine to. He turned to Bartlett. 'Norma Berryman does live here, sir, but she's gone away for a few days. We've been invited to look at her room if we want but she's definitely coming back next week.'

'Well. I don't think we need to see her room, Boase – she's obviously around so we can come back. Make sure you ask this lady to contact us if Norma decides to leave – but don't let her say we've been here. Oh, and tell her Norma hasn't done anything wrong; just helping us with our enquiries – I don't want the mademoiselle to think she's harbouring a criminal or anything like that.'

In perfect French, Boase obliged and the two men descended the steps, the 'Mademoiselle' smiling and waving to the younger man.

'Well, where did you learn that my boy?'

'Oh, it's just a bit of schoolboy French, sir.'

'Well, you certainly had a better education than I did,' came the reply.

At half past six exactly, Archie Boase knocked at the Bartletts' front door and stood waiting with an enormous bunch of spring flowers. Spring came early to this part of the world and snowdrops and daffodils and tulips poked their heads up several weeks before the rest of the country, often completely finished before the north of England had seen its first bloom. Caroline came to

174

open the door.

'Archie, how lovely to see you again – come in, Irene's just finishing getting ready.'

Boase followed Caroline through to the parlour where Bartlett was sitting smoking his pipe. Topper looked at Boase, his head cocked on one side – he didn't need to get up, this chap was no threat to his master.

'Hello, my boy, sit down. We even had dinner early so Irene could go the fair with you.'

'Oh, I'm sorry, Mrs Bartlett, I didn't mean to inconvenience you.'

'You didn't in the slightest – and call me Caroline. Now where is that girl? Irene, Irene, Archie's here waiting for you.'

A few minutes later Irene came into the parlour. Boase couldn't take his eyes off her. She wore a green woollen dress which matched the colour of her eyes with a short black fur-trimmed jacket over the top and a cloche style hat which came down over her ears and made her face look like that of an angel. She was wearing Archie's bracelet which he had given her for Christmas – she wore it every day. He stood, just staring at her.

'Well, come on then, Archie – we don't want to miss all the fun.'

Boase offered her his arm.

'Are you sure you'll be warm enough – it's quite cold out?'

George and Caroline Bartlett looked at each other. There was no doubt that Archie Boase cared a lot about their daughter and they were pleased. The young couple reminded them of themselves years before; they hoped that they would be equally happy if they decided to make their relationship more permanent.

The fair was in full swing when the couple arrived and they had such a lovely time. They rode on everything, they ate nearly everything and they won almost everything. At half past ten, Boase walked Irene to her door. As they stood on the step, Irene gave him a big hug. As he caught the scent of lilacs in her hair, Boase held her close, her soft cheek next to his. She turned her face and kissed his lips.

'Goodnight, Archie – thanks for a lovely evening.'

As she turned her key in the lock and opened the front door, Topper appeared – he never went to bed until his family were safely in their beds. The dog licked Boase's hand and disappeared inside with Irene. The door closed and the key turned. Boase's legs were trembling – he'd never kissed a woman before, not on the lips, anyway. He never wanted to kiss another, of that he was positive.

Chapter Eight

Annie Bolitho came around the corner of Penvale Manor on her way back from the kitchen garden, a basketful of vegetables in her hand.

'BOO!'

She jumped and dropped the basket, its contents falling to the ground. She had come face to face with Patrick McGinn.

'How could you – I almost jumped out of me skin,' she knelt to the ground to retrieve the produce.

'Now that would have been something to see, you jumping out of your skin.' The young postman was grinning from ear to ear.

'Just you get down 'ere and 'elp me pick all this up.'

Patrick McGinn obliged and tried to steal a kiss as he did so.

'You stop that now,' Annie Bolitho said crossly, getting to her feet and smoothing her uniform, 'and give me the post.'

She snatched the letters from the postman's hand, picked up her basket of vegetables, and, sticking her nose in the air continued her journey back to the house.

Once inside, she sorted the post; one letter for cook, none for any of the other servants, the rest for the masters. She placed those remaining four letters on the silver tray and left it on the hall table as usual.

At half past nine, Rupert Hatton came down the stairs and, on his way to the breakfast room, stopped to collect the post. Only one was for him and, feeling hungry, he took it to the table with him to open after his breakfast. He helped himself to a very large plate of food from the silver dishes on the sideboard and took it to his usual place at the table. As he ate, he looked at the envelope – he thought he recognised the handwriting, but he didn't know who it belonged to. Finishing his breakfast, he picked up the envelope and, sliding a knife under the seal, he opened it and read:

Dearest Rupert
I'm in a spot of bother, old man – you know I've had trouble with my landlady and my tenancy is now up. I really must see you as I need your help. I don't want anyone to see us as I know you still want to keep us secret. Meet me at Swanpool – I shall be waiting at the western end of the pool at eleven o'clock tonight (Monday). Please, please come – I need you.
Yours always
Harry

Rupert folded the letter, replaced it in its envelope and quickly put it in his pocket. What could be wrong with Harry? Why, hadn't he told him only last week that he could come and live with him at Penvale Manor? It was probably nothing – Harry did tend to overreact; Rupert put it down to his musician's temperament. Anyway, he would go and meet him, in fact he was looking forward to it – perhaps Harry would come back to the house with him and have a few drinks, maybe stay the night. Rupert continued with his breakfast and made his plans for the evening ahead.

With the rare opportunity of a day off presenting itself, Archie Boase packed a pair of binoculars and a travel watercolour box and pad. Today he would try and relax and think – think about Irene Bartlett of course. He was still in shock at the events of last night and couldn't believe that he, Archibald Boase, had, a few hours ago, kissed the most beautiful girl in the world; no, she had kissed him. There was no way he could have worked today even if he had had to. No, today he wanted to be alone with his thoughts, and there was no better way than to do a spot of bird-watching and maybe some painting or sketching. Setting off from his lodgings in Melvill Road, he walked the circular route along the sea front, down past the cemetery

179

and headed towards Swanpool. Reaching the beach he sat for a few moments but couldn't see anything he really wanted to paint – there were too many people around anyway so he set off again to find somewhere quieter. He made his way across the cliff path that led from Swanpool and gave uninterrupted views of the bay. Feeling better for the exercise and his head clearing, he continued on towards Maenporth. He soon arrived at the small beach and, seeing no sign of human life, but much bird activity, he settled down to paint. Maenporth had always been one of his favourite beaches, not much more than a cove really with a couple of cottages looking out to sea and dominated by the Crag Hotel above, this was the ideal place to be alone with one's thoughts.

Boase wondered what he should do next about Irene – what did men do when they had kissed a girl on the lips? Perhaps he should leave it to Irene; she always seemed to know what to do. She must like him to have done that. He felt in his pocket and pulled out the multi-bladed knife that she had given him for Christmas. He opened the largest blade and proceeded to slice an apple which he had brought for his lunch, together with a pork pie, a large piece of cheese, a slice of ham, and a currant bun.

Boase finished the food and washed it down with a pint of milk. For the first time ever, he couldn't concentrate on his painting – the thing he loved most in life, painting birds; well, it *had* been the thing he loved most in life, now things were different; there was nothing above Irene Bartlett. What was happening to him? He had never felt like this before; it was a nice feeling but it worried him slightly. How could a woman have such a strange effect on a man? Puzzled by his own thoughts, Boase picked up his bag and headed for home, back along the cliff path towards Falmouth. As he rounded the bend in the cliff path, passing Henry Scott Tuke's cottage, he saw Swanpool in front of him. He jumped down onto the sand from the rocks. As he looked up he could see Norman Richards at the other side of the beach with a man. Boase squinted as he walked in their direction. He had known Norman for a year or two, only through buying Mint Imperials for his landlady as a weekly treat on a Friday – they were her favourites and Boase thought it was a nice gesture, she was always so kind to him. Norman always had a strange assortment of friends, Boase had thought and that man was someone he was sure he recognised but he couldn't quite remember who it was. He carried on his way, puzzling over the man's identity.

As Boase walked across the beach he paused halfway. This was the exact spot where the body of Ivy Williams had been found. Boase looked around him. Who did it? Why didn't Bartlett know yet – why didn't he himself know yet? There was something missing, probably something obvious. They'd have to do better than this, this case was going on too long now; the murderer must be caught. Neither he nor Bartlett wanted Greet to send someone down from up-country to work on this case, but that was looking more and more likely the longer it went unsolved. It was only being left to them now on account of Bartlett's outstanding work in London previously – Greet had a good man and he knew it, but pressure was mounting now from all directions.

There were several people walking across the beach, some with dogs, others with children. The tide was coming in now and the weather was turning worse. As Boase reached the other side of the small beach, he stood on a large rock looking out to sea and the rain began to fall. First it started slowly, just a slight drizzle, then, in an instant, it absolutely poured out of the sky. It was torrential. That seemed to be a strange feature of this town – rain appearing almost out of nowhere, with no warning. Boase didn't mind, in fact, he quite liked it. No one else at Swanpool today seemed to though – they all disappeared hurriedly, like cockroaches when a light goes on.

At precisely twenty-five minutes to eleven, Rupert Hatton walked across the courtyard at the back of Penvale Manor and entered the stable block. Almost all of the buildings had been converted to motor garages to house the twins' rapidly growing collection of cars. The stable block was quiet and the moon lit the interior through the semi-circular windows up near the roof. Rupert felt in his pocket for his keys and, after unlocking the vast double doors and slipping through a narrow gap, he turned, pushed them wide open, and approached a small two-seater motor car. He fumbled in the darkness to start the car and, after a couple of attempts, success was his. The engine rumbled as befitting a powerful little racing car and Rupert stopped in the courtyard and ran back to close the doors – he didn't want anyone to ask the next morning where he had been. He paused before closing the doors and looked up at the array of windows which faced down on to the courtyard – they were all darkened. He looked up at the moon which was just disappearing behind a cloud and then he was in complete darkness. With some difficulty he returned to the car wishing he had put its lights on. Slipping into the seat he set off down the long drive at top speed. Shortly before five minutes to eleven, Rupert Hatton's motor car purred along the sea road at Swanpool; he stopped at the west end of the beach behind the pool and got out of the car. The moon was illuminating the dark, murky water and Rupert stopped to light a cigarette. He fumbled in his pocket for his cigarette holder but it wasn't there.

He lit anyway.

Extinguishing the light and dropping the match to the ground he walked on in the direction of the pool. There was no one around and the nearby houses were all in darkness. A dog was barking in the distance and the only visible lights were those coming from a ship in the bay. Rupert continued on and stepped into the dense shrubbery which bordered the edges of the pool. He felt a little nervous – he hadn't seen Harry's car anywhere; perhaps he had decided to walk, maybe he was going to be late. More likely he had changed his mind; Harry could be so impulsive. Rupert decided he didn't want the cigarette and dropped it onto the mud beneath his feet. Now he lit another. There had been rain early that morning and although the sky had become clear now, the ground was damp and the mud clung to his calfskin boots. He looked around him although the bushes were thick and he could see nothing. He had heard men in the trenches whistling to keep their spirits up but he didn't want to break the deadly silence. He walked forward a few yards and reached a small clearing from where the pool was visible. As the moon emerged from behind a cloud he reached for his gold pocket watch and, opening it, squinted at the hands – two minutes past eleven. He couldn't believe Harry could mess around like this. If he didn't come within the next few minutes he was going home. As thoughts churned over in his mind he wondered what could be done about Frank Wilson and the money he was demanding. He wanted it on Friday night. Rupert shuddered as he remembered the night he had left the Magnolia Club and Wilson had threatened him.

More than ten minutes had passed now.

As he stood and prepared to light yet another cigarette he heard something close by him. He turned and the moon instantly came out brighter than ever. A figure was beside him. Rupert dropped his unlit cigarette.

'What the hell are you doing here? How did you know I'd be here? Go away, I'm waiting for someone.'

The moon disappeared behind the clouds and the pool was again in darkness.

Boase was back at his desk early the next morning. He stood and stretched then wandered out to the main desk and picked up Bartlett's newspaper. He glanced at the headlines then threw the paper back down. He'd just remembered something; that man with

Norman Richards – that was Jan Rowe! He knew it. Mrs Williams's godson. But wasn't he in prison? Well, no, obviously. Boase remembered him from before, he was a bad lot, all right. He was always trouble for his godmother. He remembered at least four occasions when he had been drunk and disorderly and in the station. But, if he was out of prison, why would he come back here? Boase smiled to himself, thinking that nothing would surprise him about that man. At that moment the front door of the station was flung open and Ernie Penhaligon ran up to Boase.

'Sir, I was just on my way back to the station when a young woman who had been walking her dog out at Swanpool came up to me in a hysterical state. She said she found a body by the side of the pool.'

'Where is she now?' Boase asked.

'She's outside with her dog – she's a bit shook-up too – shall I bring her in?'

'Yes, of course, bring her in – immediately.'

Just as Boase finished speaking, Bartlett arrived.

'Well then, Boase, what's all this mayhem?'

Boase explained what he knew and the young woman was taken into Bartlett's office while Penhaligon looked after her dog in the lobby.

Boase offered the woman a seat. Bartlett sat next to her.

'Now, miss. I'd like you to tell me your name and what's happened – as clearly as possible please.'

The young woman took a deep breath.

'My name is Betty Trevaskis and I live at number two St Thomas Street, Penryn. I'm a waitress at George's Cafe in Arwenack Street. For the last three days I've been staying with my aunt – she's a cripple and she hasn't been very well so I offered to help look after her. She lives round the back of Swanpool, you see. She's got a greyhound called Polly and usually her neighbour, a very nice man, walks Polly, but he's gone away for a month and my aunt couldn't manage. Anyway, this morning, I was taking Polly around the pool for her constitutional before I left for work. Polly ran off – which she never does – and she ran into the bushes. I followed her but she wouldn't come back. Anyway, when I found her–'

Tears began to trickle down Betty Trevaskis's face.

'Go on please, miss,' encouraged Bartlett.

'Well, there was a man, dead, just lying by the side of the pool – it was horrible. I didn't know what to do so I just ran, then I bumped into that nice young constable while I was running along and he brought me here.'

'And where was this, Betty?'

'I met him on Western Terrace – that's how far I had come when I saw him.'

'Would you take us to where you saw the body?'

'Well, I don't mind but I'm supposed to be at work – I'm so late already, I can't afford to lose my job.'

Bartlett patted the girl's shoulder.

'Don't worry – I'll send someone down to George's, you won't be dismissed. Besides, you shouldn't go to work – you've had a nasty shock.'

Bartlett and Boase took Betty Trevaskis to Swanpool; she led the way and, sure enough, the body was exactly as she had left it, almost hidden in the undergrowth. Bartlett arranged for someone to take her home and to make sure she was all right – there would be nothing more she could tell him at this stage. She had already said she hadn't seen anything or anyone around – it was early when she went out and Swanpool had been quiet.

Bartlett and Boase inspected the area and the body themselves. Boase took a notebook from his pocket to make some sketches and to note details. As he did this a photographer arrived and began taking pictures, under Bartlett's instruction. Boase bent over the body and looked up at his superior.

'Oh my word, it's one of the Hattons, sir – I've no idea which one.'

'Well, unless they've swapped cars, it's

Rupert. One of the constables spotted the motor parked across the lane – it's his but we'll need a positive identification.'

Bartlett and Boase continued to survey the murder scene. The discarded cigarettes were observed as was the bullet wound through the victim's head. Boase bent to the ground and, with the assistance of a large white handkerchief, picked something up. He wrapped the object carefully.

'Sir, it's a revolver. A Mark VI Webley. I'll see if we can find out anything about it.'

'Right you are, Boase.'

Bartlett continued to tread carefully around the vicinity of the body, his eyes scanning the ground.

'Looks like he was here a while waiting for someone, judging by the cigarettes he smoked,' remarked Bartlett, pointing to another stub.

'I know, I've seen them, sir – maybe two people stood here smoking – we'll check for footprints. Do you think he killed himself, sir?'

'Unlikely – check for the footprints, and whatever you do, don't disturb too much or you'll lose any evidence,' came the reply.

The body was removed and Bartlett and Boase took a trip to Penvale Manor. On the way there Bartlett asked of his assistant, 'Did you notice anything unusual, Boase?'

'How do you mean, sir?'

'Well, you asked if he killed himself and I said I thought it unlikely but, you checked and told me there were no other footprints in that mud except the victim's. Isn't that a bit strange to you?'

Boase had to admit that it was and maybe they were, indeed, looking at a suicide case. No doubt time would tell. The two men arrived at Penvale Manor and on ringing the door bell, Annie Bolitho answered their call.

'Good morning, miss – are either of the Hatton twins at home?' Bartlett enquired politely.

'Yes, one of them is – he's taking breakfast with Lady Hatton but I didn't actually see which one; I just saw his back as he went through the door to the breakfast room. Sorry.'

'That's all right, miss but it's very important that we speak with him and his mother.'

Annie Bolitho asked them to wait while she went to interrupt the Hattons. Presently she returned and asked them to follow her to the breakfast room. She showed them inside where one of the twins was at the table, eating with his mother. They both stood up as the men entered the room. Lady Hatton walked over to Bartlett.

'Good morning, Mr Bartlett, what brings you here this fine day?'

Bartlett looked at her son.

'Forgive me, sir – which are you? You're so

like your brother.'

The twin stepped forward.

'I'm Algernon – is there anything we can do for you, Bartlett?'

'I'm afraid I have some bad news for you both. Early this morning a body was found at Swanpool; we have reason to believe it is Rupert's.'

Lady Hatton sank down into an armchair and Algernon gasped.

'No, you must be mistaken – not my brother, no, I don't believe you. Look you damned fool, what's going on here? Coming round here with these ridiculous ideas and stories about bodies – why are you doing this?'

His mother looked up at him, her eyes wet and red. 'Shut up, Algernon, for once in your life, shut up.'

Algernon looked shocked at his mother's tone and he obeyed. Bartlett addressed him quietly.

'I'm so sorry, sir, but I will first need someone to identify the body and I really don't think it would be fair to expect your mother–'

'No, she can't do it, I will. I can't believe this, Inspector Bartlett. Everything was all right yesterday, how can this have occurred? Do you know what happened?'

'We know nothing just at the moment, sir, but obviously we'll keep you informed.

When you've seen the body, I'd like you to come to my office – if you don't mind, sir, just to fill in any details which might be helpful.'

Algernon nodded.

'Yes, of course I'll come.'

The two policemen left the room while Algernon comforted his mother.

Later that afternoon, Algernon Hatton came to see Bartlett in his office. He had identified the body as that of his brother, Rupert.

Bartlett offered him a seat and a cup of tea; the latter was declined.

'Can you tell me if your brother had any enemies, sir, anyone who would want to hurt him? Had he upset anyone recently?'

Algernon Hatton's lip curled as he snarled, 'Oh yes, Inspector, yes I think I know of someone.'

'Go on please, sir.'

Hatton now felt he had nothing to lose.

'When my brother and I were in France, we spent the whole four years there. From 1914 to 1918. I had a batman by the name of Francis Wilson, as I believe I told you last time.'

Bartlett's ears pricked up at the mention of this name; he had been wondering when it would come up.

Hatton lit a cigarette.

'I'm sorry – do you mind if I smoke? I'm a

bit on edge at the moment, you understand.'

'I understand perfectly, sir, you go ahead.' Even Bartlett couldn't help feeling sorry for the over-privileged cad.

'Well, where was I? Oh, yes, well, he was my batman and he seemed a decent enough sort of fellow, we rubbed along all right together and looked out for each other. Those were terrible, dark days, Inspector – I couldn't wish it on any man.'

Bartlett nodded, half thinking that the likes of Hatton had probably had quite an easy ride compared to his dear son John. John didn't get the chance to come back alive; wouldn't ever have the chance to fall in love and have children, would never have the chance to wake up with the woman of his dreams in his arms. He continued to listen as Hatton went on.

'Anyway, one day in June 1917, there was a bit of trouble and, well, to cut a long story short, Wilson was charged with the murder of a man – Private Tremayne was his name. He denied everything, and he'd been loyal to me – very loyal, saved my life once in fact – so naturally, I felt I should intercede. Luckily I was in a position to do this and he was let off. We hadn't really heard much about him until the end of last year when he started to ask for money – I said that enough was enough, I'd got him off a murder charge, yes – but that didn't mean we would be the best of chums for the rest of our lives. I turned him down flat for the money and then the next thing we knew, he pitched up here at Christmas, threatening my mother, my brother, and myself with a gun.'

Bartlett wasn't going to let on that he had already heard part of this story – he wanted to hear Algernon Hatton's version of it.

'I told him the same again – no money, and there was no point in him coming back again. Rupert said after that he thought we should give him something to make him go away – but where would it stop, Inspector? What if he kept coming back for more? Anyway, we later received a letter from him demanding that we leave money for him–'

'Have you still got the letter, sir?' Bartlett enquired.

'No, I threw it on the fire. Later, Wilson accosted my brother when he was leaving his club. He apparently threatened him again and said he wasn't happy to find we wouldn't pay him. He told Rupert to follow the instructions in the letter and said that if we didn't comply, he would come after Rupert, myself, my mother, and even Rupert's friend.'

'Rupert's friend – who would that be, sir?'

'He's a chap called Harry Watson-Booth, he's a bandleader, plays at the Magnolia Club usually. He and my brother had become quite good friends by all accounts.

Anyway, Wilson said that he still wanted the money and that we were to leave it at the original place that he had instructed.'

'How much?'

'Five hundred.'

'And when were you supposed to drop this money?'

'It's tomorrow night – midnight at the cemetery. Do you think you might catch him there, Inspector? If you do, you might save the rest of my family from the hands of a killer.'

Bartlett stood up.

'Well, sir, I'd be very interested in meeting up with Francis Wilson, for a number of reasons, but I don't think we should jump to any conclusions at this early stage.'

'But doesn't all the evidence point to him, Inspector? And we know that he was the last person to be seen with the murdered woman too. He's a bad lot, mark my words.'

'Well, we won't trouble you any further today, sir. Just you take care of Lady Hatton and we'll be in touch. Good day, sir.'

Bartlett opened the door of his office and Algernon Hatton left, Bartlett settled back into his chair.

'Boase, I'd like you to go and see this Harry Watson-Booth – try and find out what he knows about all this business – about Wilson threatening Hatton. If you go now you could have a drink at the Magnolia

Club – you needn't come back here then, not unless you've got some really interesting news that won't wait until tomorrow. Mind you're in early in the morning though – I want to plan something for tomorrow night at the cemetery. Frank Wilson is bound to turn up looking for his money and I'd really like to speak to him. See you tomorrow, my boy; good luck at the Magnolia Club.'

Boase took his hat and coat and left the station.

Chapter Nine

Boase arrived at the Magnolia Club, which was just opening for the night. He approached a young girl at the cloakroom desk.

'Excuse me, miss, I'd like to speak to Harry Watson-Booth, is he here at the moment?'

The girl put down the coat she was holding.

'No, I'm sorry, we haven't seen him for a couple of days. He didn't turn up last night to play either.'

Boase looked puzzled.

'How strange – I understood he played here most nights.'

'That's right, but we haven't seen him or heard from him.'

At that moment a tall, slim man entered through the revolving door and approached the desk. He was, Boase thought, about twenty-eight years old, clean-shaven with curly, jet black hair and small round glasses. He carried an instrument case.

'I say, Patricia, could I just leave my clarinet here while I make a telephone call? I really don't want to lose it again.'

Patricia agreed.

'Freddie, this gentleman was asking about Harry...'

'Who might you be?' asked Freddie, looking Boase up and down.

Boase, who had already glanced at Patricia's name badge when they met said politely, 'Thank you for your help, Miss Penrose.'

He pulled the young man across the lobby.

'I am Constable Boase and I want to ask some important questions about Harry Watson-Booth. Can I talk to you?'

Freddie apologised.

'Of course you can talk to me, I'm sorry – Freddie Giles, I didn't realise who you were. In fact I'd be very pleased to tell you about Harry. Let me buy you a drink.'

The two men sat at a corner table in the bar.

Freddie took a sip of his drink.

'I wondered how long it would be before you came.'

'What do you mean, sir? Is there something you wish to tell me?'

'You're looking for Harry, right?'

'Right.'

'Well, he's gone and he's not coming back. He's left the band, gone away – I don't know where, but I'm the only person who knows why he went.'

'Go on.' Boase was becoming more interested.

'Harry told me he was threatened by someone and couldn't stay – he was fearing for his life. He didn't say where he would go. He didn't even say if he was staying in the country. But he did give me this to show you if I thought anything was wrong – in fact he said to show it to the police if he was found dead. I hope I'm doing the right thing.'

Freddie Giles pulled a sheet of paper from his jacket pocket and handed it to Boase. It was a small, square blue piece of paper with black writing on one side. It read:

I know about you and your boyfriend. I've seen you together. Men like you make me feel sick. Rupert Hatton should know better, a man of his standing. I've always hated him and now I hate him even more. He wronged me many years ago. Unless you want some of what he's got coming, you'll go away and never come back. You'll read about him in the papers and be glad you didn't hang round.

Take some good advice when it's offered.

Boase read the letter with interest.

'Do you mind if I keep this, sir?'

'No, please do. I say, Constable, do you think Harry's in danger? What does this letter mean?'

Boase smiled. If anyone couldn't read between the lines of a letter like this, they must be pretty thick. He stood up.

'I can't say if Harry's in any danger just at the moment, sir, but you did right to give me this letter. Thanks for the drink. You'll let me know immediately if he shows up again?'

'Yes, of course I will.'

Boase left Freddie Giles standing in the lobby of the Magnolia Club and headed for home.

At eight o'clock the next morning, Bartlett and Boase stood in their office. Bartlett lit his pipe.

'About tonight, Boase. I hope you haven't made any plans? I intend to be at the cemetery at midnight to meet up with Mr Wilson. I'm going over to Budock to see Hatton this morning and I shall arrange for him to make his drop at the required place as instructed. When Wilson turns up for the money, we'll have him. We'll have to be careful though, he might be armed and he'll probably be watching when Hatton leaves the package – we can't afford to be seen. I want you to meet me here at eleven o'clock tonight – I'll give you the final details then.'

'Right, sir, I'll be here. Before you go out, I need to speak to you about last night at the Magnolia Club – I didn't come back here because I thought it would keep until today, and anyway, it was getting late when I left. You need to know about this, sir. I met a man who plays with the Havana Orchestra, with

Harry Watson-Booth. Freddie Giles he's called. He said Watson-Booth hasn't been around since he got this threatening letter.'

Boase handed the letter to Bartlett. He read it quickly.

'Go on, Boase.'

'Well, apparently, Watson-Booth showed this to Freddie Giles but told him not to tell anyone unless anything happened – or if he was found dead. He obviously felt the threat was a serious one and he's gone. No one knows where.'

Bartlett, who had stood to put on his hat and coat, sat back down.

'Who do you think wrote this, Boase?'

'I'm really not sure, sir. I suppose it could be Frank Wilson.'

'Why?'

'Perhaps he wanted Watson-Booth out of the way so he could kill Rupert Hatton. If he'd already murdered Ivy Williams, he didn't really have much to lose.'

'But why would Frank Wilson kill Rupert Hatton?'

'Because the Hattons wouldn't give him the money, sir?'

'If you're right, Boase then it means that Algernon Hatton could be the next victim. For some reason, the killer let Harry Watson-Booth go. Why? Is Watson-Booth someone to the killer? We need to find that out. But why kill either of the Hattons? Didn't Algernon say that when his brother was threatened by Wilson, he gave him another chance – to-night – to drop the money? Why kill him? This person is playing strange games and I don't like it Boase, and that's a fact.'

Bartlett finished getting ready to leave.

'While I'm at the Hatton place, I'd like you to enquire about Norma Berryman again. That French bit in Truro said she had only gone for a couple of days so she should be back by now. I hope you catch up with her – try and get her back; it would mean so much to the Berrymans.'

'Well, I'll try, sir but I can't make her come back, can I?'

'Make her. It's more important than you know.'

Bartlett left the station and Boase settled down to plan how he was going to find Norma Berryman and then get her to come home to her parents.

As Boase drank his last cup of tea before heading for Truro, the desk sergeant knocked on the door.

'Excuse me, Archie. These post-mortem details were just hand-delivered.'

He handed Boase a large brown envelope addressed to Bartlett. Hoping that the senior man would want him to open it, Boase did so. They really had already known the results, this was now just confirmation; Rupert Hatton had been killed by a single shot through the head. Inside the envelope was a smaller one marked *Found on deceased's body. Give to police.* Boase opened this also. It was the letter to Rupert Hatton arranging for him to meet his killer. It was signed by Harry Watson-Booth. Boase thought intently for a minute or two, then, putting the letter in his pocket, made his way to the Magnolia Club.

Arriving about fifteen minutes later at the club, Boase knocked repeatedly on the locked door. It was quiet now, so early in the morning – although some revellers often didn't leave until the early hours. He tried to peer through the glass doors, suddenly out of the corner of his eye he saw some movement. He hammered on the door again and the figure stopped and looked towards him. It was a cleaner. She came to the door and Boase held up his identification to the glass. The cleaner hurriedly unlocked the door and he entered.

'I'm so sorry to bother you, miss, but I really must speak to Mr Freddie Giles.'

'None of the band is 'ere now, they've all gone 'ome, they don't 'ang round once they've finished,' the cleaner replied.

'This is police business – can you tell me Mr Giles's address?'

'Well, I don't know it – I don't 'ave nothin' to do with the band, I just clean up after 'em, an' a right mess they can make at times, I can tell you.'

Boase was growing uncharacteristically impatient.

'Could there be a written record of the players' addresses kept in the club?'

'Well, sir, I don't know. There's some books up in the office but I don't know what they are – you could 'ave a look if I unlock it.'

'I'd be much obliged.'

The cleaner led the way up a steep flight of stairs. At the top was a door. She slowly went through a large bunch of keys on an enormous ring. Boase sighed.

'I'll be there in a minute, just you 'ang on – I always 'ave trouble with these keys, 'ere you are, this is it.'

She unlocked the door and Boase entered the small room.

'I'll leave you to it,' the cleaner said, 'but I'm goin' 'ome in fifteen minutes, you shall 'ave to go when I do.'

Boase was already wading through a large pile of papers and ledgers. After nearly ten minutes he saw a file marked *Contact Details/Addresses*.

'Please let it be here, please, please,' he said to himself. He leafed through several pages and there it was:

Freddie Giles, Clarinettist

14, Norfolk Road, Falmouth.

Boase heaved a sigh of relief and, leaving the office, ran back down the stairs, thanking the cleaner on his way out. He made his way through the alleys and up the steep hills until he reached the smart Edwardian terraces which were Norfolk Road. Reaching number fourteen, the second house in the row, he knocked on the door. Presently a large, round woman opened it.

'I'm sorry to bother you, madam, does Freddie Giles live here?'

'Of course he does, he's my lodger. I'll call him. Mr Giles, Mr Giles – someone to see you.'

Freddie came to the door.

'Hello again, Constable Boase, nice to see you.'

On hearing this address, the landlady stepped forward.

'I don't want any trouble here, Mr Giles – this is a respectable house.'

'I can assure you, madam, that Mr Giles is in no kind of trouble, believe me, he's merely helping me with my enquiries.'

'Hmmm – that's what they call it now, is it? Helping the police with their enquiries. Well, I'll leave you to it, but, any trouble, you'll be out.'

Boase wasted no time in showing the letter to Freddie Giles.

'I need to know if you think this is Harry's handwriting, and is this his signature?'

'No, that's not his writing. It's similar, I suppose. I should know – when I went overseas for six months, we used to correspond and I'm quite used to his handwriting. No, that's not his.'

'Are you absolutely sure?

'Look, I'll give you one of his letters if you like – to compare. I kept a couple of them. Wait, I'll go and get one.'

Freddie Giles returned with a letter which was about one year old and gave it to Boase.

'You can keep that if you like, if it'll be of any help to you.'

Boase took the letter.

'Thank you, sir, you've been more help than you can imagine.'

Boase left. He still had to catch up with Norma Berryman today. He'd call in at the station first; he wanted to make sure these letters were safe and it might be a good idea to pick up his pork pie and chicken leg since it was almost lunchtime.

As Boase entered the police station, Bartlett met him in the lobby. Boase took off his hat.

'I've got some really interesting news for you, sir.'

'It'll have to wait for now, Boase. I've seen Hatton and arranged everything for tonight but, listen, there's someone you should see in my office. Go in.'

Boase walked through the door and a young woman rose from his chair. It was obvious to Boase immediately. It was Norma Berryman.

'What good news, my boy, eh? What good news.' Bartlett was ecstatic.

'Norma and I have had a long chat which I'll tell you about in a minute. Meantime, she was just saying how she'd like to powder her nose and we're going to get a bit of something for her to eat and then we're taking her home.'

He turned to Norma.

'Off you go, young lady, your food will be here in a minute.'

The girl smiled at Boase, picked up her handbag, and left the office.

'You won't believe this, Boase. That French girl we were speaking to in Truro, well, should I say, you were speaking to, gave Norma your card and when she returned to her room, she decided to contact us. I'll tell you something, you wouldn't believe what that girl's been through. She was shopping in Truro, just minding her own business – and when she was crossing the street she was hit by a motor car. Well, she was taken to hospital in a very bad way – in a coma and not expected to live. She wasn't carrying any means of identification so no one knew who she was – couldn't contact her next of kin or anything. Anyway, it turned out that she made a good recovery, under the circumstances, but had no memory of her own life; didn't know who she was, who her parents were, where she lived – nothing! When she got better the matron on her ward set her up with a job at the livestock auctioneers and arranged for her to take the room she was living in. It seems that when she heard about us and saw your card, something happened to slowly bring back her memory – after all that time – would you believe it, Boase? As soon as she's eaten, I'm taking her home to her parents; she's a bit worried about seeing them on her own so she asked me if I'd go with her. Personally, I can't wait to see their faces.'

Boase was trying to soak all this up when Norma Berryman returned with some sandwiches the desk sergeant had fetched for her. She spoke as she ate, 'I saw the stories in the newspapers about Ivy Williams and it was only a couple of days ago that I remembered who she was.'

'You knew Ivy Williams?' Boase stared intently at the girl.

'Yes, I knew her very well. I think there's something you should know – if you don't already. Ivy Williams wasn't very clever, she couldn't read or write particularly well but she got by. She regularly came into the library when I was working there to try to improve herself and she used to ask me to help her choose suitable books that she might like to read. Anyway, one day last year, I probably said something out of turn to her. I knew that she was always wondering who her natural parents were; her mother was dead and it wasn't something she would speak to her father about – he would be too upset and she knew, deep down, what good parents they had been to her. Still, she wanted to know more about her background. She said she'd always suspected that she had been adopted but knew no more than that. I, at one time, had had to help out at the Union workhouse – the library put me forward to help with their record-keeping which had got into a bit of a mess and so I worked there for about two weeks. Well, when I was there I happened to find out about Ivy's birth, in the workhouse – I wasn't snooping, I just came across it. What I found out amazed me. Her mother had been sent there as a girl of sixteen from the Hatton place out at Budock and the records said that the girl, Maude Mockett she was called, always maintained that one of Lord Hatton's sons was the father; the birth certificate, however, was blank on the paternal side.'

'We know most of this already, Norma,' Bartlett told her politely.

'No, there's more. One day, shortly after I found this out, Ivy came into the library, very upset. She said she couldn't go on not knowing about her parents – she even showed me a little photograph she had kept for years; she said she thought her mother might be in the picture. She felt she had to find out, it was so important to her, so...' Norma paused, 'so I told her what I knew about the Hattons, everything.'

Boase raised his eyebrows.

'I really had no choice – she was desperate and then the last I knew was she told me she was going to make them pay. Have I caused lots of trouble, Mr Bartlett?'

Bartlett didn't feel like telling Norma that she had probably caused immense trouble; that possibly even a murder had occurred because of this.

'No, don't worry, Norma, don't worry.'

'There's something else,' she went on, 'when I found the records and the birth certificates ... well, there were two.'

'Two?' Bartlett was really surprised now. 'What do you mean, two?'

'Ivy Williams was a twin – there were two certificates. The other baby was called Gloria.'

Boase's thoughts immediately jumped back to Claude Bennett's office – he might have thought Ivy Williams had been to see him; could this be possible? He looked at Bartlett who sat looking astounded. Thoughts of every description were racing in both men's heads now. All this new information made things look very different indeed; it also possibly changed Norma's position – not for the better. This girl knew a lot that might put her in danger. For now, though, Bartlett was content to return her to her parents.

Bartlett and Norma Berryman walked up the path to the house Norma had grown up in. Bartlett knocked on the door while Norma stood anxiously behind a small bush outside the window. The girl's father opened the door and Bartlett heard a voice call from inside.

'Who is it, dear?'

'It's Mr Bartlett. Hello, Mr Bartlett, will you come in?'

Mrs Berryman came through the passageway, wiping her hands on her apron.

'Come in, won't you, how are you?'

'I've brought someone to see you both.' Bartlett beckoned Norma to come forward. She emerged timidly from behind the bush.

'Hello, Mum, hello Dad.'

Mr Berryman smiled the biggest smile that Bartlett had ever seen on anyone's face while his wife just stood in the doorway, motionless. In a moment she held out her arms to her daughter.

'Come 'ere, you bad girl. Where 'ave 'e bin? You don't know 'ow worried we've bin. Come 'ere to your Ma.'

Mother and daughter embraced and sobbed. Mr Berryman held out his hand to Bartlett.

'I don't know what to say to you, Mr Bartlett, sir, indeed I don't. You've given me the best gift I've ever 'ad and I can't thank you enough.'

Mrs Berryman looked up, unable to speak, but her face told Bartlett everything he needed to know. Quietly he turned and walked back up the garden and through the gate.

Chapter Ten

Returning to his office, Bartlett found his assistant at his desk making notes.

'Hello, Boase, you'll be pleased to hear there was a very happy reunion – very happy indeed. We now have one less thing to worry about – although we need to keep an eye on Norma, she knows too much. What are you up to?'

'Sir, we've just been sent the post-mortem results which were exactly as we expected, but also this letter was found on the body.'

Boase handed him the letter.

'I went straight round to speak to Freddie Giles and he gave me an original letter written by Harry Watson-Booth – the writing is similar, but it's not by the same hand. This was sent to Rupert Hatton to arrange a rendezvous and he obviously didn't suspect that there was anything strange about the writing; at least, if he had, why would he have turned up? Someone else, the killer, wrote this and sent it to set up Hatton's murder. Apart from Frank Wilson, who else could it be?

Bartlett listened thoughtfully.

'I admit, I have absolutely no idea what's

going on – perhaps everything will become clearer if we pick up Frank Wilson tonight; let's wait and see. In the meantime, I think we should keep an eye on both Norma Berryman *and* Algernon Hatton – they might both be in danger for very different reasons.'

At five minutes to eleven, Bartlett and Boase let Algernon Hatton into their office. Bartlett asked him to sit down.

'Now do we all know what we're doing? Mr Hatton?'

'Yes, yes, I think so. I'm so nervous, Inspector Bartlett – what if anything goes wrong?'

'Don't you worry about anything except dropping the money as we've arranged, that's all you need to do. All right, Boase, are you ready?'

'Ready, sir.'

Bartlett buttoned up his coat.

'Good, then let's go.'

Boase stopped the car about a ten-minute walk from the cemetery and the three men split up and approached it from different directions. They were all to get a good view of the foreign monument, which was large and tall and so could be easily seen above the others. Hatton walked down the hill a short way and stopped at a small gate which led into the cemetery; the grave was quite near. The moonlight shone across this grave and the few immediately surrounding it. Bartlett walked down the hill towards Swanpool to approach from a lower gate while Boase entered right at the top. The cemetery was large and, thankfully, had several entrances. By half past eleven, all three men had a good view of the stone. Hatton looked at his watch then walked towards the grave carrying the package. As he reached it, he looked around him – Bartlett and Boase were well hidden; he hoped they were still around, he was feeling rather more nervous now. He dropped the package between the grave and the hedge and, leaving by the nearest side gate, as instructed by Bartlett, began the walk back to the car. Bartlett and Boase watched all this and remained still. The moon continued to light up this part of the cemetery and the white package could be clearly seen. Bartlett looked at his watch; it was a quarter to twelve. He hoped this would all go to plan. A couple of party-goers, seemingly the worse for drink, stumbled down the hill, laughing and joking. Still no sign of anyone else. The wait continued.

Boase felt a sneeze coming on and he pinched his nose hard to stifle it which action was, happily, successful. He had installed himself into such a small, awkward vantage point that his knees were beginning to feel extremely cramped. How he wished that something would happen, or that he could at least stretch his legs, just a little. He managed to look at his watch; two minutes past midnight. He hoped the wait wouldn't be much longer. He couldn't see Bartlett – he assumed he must be nearby. A rat ran swiftly across Boase's feet and he jumped. He saw the rodent scuttling across the nearby graves and smiled to himself in relief. He heard a noise. Bartlett had heard it too. It was the sound of the top gate opening – Boase recognised it as it had made the same sound when he had entered by it earlier. Both men listened intently. The wind had begun to blow and it moaned quietly between the headstones. Boase's heart was racing now. The two men expected to hear footsteps or the rustle of a raincoat – something, anything. But nothing came.

Fifteen minutes after midnight and still nothing. Boase looked up to see Bartlett standing beside him. He spoke in a low voice.

'I don't want to spend all night here, Boase. You go back to the station, get a constable to stay here for the rest of the night and let Hatton go home. Come back with the relief and then you can pick me up. I'll wait here. I don't want to take that package in case Wilson turns up later on. Give the constable strict instructions on what to do if he shows up.'

Boase stood up and prepared to leave the cemetery. Bartlett returned to his original place and waited. About twenty minutes later, Boase returned with Constable Penhaligon who, having already been briefed, took up his place from where he could readily see the white package.

'No falling asleep on the job now, Penhaligon,' joked Boase.

'No chance, sir,' came the reply.

Bartlett and Boase returned to their homes soon afterwards. Bartlett felt the next day would be hectic and thought a few hours sleep wouldn't go amiss.

At nine o'clock in the morning a weary Bartlett and Boase turned up together at the police station, later than usual. About ten minutes later Constable Penhaligon arrived – carrying the package.

'No show, sir,' he said handing the money to Bartlett – I waited until almost nine o'clock.'

'Thanks, Penhaligon,' said Bartlett taking the money and putting it on his desk. 'You go home and get some sleep now – you deserve it.'

Penhaligon stifled a yawn and left the station.

Boase handed Bartlett a strong cup of tea. 'What now, sir?'

'You tell me, Boase. I've no idea – why didn't Wilson show up?'

'I can only think that he changed his mind about the money, killed Hatton, and now...'

'Go on,' prompted Bartlett.

'And now, he's going to kill the other one.'

'Do you really think so?'

'I don't know what to think, sir. Who wouldn't want five hundred pounds of easy money? At the moment we don't know if the killer of Ivy Williams is the same as that of Rupert Hatton – or even if there's going to be another murder.'

'That's our worry now, Boase – we're going to have to protect Algernon Hatton, just in case you're right. We also need to look out for Norma Berryman – she knows a lot, probably too much. This is all a mystery to me. This afternoon I think we should go back to Swanpool and have another look at the Hatton murder scene, see if there's anything we've missed.'

At midday, Algernon Hatton came into the station asking for Bartlett. The desk sergeant announced him and he was shown into the inner office.

'I was just wondering,' he began, 'if the money was collected last night?'

'No, it wasn't,' replied Bartlett. 'You may as well have it back, sir – here it is.'

Algernon took the package.

'I was just passing, I'm taking my mother to her lunch club and I thought you might like to know that, following the inquest, my brother's funeral is going to be held on Wednesday. We'd like you to come, if you can, that is.'

'We'd like that too, sir,' replied Bartlett

holding the door open for Algernon Hatton.

'Good day, sir.'

'Good day, Inspector Bartlett.'

'Would we?' Boase looked puzzled.

'Would we what?' Bartlett was settling back into his chair.

'Would we like to come to the funeral?'

'Of course we would, my boy – we can have a look, see who's there, see if there's anything unusual going on. Strange that the coroner is allowing a funeral so soon though. But, you never know, Boase, what you might see or hear. We'll be there.'

At two o'clock in the afternoon, Bartlett and Boase took a trip to Swanpool to have another look at the scene of the murder. It was a bright sunny afternoon and many people were walking their dogs on the beach.

'Nice day for Topper,' observed Bartlett.

The two men reached the west side of the pool and began having a look around. This had already been done but Bartlett couldn't believe there wasn't something else that could help.

'I don't understand, sir.' Boase was looking on the ground. 'No other footprints what-soever, not even the next morning – there was nothing besides the one set.'

'I don't know the answer to that. As you say, absolutely nothing. Someone came up to Rupert Hatton, here at this very spot, shot him through the head and left. No footprints.

No traces of anything. All there was to be found were a couple of Rupert's cigarettes and his own footprints, which prove nothing – he was kept waiting so he had a couple of smokes and paced – so what?'

'We're sure it wasn't suicide now – not after reading that note arranging the *rendezvous* – and, with the best will in the world, I don't think Hatton was clever enough to construct a double bluff by sending that letter to himself to make it look like someone had killed him. Anyway, what would be the point in that; come to that, what's the point in anything?'

Boase quickly changed the subject – if Bartlett was going to get all philosophical now, he wasn't interested; that kind of talk didn't do anyone any good.

As the two struggled to make sense of the whole thing, life in Falmouth was going on much the same as usual for everyone else. It had become routine on Saturday nights for Kitty and Eddy to have tea at the Pengellys'. This was usually followed by a few card games. Although Kitty wouldn't want to be with anyone else besides Eddy, she desperately missed her own family. It was going to take some getting used to, she could see that. Eddy realised this and was quite happy to accompany her home every Saturday night. Tonight was no exception.

Kitty and Eddy knocked at the door at half

past six.

'They're 'ere, they're 'ere,' squealed Ruby to her mother as she ran to open the door.

'Come in, you two – you don't need to knock, Kit, this is still your 'ome.'

The three went into the kitchen where Rose Pengelly was putting the plates out on the table.

''Ello, you two, ev'rything all right?'

Kitty gave her mother a big bunch of flowers.

'Everything's fine, Ma,' she said kissing her mother on the cheek.

'Da and Jack not back yet?'

'No, they'll be 'ere in a minute or two. Ruby, put an extra chair for Eddy, will you, love?'

Within half an hour the entire family was sitting down together, eating dinner and exchanging stories. Jack finished his food first, as usual.

'I 'eard there was another murder at Swanpool last week. One of them posh twins from Budock, they say. Ruby, you should get your policeman friend round 'ere an' 'e can tell us all the gory details.'

'Shut up, Jack. I don't want such talk at my table, thank you.' Rose liked a bit of gossip but not this kind.

'Anyway, 'e's not my policeman friend, as you put it, actually.' Ruby looked indignant.

Jack persisted.

'Yeah, 'e is – you was in that dancin' competition with 'im.'

'So?'

Kitty put an end to the bickering – Eddy was an only child and all this was new to him.

'What did you spend your fifty bob on, Rube?'

'Well, I bought a lovely new 'at – it was ever such a bargain, only nineteen and eleven. You should see it, Kit, it's a cloche in blue taffeta; I'll go an' get it in a minute if you like – you can try it on. An' I bought a pair of shoes and two pairs of silk stockings. I was able to open an account at the West End store and now if I want anything, I just put it on me account – you should get one, Kit, all you 'ave to do is pay a shilling a week an' then you can go an' buy things when you want to.'

Rose snorted.

'What a fine thing that is, getting in debt before you've even started out. It'll all end in tears. An' whoever 'eard of a nineteen and eleven 'at, for goodness' sake?'

'I'll be careful, Ma, I promise – ev'ryone likes new clothes.'

''Ow you settlin' into that nobby place of yours, Kit?' asked Jack.

'Ooh, Jack, it's lovely an' you still 'aven't bin to visit us yet. I know, why don't you all come for tea tomorrow and then I'll show you round?'

Kitty looked at Eddy, momentarily forgetting he was there, so quiet was he.

'Would that be all right, Ed?'

'Of course – it'd be lovely.'

'That's settled then, come at three o'clock – you'll come won't you, Da?'

'Just you try an' stop me.' Bill began to fill his pipe. 'I'm just off outside for a smoke. D'you want to join me, Eddy?'

The two men went out into the yard where Eddy lit a cigarette. Bill turned to him.

'I've seen a change in my Kitty since she married you – I don't think I've ever seen 'er so 'appy. You carry on like that and we'll always rub along very nicely, me an' you.'

'I promise I'll always look after her, Mr Pengelly.'

'I think, young man, it's about time you called me Bill.'

'All right then, Bill.'

Inside Jack and Ruby cleared away the tea things while Kitty and Rose sat and talked. Rose picked up her knitting.

'Eddy's such a nice young man, I really like 'im – an' 'e's good to you.'

'I really love 'im, Ma.'

'Anyone with eyes in their 'ead can see that.' Rose smiled. She was so happy for Kitty. She hoped that Ruby would find someone as nice as Eddy.

'We might be gettin' a car, Ma.'

Jack came rushing in from the kitchen.

'Did you say a car? Well, you'll be too important to speak to the likes of us soon then.'

'Don't be stupid, Jack – it'll only be a second-hand one, nothing grand.'

Rose looked up from her knitting.

'Even so, no one in this family 'as ever owned a motor car before.'

The Pengellys and the Rashleighs got together for a game of cards before it was time to leave.

They all said their goodbyes and Kitty and Eddy left for home.

Norma Berryman was soon installed back in her old job at the Falmouth Library. The head librarian, a very nice woman called Alice Treleaven, of whom Norma was very fond, had had to take on someone temporary but she had kept Norma's job open. She told her that she had always hoped she would come back and that giving her job to someone else would feel like an admission that something serious had happened to her. Norma was extremely grateful. She was already feeling much better and being back home with her parents was aiding her recovery. On her first Monday back, Miss Treleaven came to speak with her.

'Norma, dear, I'm so pleased to have you back.'

'I'm very pleased to be back, Miss Treleaven – and thank you for keeping my job for me; not many would have done that.'

'You're very welcome, my dear. Now, I have a little favour to ask, but only if you're feeling up to it. The lady that took your place in your absence, although very kind and well-meaning, wasn't particularly efficient and, as a result, I have a rather large backlog to deal with. I was wondering if you're well enough to stay behind tonight to help me with it? Of course, I'll allow you an extended lunch break in addition to the overtime.'

'I don't see why not, Miss Treleaven. I'll just let my parents know when I go home at one o'clock.'

'Thank you, Norma. That will be such a big help to me. Take from one till three if you wish.'

Norma continued her day until the library closed, then she sat with Miss Treleaven to have a cup of tea and to get her instructions. There was certainly a lot of work which had been left undone and the two women just about finished at half past nine. Miss Treleaven locked up the library and said goodbye to Norma as she went towards her home in Lister Street. Norma left the library and walked in the other direction. She carried on until she reached the top of the thoroughfare known locally as the Rope Walk. As she started on to this road she heard footsteps behind her. It was dark now and she felt a little nervous. She quickened her step, breathing rapidly. Still the footsteps came behind. Then nothing. She gained enough courage to look behind her. There was no one. She stopped and smiled to herself she had imagined it – after all she still wasn't completely recovered from her illness. She carried on in the direction of her home which was quite close now. Then she froze. She distinctly heard a voice. A very audible voice but yet a whisper.

'Norma.'

She hurried on now, a feeling of terror inside her. She was running, she didn't look behind. The footsteps were there again, quicker now.

'Norma.'

She could see her house. She ran faster than ever, flying through the garden gate and up to the front door. She couldn't find her key. She hammered on the door, still fumbling in her handbag. A light appeared in the small glass panel at the top of the door which was quickly opened. There stood her father.

'Hello, Norma, love, I was just coming to meet you – it's getting a bit late. Come in now.'

Norma went inside, not daring to look behind her out into the garden.

Chapter Eleven

The day of Rupert Hatton's funeral arrived and it was a warm and sunny one. The service was to be held at Budock Church, followed by interment in the churchyard there. The church was very close to Penvale Manor and this was where the family worshipped. Sir Charles Hatton had himself been buried here quite recently. Bartlett and Boase arrived at ten minutes to eleven and sat at the back of the church. Bartlett didn't want particularly to meet anyone but was interested in who might show up. The funeral service began at eleven o'clock. Lady Hatton sat at the front next to her son's coffin, her one remaining son by her side. Shortly after, the funeral procession was led outside and there Rupert Hatton was laid to rest in the family grave. Bartlett looked at his assistant.

'I don't see anything or anyone unusual here, do you, Boase?'

'Don't think so, sir.'

As the mourners prepared to follow Algernon Hatton and his mother back to Penvale Manor, Boase walked across the neatly cut grass to the chauffeur-driven car. Hatton, seeing Boase approaching, got out of the car.

'Thank you so much for coming, Constable Boase. I hope you and Inspector Bartlett will come back to the house for a drink?'

'Thank you, sir, that would be very nice.'

Boase walked back across the grass to where Bartlett was standing.

'What was all that about?'

'He asked if we would go back to the house for a drink. I hope you don't mind, I said we would. We've found nothing here – I thought we might get the opportunity to snoop a bit at Penvale Manor.'

'All right, Boase, we'll go.'

When they arrived at the manor house, many of the mourners had already arrived. Maids and footmen wearing black armbands lined the entrance hall bearing trays of glasses. There was everything – mulled wine, whisky, sherry, brandy, Boase had never seen so much drink. He walked through into another reception room which was laid out as if for a banquet. There were about fifty people milling around, talking, drinking, eating. Bartlett and Boase had a look around and weighed up the guests. Nothing out of the ordinary seemed to be happening. Bartlett couldn't help but think that he had never seen so many wealthy people in one place; no one here was short of a bob or two. These were exactly the same types as those who had taken advantage of Maude Mockett. Their sort never changed. No, Bartlett had no time for these people; he didn't like them and he didn't feel comfortable with them. He had grown up in an area where people didn't have enough money to eat, couldn't feed or clothe their children, and where the infant mortality rate was so high that in many families a child was lucky to see the age of five.

Bartlett had asked one of the maids if he and Boase might have some tea and this was promptly brought to them and placed on a side table where, conveniently, there were two chairs. The two men sat down and watched the people moving around. Finishing his tea, Boase stood up.

'I think I'll get some fresh air, sir.'

'I'll join you, Boase.'

They both left by the front door. Bartlett lit his pipe and stood at the front of the house admiring the parkland. Boase took a walk around the back. He wanted to see the rest of the grounds. By going around the side of the house, he found himself in a courtyard which was lined on one side with the stables. All the doors were open and some very expensive-looking motor cars were parked inside. Boase strolled over to them. There were about ten cars in the stables. No one was around so he wandered amongst them – he wouldn't get the opportunity to see so many fancy cars like this again. As he was admiring a fast-looking little two-seater, his coat brushed against something hanging from the wing mirror. He stood back to see what it was. It was a green, rubber bag, like a sort of washbag which sealed shut. Boase had never seen such a neat little bag before. It appeared airtight and watertight. He wondered what this had to do with motor cars; perhaps it was for tools or something. He picked it up and looked at it and then replaced it on the mirror. He could have done with something like that in the trenches to keep his things dry – just the job that would have been. He carried on walking to the end of the line of cars then went back to the front of the house to meet up with Bartlett.

'See anything?' Bartlett asked.

'No, not really, sir, just some very nice cars garaged up in a stable block.'

The two said their goodbyes to the Hattons and left to return to the police station.

At Mrs Williams's tobacco shop in High Street, Norman was in trouble again. Mrs Williams had asked Kitty to check the day's takings and they were found to be short.

'Norman, come in 'ere,' Mrs Williams' voice boomed from the shop. Norman dropped the broom with which he was sweeping the stockroom floor and ran into the shop.

'Yes, Mrs Williams?'

'Norman, we are missing two and four-pence – can you account for it?'

'No, Mrs Williams ... well...'

'Well, what?'

Norman started to shake and get confused.

'I'll try an' sort this out, Mrs Williams, you go up and 'ave your tea,' Kitty offered.

'I will not. This idiot is always making mistakes and costing me money and now 'e's gone too far.'

The miserly shopkeeper frequently forgot that she had to make allowances for Norman, and also that she was paying him next to nothing anyway.

'A man came in for some tobacco, an' 'e gave me a ten bob note, an' then 'undreds of people came all at once, an' I must 'ave got mixed up.'

'Well, we're two an' four short and it's comin' out of your wages each week until it's paid back.'

Mrs Williams left the shop and went upstairs.

Norman look devastated. Kitty put her arm around him.

'Don't worry, Norman, I'll make a deal with you. Seem' as it was partly my fault too 'cos I was too busy to 'elp you, I'll go 'alves with you, all right?'

'It wasn't your fault, Kitty. I can't let you do that.'

'Yes you can – anyway, I'm a married woman now, I've got pots of money.' She winked at him and he smiled.

Back at the station, Boase was putting on his coat to go home. Bartlett looked up.

'Doing anything tonight, my boy?'

'No, sir, nothing.'

'Come round for your tea if you like – Mrs Bartlett mentioned it this morning and I forgot to ask you; half past seven all right?'

'Yes, sir, thank you, sir.'

Bartlett knew that Boase wouldn't refuse – he also knew that if he had told him that morning, the young man would not have got half as much work done as he had. Caroline Bartlett had told her husband what a special relationship Boase and Irene had. 'As if I hadn't noticed,' Bartlett had thought to himself. No one really would ever be good enough for his beloved Irene, but Archie Boase was a very good candidate.

Boase arrived at the Bartlett house at half past seven, eager to see Irene again; he hadn't seen her since the night of the fair when they had kissed. How would she be with him tonight? Irene answered the door. She looked lovely and she beamed when she saw him standing on the step.

'Hello, Archie, I'm very pleased to see you,' and she kissed him on the cheek.

'Hello, Irene. You look nice.' He stood there, not quite knowing what to say.

'Well, come on in then, you silly goose,' she laughed and pulled him into the hall where she took his hat and coat and hung them on the hall stand.

'Mum and Dad are in here. Supper's ready.'

They both went into the dining room. Topper came over to Boase, sniffed his hand and lay back down again by Bartlett's chair.

Caroline came in from the kitchen carrying two plates of food.

'Hello, Archie. How are you? You can come to the table now if you like – everything's ready.'

The three Bartletts and Archie Boase sat down to a supper of fish, boiled potatoes and peas followed by a homemade treacle pudding with custard. Boase stood up to clear the table.

'That was lovely, Mrs Bartlett, thank you.'

'I told you before, Archie, it's Caroline – and don't thank me, Irene did nearly all of it – she's becoming quite a good cook these days, aren't you dear?'

'Stop it Mum.' Irene looked embarrassed.

Bartlett stood up from the table.

'Don't you be ashamed of being a good cook, my girl, never. Since the war, and don't any of you get me wrong, but since the war, with all these women going out to work and taking on men's jobs, well, they seem to have lost interest in domestic life. We couldn't have won the war without them, I daresay, but there's something right about coming home to a good woman and a good dinner on the table. These days, young couples, both working, hardly ever see each other. Do you know, there's one man in Falmouth, comes home from work every night and cooks for his wife and the nippers while she's out cleaning offices. Can you believe it? She comes home and her dinner's ready and the children have already been put to bed by him. I ask you – who ever heard of such a thing, and making a fool out of her husband like that; why, he must be the talk of Falmouth. So, no don't you be ashamed to cook, especially good, plain, English food. Now, there's another thing...'

Irene nudged Boase and stifled a giggle. Her dad was starting on something now. He had very fixed ideas and opinions and didn't mind who knew!

'...yes, another thing,' he went on. 'What's all this business about foreign food, eh? Tell me that. I heard that in London now they eat snails. Can you believe it, slimy snails, of all things? I wouldn't give you a thank you for them – I've got them all over the garden and they're a perishing nuisance, that's what. I'd rather starve. Give me a nice bit of steak and kidney pudding anytime.'

'Oh, do stop going on, George.' Caroline had had enough. 'The youngsters don't want to listen to you moaning on. Sit in your chair and I'll get you a nice drop of Leonard's –

that's English, I take it?'

'Don't you mock London beer, Princess, there's nothing like it, get one for the boy as well. You'll join me won't you, my boy?'

'Yes, thank you.'

Caroline brought two bottles of Bartlett's favourite tipple. He had drunk Leonard's London beer for years and was never known to drink anything else. Brewed in the East End, it was a strong, dark ale – a real man's drink, Bartlett called it. Sadly there was only one public house in the area that sold it – happily, the Seven Stars was about a one-minute walk from the police station. Bartlett never sat and drank in pubs but he always liked to have some beer at home, so he often called into the Seven Stars on his way back from work to pick up half a dozen bottles for himself and a couple of pale ales for Caroline; it would do her good, he told her, and she often had one before going to bed at night.

Bartlett and Boase sat beside the fire drinking, with Topper lying across the hearth rug enjoying the warmth. Bartlett put down his glass.

'I hate to talk shop, my boy, but what did you make of that funeral today? I really expected to see someone or something that might help us.'

'I don't know what to think; all I saw was some expensive motor cars, as I told you –

they must have an awful lot of money to burn, that's all I can say. You'll laugh, but I found a bag hanging on one of the car mirrors and I was just thinking what a handy thing that would have been in the trenches. I've never seen anything like it – completely airtight and watertight, a really good invention. Couldn't think what it was used for though. Tools, maybe, although I don't know why you'd want to keep your tools dry and airtight.'

'Don't know either,' mused Bartlett. 'How big was it?'

'Well I'd say ... wait a minute.' Boase put down his glass and leaned forward in his chair. Topper sat up and looked at him.

'I'd say it was revolver-sized.'

'What? What do you mean, revolver-sized?' Bartlett looked at him enquiringly.

'Well, I've just had a really mad thought. Just listen before you say anything. There were no footprints on the bank, right? What if the murderer swam through the water with the gun in that bag, or a bag like it? I had real trouble keeping my gun dry in the trenches and that crossed my mind when I saw that bag hanging on the car mirror. The killer could have shot Rupert Hatton from the water and then swam away again, leaving no footprints.'

'Seems a bit far-fetched to me.' Bartlett finished his beer. 'So, are you saying that the murderer used that bag to keep a gun dry then hung it on a mirror on that car in the Hatton's motor garage?'

'Why not?'

Bartlett looked perplexed.

'So you think someone who lives or works at Penvale Manor killed Rupert Hatton?'

'Maybe – maybe not. We know that Frank Wilson turned up there some time ago demanding money and threatening the Hattons. Maybe he went back there and left it to try to implicate Algernon Hatton. He got rid of one of the twins, perhaps he thinks he can despatch Algernon by laying his brother's murder at his door.'

'Perhaps. But where does that leave us?'

'I don't know. Maybe we should go down to the pier and river to see if anyone's seen Frank Wilson – they must all know him, he's been running ferries and tugs there for years. Someone might have seen him; we know he's still around.'

'That's not a bad idea, my boy. We'll go down there tomorrow, ask some questions.'

The clock in the hall chimed eleven. Boase stood up.

'I really must be going now.' He turned to Caroline.

'Thank you again, Mrs Bartlett.'

'I've told you before, Archie, call me Caroline. And you're very welcome. I hope you come again soon.'

'Goodnight, sir, see you in the morning.'

'Goodnight, my boy. Irene, see Boase out, will you?'

Irene was already waiting with Boase's hat and coat. She handed them to him and he put them on. She opened the front door and they both stood there.

'Thank you for a lovely evening, Irene, and for the food.'

'You're very welcome, Archie. I hope you'll come again soon, it's so nice having you here. Come here – you must do up *all* of your buttons – you'll freeze.'

Irene did up the remaining coat buttons and the couple stood until Irene reached up and put both her arms around Boase's neck and kissed him. She was small and slim, only about five feet in height, and she had to stand on her tiptoes to reach him. This time he wrapped his arms about her narrow waist and kissed her too. They stood for a moment, enjoying their newly found closeness. Boase whispered goodnight in her ear. He didn't want to leave her. He could smell lilacs in her hair; it was lovely. He walked home thinking only of Irene and how lucky he was to have met such a girl.

By nine o'clock the next morning, Bartlett and Boase were at the Prince of Wales Pier hoping to find out more about Frank Wilson. Bartlett lit his pipe and Boase opened a large white paper bag containing one hard-boiled egg and a pork pie.

'Right, Boase, I think we'd be better off splitting up, that way we'll be able to cover more ground. You take a walk up to Customs House Quay and I'll stay around here. Remember, we want to find out if Wilson's been around lately – if he's spoken to anyone, brought a boat in, anything at all.'

'Right-oh, sir.'

Boase walked through the main street until he reached the Quay where several small boats were coming and going and a few men were mending nets. He approached one of them, a swarthy man of about fifty, who sat with a pipe in his mouth, sharpening a piece of wood to make a peg.

'Excuse me, I'm Constable Boase and I was wondering if you could help me?'

'Sit you down, young man,' said the fisherman, pointing to a lobster pot next to him. 'I'm Tommy Medlyn, what can I do for you – looking for a criminal?'

He laughed the loudest laugh Boase had ever heard and all the other fishermen within earshot laughed too.

'Actually, I was wondering if you'd seen Frank Wilson lately, I wanted to speak to him but no one seems to know where he is?'

'Frank Wilson, I 'aven't seen 'im for ... well, must be six months. I tell 'e who might know an' that's Binny Vivian. Look 'e's over there – 'e was quite friendly with Frank for

239

a while, I know. See – 'im with the navy jersey on.'

Boase thanked Tommy Medlyn and made his way across the quay. He approached the man they had talked about. He looked about sixty with a grey beard and very red cheeks. He wore a navy fisherman's jersey, navy trousers and a navy cap. He sat repairing a net.

'Binny Vivian?'

'That's me – who wants to know?'

'I'm Constable Boase, Tommy Medlyn said you might be able to help me.'

'Me? 'Elp the police, it'll be the first time.' Binny Vivian chuckled. 'Sit down, lad. Now, what do 'e want to know then?'

'Do you know where Frank Wilson is?'

'Oh, it's Frank you're looking for, is it? Well I don't know where 'e is at the moment. I saw 'im, I s'pose about a fortnight ago. He came alongside 'ere and asked if I could 'elp 'im with a repair to one of 'is boats.'

'Did you help him?'

'You must be jokin' – it was dark. I'd just come out of the pub and I saw 'im. "Binny," 'e says, 'can you 'elp me with a repair job quickly?' I said I would but not until morning – we wouldn't be able to see. He didn't like it much an' that's the last time I saw 'im. I'm sorry too. I like Frank very much, 'e's a nice boy and was very kind to my wife years ago when she was ill. No, I won't forget his kindnesses. But, young man, I can't tell you anything else because that's all there is.'

'I see,' there was disappointment in Boase's voice, 'well thanks very much, Binny.' As he turned and walked up the quay, a thought came to him. He went back.

'Just one other thing, Binny – how good a swimmer is Frank? Pretty good I imagine, spending his life on the water?'

On hearing this Binny and two other fishermen, who had just joined him, began to laugh. They laughed so much they couldn't tell Boase just what was so funny.

When they had regained their composure, Binny spoke, 'Frank Wilson, a good swimmer? Why 'e couldn't swim if 'is life depended on it – an' it nearly did once. I remember one summer, a few years back, we was all messin' around on the Prince of Wales Pier and Frank got pushed in the water. Well, we was all laughin' until, that is, we suddenly realised 'e couldn't swim a stroke. All his life, as you say, on the water an' 'e can't swim. Who ever 'eard of such a thing, I ask you?'

'Thanks very much, Binny.' Boase couldn't wait to tell this to Bartlett. If Rupert Hatton was shot from the water, it certainly wasn't Frank Wilson in the pool that night.

Boase caught up with Bartlett in the town and together they took the short walk back to the station. Bartlett had gleaned no inform-

241

ation. Boase told him about Frank Wilson not being able to swim. Bartlett listened.

'Well, it may surprise us that he couldn't swim, but what if he went across in a boat?'

'But there was no boat around,' replied Boase, 'we searched the whole pool – we would have seen a boat.'

'I suppose you're right. None of it sounds very convincing. I've arranged to meet Norma Berryman this afternoon – it's her half day. I want to ask her more about Ivy Williams.'

At one o'clock Bartlett met Norma Berryman in George's cafe. They had a cold lunch of veal and ham pie, bread, and pickles. Bartlett asked about Ivy Williams.

'Tell me more about what happened when Ivy found out that one of the Hattons was her father.'

'Well, Mr Bartlett, I can't really tell you any more. I did find it a bit strange when she told me that they would have to pay for what they'd done, I didn't really know what she meant by that.'

'Did you tell her that she was a twin?'

'No, I felt like I'd shocked her enough – I thought that maybe I'd tell her in the future, but it's too late now and she'll never know. It's just too sad, don't you agree, Mr Bartlett?'

'Yes, I agree, Norma. Can you remember anything else?'

'No, really I can't. But there *is* something I want to tell you.'

'Go on.'

'Well, I hope you don't think I'm being silly, but when I left work late the other night, I thought I was being followed. I got as far as the Rope Walk when I heard footsteps behind me. They quickened when I walked quicker then, twice, someone said my name, sort of hushed but loud. I was very frightened, Mr Bartlett. I was lucky I was quite near to home so I ran the rest of the way. I know I'm still not fully recovered yet and when I got home I just thought that it was, well, in my mind – that it never really happened. But I was so scared, Mr Bartlett, I really was.'

'Did you tell your parents?'

'Oh, no. They'd be so worried.'

'Norma, I want you to do something for me; I want you to promise me now, that while all this unsolved business is still going on, you won't stay out at night on your own – not even working late; make sure someone meets you. I don't want to alarm you, but I want you to be careful. Your parents have only just got you back and I want to keep you safe for them.'

'Am I in danger, Mr Bartlett?'

'I don't think so, Norma, but you do know a lot which isn't a good situation to be in. Just be vigilant, all right?'

'All right, Mr Bartlett, I will, I promise.'

'Fancy a trip out to Penvale Manor, Boase?'

'What for, sir?'

'Well I spoke with Norma yesterday and something's been playing on my mind ever since. She said that when she told Ivy Williams about her father, Ivy said that they were going to pay for what they'd done. I wonder if one of them is responsible for her murder.'

'Why have you changed your mind, sir?'

'What if Ivy Williams was blackmailing the Hattons? What if she was tapping them for money and they'd had enough of her?'

'I suppose it's possible, sir. I hadn't thought of that.'

'Neither did I when Norma first told me – when she said it again yesterday I just had a feeling about it all. That's why I want to go over to see Hatton. Coming?'

Algernon received his guests in the blue drawing room. There was a fire blazing in the huge marble fireplace, which was very welcoming on such a cold February day. Bartlett stepped nearer to it.

'I'm sorry to bother you, sir, so soon after the funeral.'

'That's all right, Inspector, how can I help you?'

Bartlett had nothing to lose now.

'I was wondering if you had any contact with Ivy Williams before her death?'

'Ivy Williams? Why should I?'

'This might be a good time, sir, to tell you that I know that you and your brother were related to her, so you don't need to hide it from me.'

Algernon walked over to a drinks cabinet and poured himself a large whisky. Bartlett and Boase declined his offer to join him. He sat down in a big leather armchair and Bartlett sat in the chair opposite him.

'Well, if you know, I suppose there's nothing I can do to cover any of it up, is there?'

'No, sir. Please tell us everything you know.'

Boase continued to wander around the large drawing room studying the paintings and photographs which hung on the walls.

Algernon began, 'Some time last year, this woman wrote a letter to us asking for money. She said she knew about my brother and me, that one of us was her father and that the least we could do was to pay her a regular income or she would bring shame and scandal on our family. Naturally, we both knew what unfortunate events had taken place here at the house so many years ago and my brother and I discussed what to do, at length. Rupert was always for a quiet life. I said that we shouldn't pay her – he said we should, that we owed her that much considering the hardship she had suffered. Rupert would go out of his way to keep the peace, he was a very nice man.'

Hatton paused and lit a cigarette.

'My brother didn't want my mother to find out – the shock and the shame would probably have killed her; that's what made up my mind. As you may know, my father was involved at the time and knew everything, but my poor dear mother, well, it would just be too much for her to bear.'

Algernon Hatton poured himself another large drink and continued his story.

'We agreed to pay her ten pounds a month, which I thought was excessive, but we did it anyway. We set up an account with our bank and had the money put in for her so she could take it when she wanted.'

'How long did the payments continue, sir?'

'Just two months – but, I promise you, Inspector, we didn't kill her. It doesn't look very good though, does it?'

Bartlett had to agree.

'Can I ask you a personal question, sir?'

'I suppose so.'

'Which of you was her father?'

'Well, that's something that's known only to my brother and me, well, only to me now. Oh, what the hell – it was me, I was her father. My brother told me to leave Maude Mockett alone but I was stupid. I would have done anything in those days, just for fun – and I admit I've hurt people through my selfishness and stupidity but – murder? No.'

At those words the door opened and Lady Hatton stood there. She walked into the room.

'Hello, Inspector Bartlett, Constable Boase.' She turned to Algernon who had stood up when she entered the room.

'Oh, Mother, were you listening?'

'Yes, Algie, I was. But don't worry – I know about my grandchild.'

'But ... but how?'

'It's a long story, Algie, darling, but believe me, I know. You boys were always keeping your little secrets – but this? I'm sorry it was all hidden from me but, well, I can understand your father not wanting anyone, including me, to know. You must feel very sad to have lost your daughter. I'm sorry.'

'I'm sorry too, Mother. I really didn't have anything to do with her murder – you must believe that.'

'I believe you, dear – but it's not what I think that counts.'

Boase had finished looking at the pictures and now sat at the back of the room, listening to all that was being said.

Bartlett stood up.

'Thank you for being so honest with us, sir, I'm sure it wasn't easy but there is just one more thing.'

'What, Inspector?'

'Could you tell me where you were on the night of Ivy's murder?'

'I can't even remember when it was.'

'I'll remind you, sir – it was the night of the twenty-fifth and twenty-sixth of November.'

'I'd have to check my old diary, wait a moment please.' He left the room and returned with his journal. He leafed through to that date.

'Oh, I do remember – look. Rupert and I had supper with the Carlisles out at Mawnan Smith. We spent the night there – had a bit too much to drink. They'll confirm, I'm sure.'

'Thank you, sir, thank you, Lady Hatton. I won't trouble you any further. Good day.'

When Bartlett and Boase left the house, they stopped and looked at each other.

'What do you make of all that then, Boase?'

'Quite unbelievable, sir. There's another thing.'

'What's that?'

'Well, I know it probably doesn't prove anything, but when I was looking at the pictures in that room, there was a photograph of Algernon Hatton winning a national swimming competition in 1896. Looks like he was a good swimmer.'

'You're right, Boase, it doesn't prove anything. Let's make a move now.'

They made their way back to Falmouth to arrange to visit the Carlisles at Mawnan Smith. Bartlett felt he ought to establish an alibi, just in case – he couldn't afford to take any risks at this stage.

Later that afternoon, Bartlett and Boase were on their way to Truscott House at Mawnan Smith. Bartlett had met the Carlisles when he and Caroline had attended a charity dinner a couple of years before; he thought she and her husband were a very nice couple. Peter Carlisle had bought the house just before the war. He had met Helen in his home town of Salisbury and they married there about six years ago. Bartlett had thought it strange, though, that a man of almost fifty should be married to a young woman of thirty. Why, she wasn't much older than his Irene! Having such a big place with plenty of land allowed Peter Carlisle to indulge his passion for breeding racehorses. The couple could afford to do a lot for charity, they were very wealthy – something Bartlett didn't like much. However, the Carlisles were very nice, ordinary people, and very generous to those less well-off, so that counted in their favour as far as he was concerned.

The two arrived at Truscott House and approached it down a long drive which, in a few weeks, would burst into life with beautiful rhododendrons. The house was early Victorian and very large. Two splendid racehorses were being walked across the drive as they reached the house. To the right was a vast stable block and plenty of people hard at work cleaning, grooming, and all the associated equine-related tasks. Bartlett and Boase walked up to the front door but as they were about to ring the bell they heard a voice.

'Hello, can I help you?'

They turned round and Bartlett at once recognised Helen Carlisle walking towards them across the lawn. She wore a long grey coat and, much to Boase's surprise, grey trousers with knee-length boots.

'George, how lovely to see you again.' She shook his hand.

'Hello, Helen. How are you? This is Constable Boase – Archie.'

She shook Boase's hand too.

'Hello, Archie. What brings you all the way out here, George?'

'Well, I was hoping you could clarify something for me, Helen.'

'Why don't you come into the house and have a cup of tea?'

'That would be very nice, thank you.'

Bartlett and Boase followed her into a large hallway and through to the kitchen at the back of the house – this room alone was almost the size of Bartlett's entire ground floor at home. They sat at a long wooden table and Helen made tea. Through a doorway a maid was preparing vegetables in the scullery.

'Peter's out at the moment – he would

have loved to have seen you again. How's Caroline?'

'She's a bit under the weather sometimes, but not too bad at the moment, thank you.'

'Your wife is such a lovely lady. Wish her well from me, won't you?'

'Of course I will.'

'You must come over for dinner some time – catch me up on all the latest police work you've been doing. What can I do for you today, anyway?'

'Well, I was just wondering if you could verify that Rupert and Algernon Hatton stayed with you one night last November?'

'Ooh, is this an alibi?'

'Sort of.'

'Yes. They did stay here. It was the twenty-fifth of November – I remember because it was my mother's fiftieth birthday and I really wanted to go up to London and see her, but Peter had some people over, including those blasted Hatton twins. To be perfectly honest, I can't bear them; well, just the one really, I suppose, but they were investing in some racehorses, so I suppose it was in the best interests of the business to keep them sweet. Yes, they were here all right. They drank and ate so much, I thought they ought to stay; they were in no fit state to go home. You don't need to take my word for it, most of the servants were here that night – they would all have seen them.'

'Your word is good enough for me, Helen. Did you know that there is now only one Hatton twin?'

'No, whatever do you mean?'

'Rupert Hatton was found murdered recently – his funeral was last week.'

'Oh, my God. Oh, I didn't mean to speak ill of the dead.' Helen Carlisle was visibly shocked.

'Don't worry, Helen. I'm sorry I sprang it on you like that.' Bartlett patted her hand.

'And he was always such a gentleman. He was always the nicer of the two – so kind and gentle – unlike his brother, I'm afraid. They were like chalk and cheese, that's for sure. Do you know who killed him?'

'No, we don't – yet.' Bartlett looked disappointed.

'Well, I wish you luck with your investigations, really I do. And you, Archie.'

'Thank you,' Boase replied.

Helen Carlisle saw the two men to the door and they left for Falmouth.

'She doesn't think much of Algernon, does she, Boase?'

'Certainly doesn't, sir. Don't blame her either.'

'Hmmmmm. Cast-iron alibi, though, I'd say.'

Chapter Twelve

Boase brought two cups of hot tea into the office. He handed one to Bartlett, the other he put on his own desk. He rummaged in his drawer and pulled out a white paper bag from which he took an enormous slice of bacon and egg pie and a tomato. He began to eat.

'How can you carry on like that, Boase? You're going to be sorry when you're my age, mark my words. I've never known anyone eat so much as you. Doesn't that landlady of yours feed you?'

'Of course she does, sir – very well, in fact – but this is my emergency food.'

'What for?'

'For an emergency. Like me getting hungry.'

Bartlett gave up. He had a lot of time for the younger generation – many of them had sacrificed their youth in recent times – but sometimes, he just couldn't understand them. He drank his tea. 'Guess what, Boase?'

'Umm – dunno, give up. What?'

'The police in Camborne caught someone breaking into a public house in Trevenson Street last night.'

'Why would they tell us that, sir?'

'Well, the culprit was Jan Rowe.'

'*Him* again. I saw him the other day with Norman Richards at Swanpool.'

'Yes, well, he's only just come out of prison and then he goes and does a fool thing like this and, not only that, he admitted to breaking in at the tobacconist's shop before.'

'What? He robbed his own godmother?'

'Yes. She was telling me before that she gave him everything he could want – and then more. And this is how he repays her. You have to feel sorry for the woman.'

'Did Norman have anything to do with this?'

'I asked that myself but apparently he wasn't mentioned. Just as well.'

Boase withdrew a large apple from the drawer in his desk.

'I don't understand why Frank Wilson didn't come for that money, Boase.'

'Nor me, sir. And where is he now?'

'I wish I knew.'

As the two began to plan their day, the desk sergeant knocked on the door and entered.

'Sorry to bother you, sir, there's a young lady outside, would like to see you. Her name is Miss Hesketh – says it's to do with Ivy Williams.'

'Send her in.' Bartlett and Boase looked at each other. Miss Hesketh?

The woman came into the office. She was

about average height, with brown, wavy hair just visible from underneath a very expensive-looking hat; her clothes were expensive too. She wore a powder blue silk dress with a matching short jacket, matching shoes and handbag. A forlorn-looking dead animal was draped around her shoulders – Boase stared at it disapprovingly. He was firmly of the opinion that wild animals belonged in the wild. The young woman's make-up was very obvious but only enhanced her already glamorous features. Boase thought she looked like a film star. Bartlett couldn't place it, but he thought she looked very familiar. He brought over a chair for her and she sat down.

'Good morning, Miss Hesketh, I am Inspector Bartlett, this is my assistant, Constable Boase. How can we help you?'

'I know who you both are – I've been reading about your murder cases in the newspapers. My name is Gloria Hesketh. Ivy Williams was my twin sister.'

Bartlett and Boase looked at each other astounded. Bartlett now knew why she looked familiar; the two women were almost identical. He sat down in his chair.

'Well, we're very pleased to meet you, Miss Hesketh, very pleased indeed. But what brings you here?'

'I want to help you to catch whoever killed my sister. I don't know how I can help, but I understand you're no further forward with your investigations?'

Bartlett felt uncomfortable. Partly because he didn't like his professionalism being undermined, which he felt it was now, and partly because Gloria Hesketh was a very, very beautiful woman and, surprisingly for Bartlett, he felt intimidated.

Gloria Hesketh continued. 'I may be able to tell you things you don't already know. I have known that I am a twin ever since I was six years old. My parents couldn't have children of their own – my father was much older than my mother, and, having made a good deal of money as a Member of Parliament and from some prudent investments, he wanted someone to leave it to. So, when they heard from a friend who was a workhouse benefactor that a baby was available for adoption, it solved all of his problems immediately. Ideally I think he would have liked a son but, being rather forward-thinking for the time, he didn't mind women being given an opportunity. My mother, too, had always wanted a baby so I suppose it seemed the ideal solution. About four weeks after they had taken me to London, they found out that I was a twin. They tried to get Ivy as well – they would have loved two of us and they could easily have afforded it, but by the time they found out, she had been taken by someone else. I grew up in a very privileged environment with a private education and everything I could have asked for but I didn't really want it all –1 would much rather have had my sister. I always knew where she was and I hoped to meet her some day. As a little girl, I used to play games and always pretended my twin sister was playing along with me. Even when I had tea parties, I always laid a place for her. I always wanted to get in touch with her, but couldn't ever summon up the nerve to make contact, until I had the money. When I saw her picture in the paper, of course, I was horrified. I didn't know she was dead until a week or so after it had happened. I looked at the newspaper and there was me, staring back at myself. When I was nineteen I had become a nurse and went to France. I couldn't believe what I saw there. I was there for two years.'

This woman had suddenly gone up in Bartlett's estimation – beautiful, caring, and with a conscience.

'My parents died very recently – within six months of each other and I was left thinking what to do next. They left me bags of money, which is nice but by no means everything. Then I saw the solicitor's advertisement in the newspaper. I don't know what I was thinking of but I pulled it off. I suppose I was bored and it was a risk. When I was at boarding school, all the other girls knew I would do anything for excitement and to make people laugh and I got into all sorts of scrapes – anything for fun; this didn't really seem any different. Of course, I didn't need the money and I realised afterwards what a ridiculous thing I'd done. I didn't know Ivy had been murdered until after I'd arrived in Falmouth.'

Bartlett interrupted her.

'How long have you been in the town, Miss Hesketh?'

'Gloria, please. Since shortly after I collected the money. I stayed here following your progress in the papers and learning bits and pieces from overhearing gossip – I didn't want to interfere but a few days ago I decided that if there was any way I could help, then I should. I've had a fairly wretched time of it, too. People staring at me wherever I go. I spent Christmas all alone and I've been completely miserable the whole time. I blame myself for not contacting Ivy sooner. I didn't want to upset my parents, although I suppose they wouldn't have minded. Ivy didn't know about me and I feel so terrible. I can't seem to get over everything that's happened. How can I miss her, Inspector Bartlett, when I didn't even know her – why do I feel this way?'

Bartlett felt extremely sorry for the girl.

'They say, Gloria, that there's a special bond between twins that no one, not even top scientists and the like, can understand. Twins have been split up as babies and still felt close after meeting up maybe sixty years later – I've read about such things. So, you're probably feeling the same way. It's just so very tragic, my dear, that this has all turned out this way. But, you really mustn't blame yourself for any of it, it's not your fault.'

'Thanks, Inspector Bartlett, you're very kind. Anyway to go on with my story, I hadn't broken the law or anything by taking the money because I am Maude Mockett's daughter, although I wasn't living in the town they said. But, I'd always had a copy of Ivy's birth certificate. I don't really know where it came from – I think my parents may have had it from the time when they were trying to get Ivy too. Anyway, afterwards, I felt sure Ivy would be glad of the money and I came here to find her. I thought we could be real sisters and make up for lost time. I was quite happy to share the money with her – she could have had it all if she wanted it, I've got plenty. A few days after I got here, I found out about her. I can't tell you how awful I felt. Sitting in a room in a strange house, in a strange town with not a friend in the world and my only sister dead – and she never even knew I existed.'

A tear fell from Gloria's cheek and Bartlett offered his handkerchief. This was a tragic tale if ever he'd heard one.

She went on, 'So I wanted to come and tell you who I am and to say that I'll do anything to help you find out who killed Ivy.'

Bartlett stood up.

'Well, I'm very pleased you did, Gloria. How long are you staying in Falmouth?'

'I don't know; I haven't got to be any-where, haven't got anywhere to go, really.'

'Well, we'll keep in touch with you and if we feel you can help us, we'll let you know, all right? Just make sure you leave us the address you're staying at.'

'You're very kind, thank you. Goodbye, Inspector Bartlett, Constable Boase.'

Gloria Hesketh left the office.

'Well, that's a turn up for the books, sir.'

'Isn't it just, Boase?'

As the light faded, Archie Boase packed a large flask of tea and some sandwiches. He put on his thickest jumper and trousers and a warm coat and woollen hat. Tonight he was going to take a walk along the cliffs – he often did. There was something about the cliffs and the sea at night. During the day he could watch birds and paint or draw them but, at night, sometimes, he just liked to sit quietly and think. Some of his best ideas had come to him, alone, looking out at the ships lit up in the bay. He piled his food and drink into his haversack and quietly left the house. It was almost ten o'clock. Boase thought he'd probably stay out until about one or two. Bartlett had said he could go into work at eleven tomorrow so he didn't even have to get up early. He hadn't decided where to go yet, but he found himself walking out to Gyllyngvase Beach. From there he walked towards Pendennis Point and found a small path which led down the side of the cliff. He found a large boulder and settled himself down, resting against it. From here he could see several ships in the bay and a few houses with their lights twinkling in the distance.

Boase felt hungry immediately and opened his food and his flask of tea. As he ate and drank, he could see a few old rotting boats moored almost directly underneath where he was sitting. People often abandoned boats – either they had become so bad that they were beyond a state where repair was an option, or they simply couldn't sell them and they had become a liability. This particular spot always seemed to be the place where they were left – a sort of boat graveyard, Boase always thought. He could see five now, silhouetted in the moonlight.

Two had tall masts and he could hear as the boats gently clanked their sides against one another as if in conversation. He continued to eat, discarding his crusts for any wildlife that might pass hungrily that way later. As he finished his tea, he could plainly hear a courting couple nearby – this definitely wasn't something Boase wanted to witness any further; now they'd spoiled it. He picked up his bag and walked quickly away and in the direction of the abandoned boats.

Having found himself a new spot to settle, Boase sat back and looked out to sea. In the quietness of the night he could hear strange thumping sounds coming from the direction of the five boats. He listened again. Quiet now. He thought it must be his imagination. Then there it was again. He moved nearer the cliff edge and looked directly down on to the boats; he was very close now. Voices. He heard voices. He listened again then thought he saw a light – like a match being struck. Boase rubbed his eyes. It was getting late, and he should be heading for home. He picked up his bag, took a last look at the abandoned boats and made his way back to Melvill Road.

The next morning, Boase was tired. He had returned home just after midnight – the night air had strangely and suddenly turned cold and he had felt a bit restless. He had gone to bed before one o'clock but had been unable to sleep. He got up early, quite forgetting that Bartlett had given him a late start, and arrived at the station before nine o'clock. Bartlett was already at his desk.

'What are you doing here so early, Boase? You're not due in for another two hours.'

'I had a bad night, sir, couldn't sleep – you know how it is.'

Bartlett did, indeed, know how it was.

Caroline was frequently up and about at night and, although she always tried desperately not to wake him, he was a light sleeper and usually got up with her to make sure she was all right. Often, not being able to find sleep again, he would go downstairs, wake Topper and the two of them would take a walk out to the beach. Topper never minded – he was always ready for a walk with his master. So, yes, Bartlett knew what a bad night was. Boase hung up his coat.

'Cuppa, sir?'

'That would be very welcome, Boase – make yourself a strong one too. You look all in.'

Boase returned with the drinks and rummaged in his coat pocket. Pulling out a ham and mustard sandwich, he looked at it triumphantly before ceremoniously laying it out on his desk before him. He took a sip of tea and looked at the sandwich again.

'Are you going to eat that or paint a still life of it?' The older man's voice boomed cynically from the other side of the office. Boase tucked in. Just as he finished, he swept away the remaining crumbs from his desk and lap and looked across at Bartlett.

'Strange thing last night, sir.'

'Oh yes?' Bartlett was writing.

'I went out late for a walk up to Pendennis and sat just above those old rotten boats – you know the ones I mean? A couple of them have been there for years.'

'Yes, I know them – one of them actually used to belong to Alfred Toy's grandfather, no wonder it's falling apart, it must be about a hundred.'

'Well, I was just sitting watching and I saw a light – like a match being struck and I heard strange sounds and voices; I didn't know anyone ever went on those boats.'

'They don't – and they'd be very unsafe if anyone tried to. They should set fire to them – get rid of them. They're an eyesore and a hazard, especially for the nippers that wander around those parts.'

'Well. I always thought they were empty but I know I definitely heard sounds.'

'You know what they say, Boase.'

'What's that then, sir?'

'Empty vessels make most noise.' Bartlett smiled at the look on Boase's face – the young man hated to be ribbed.

'Is today one of the days that Lady Hatton goes to her club, do you know, Boase?' Bartlett was filling his pipe.

'I think that's what she said, sir – why?'

'Well, when we went to Rupert Hatton's funeral, I left a very fine pair of leather gloves at the house – I can't afford to lose them now, can I?'

What an old rogue, Boase thought to himself – the old boy never missed a trick.

'Shall I come with you, sir?'

'Most definitely.'

'So why are we going back, now – you don't really believe that Hatton killed Ivy Williams?'

'Did I say that? No, I don't believe I did. I have, however, been taking in everything you've told me, all the things you tell me you've seen and all the things you tell me you've heard as well as what you think – all crucial to becoming a good policeman, Boase. Come on – ready?'

Boase drove the car and, as they reached the entrance to the drive, Bartlett touched the younger man's shoulder.

'Drive just past here, Boase – it's such a nice day, I think we'll enjoy a walk up the drive to Penvale Manor.'

'Right you are, sir, I'll just pull up over here.'

The car parked, Bartlett and Boase crossed the cattle grid and began the walk up the long drive to the manor house. Parkland was on their right with a large wooded area on the left. Bartlett paused here and there to admire the magnificent plants. He stopped once or twice to quickly nip a couple of cuttings and hastily stuffed them into his pockets. As the two men reached a bend in the drive, a narrow lane through the wood made a short cut to the back of the house; this was regularly used by staff on their way back from the village or church. Boase

265

paused here to tie his shoelace. As he stood up, both men heard a woman's voice, loudly coming from the bushes. They listened.

'It was mean of you – no one will ever think it was me. You tried to trick me. You knew all along that I could get into serious trouble.'

Then another voice – this time a man's.

'But you had no choice. It's in your handwriting. I did you a favour – why, if my mother had found out what you did, you'd have been out of here by now, with no references. You might even be facing prison.'

The woman had stopped shouting now and had begun to sob. Bartlett and Boase looked towards the end of the lane nearest the house. They were about fifty yards away and could now clearly see the uniformed figure of the maid, Annie Bolitho. She was running towards the house. The two onlookers had already established from the voice and the content of the conversation that the second person was none other than Algernon Hatton. They watched until about a minute later he also emerged on to the lane and returned to the house.

Boase looked at Bartlett.

'What's going on, sir?'

'I thought I knew when we came here, Boase, but now, well, I'm not so sure.' Bartlett lit his pipe. The two men continued up to the house and asked to see Algernon

266

Hatton. Unsurprisingly, Annie Bolitho did not open the front door to them, but a butler answered the call of the bell. He led the way into a small drawing room near the back of the house and they waited. After what seemed like an eternity, Algernon Hatton entered the room.

'Good afternoon, gentlemen, I'm so sorry to have kept you waiting. What can I do for you?'

'I'm sure I could have asked your staff this, sir, but I wanted to see how you were anyway. When I came here after your brother's funeral, I don't suppose I left a pair of brown leather gloves behind, by any chance?'

'Oh, they're yours are they? One of the servants found them later on that day – I hoped someone would reclaim them. They're just out on the hall table. I'll go and get them. Wait a moment.'

As Algernon Hatton left the room, Boase, who had been looking around, quickly ripped a sheet of paper from the top of a writing tablet which was open on a desk in the corner of the room. He stuffed it into his pocket. Bartlett looked at him enquiringly but, before he had time to say anything, Hatton had returned with the gloves.

'Here you are, Bartlett.'

'Well, I can't thank you enough, sir, really I can't. My wife bought them for me and I really didn't want to lose them; I was hoping they'd be here. Funny, things are always in the last place you look!'

Bartlett was playing for time while he weighed up Algernon's mood.

'How are you and your mother bearing up?'

'Well, we're managing to get by, that's the main thing I suppose. Mother's at her club – she didn't really want to go but I insisted. I thought it would do her the world of good, you know, to see all her friends.'

'Of course, sir, I'm sure you did the right thing.' Bartlett put the gloves into his pocket.

Boase was thinking that whatever Algernon Hatton was up to with Annie Bolitho earlier on, having his mother out of the way would probably have facilitated it.

As he reached the drawing room door, he turned and addressed Hatton, 'I hope you don't mind me saying, sir, but the last time I was here, I met your cook and I complimented her especially on her fruit cake – she said she'd give me the recipe to pass on to my landlady. Would you mind if I run down to the kitchen before I leave – I won't keep her?'

'No, no, Boase, you go ahead. We're very lucky to have Mrs Rowe. She's an excellent cook – never lets us down, don't know where we'd be without her.'

'Thank you very much, sir.'

Bartlett wasn't sure just exactly what Boase

was up to, nevertheless, he followed him down to the kitchen where Annie Bolitho was sitting at a vast table drinking a cup of tea. She stood up when they came in.

'Please sit down, miss, finish your tea.' Bartlett didn't want any woman standing up when he came into the room.

'My assistant, I believe, was looking for your cook, Mrs Rowe.'

'Cook's gone out – she's gone to the village for a couple of things. She should be back soon. Can I get you a cup of tea?'

Boase sat down next to Annie.

'Mrs Rowe makes a lovely fruit cake and said she'd give me the recipe...'

'Can you cook, then?' Annie Bolitho looked surprised.

'Most definitely not,' Boase laughed, 'but my landlady can and I'd like her to make it for me.'

'Oh, I see, well I couldn't tell you what she puts in it.'

'Does it have a name?' Boase asked, willing it not to be called 'Fruit Cake'.

'Yeah, she calls it "sixty-minute boil fruit" – whoever 'eard of such a daft name?'

Boase, amazed that anything so delicious could sound so repulsive, was nevertheless thankful that it was.

'Oh, I'll never remember that. I could at least tell my landlady what it's called, that is, if you could write it down for me.'

'All right, I'll fetch a pencil and paper.'

Annie collected what she needed from a large drawer in a dresser and sat back down at the table. She almost lay over the work, as a child at school would, for fear of having her work copied.

'Me writing's not very good, mind – 'ere I 'ope you can read it.'

She handed Boase the paper.

'That's perfect, and very kind of you, Annie – it is Annie, isn't it?'

'Yes. And that's all right. You'll 'ave to come back again for the recipe.'

'Yes, I'll do that. Thank you again, Annie.'

Bartlett and Boase left the house and headed back down the long drive. Bartlett couldn't wait a minute longer.

'What was all that about – can I have Mrs Rowe's recipe for sixty-minute boil fruit?'

'Have patience, sir. I'll tell you when we get back to the station,' grinned Boase.

'Right, Boase, you make us both a nice cup of tea and then you can tell me what all that earlier on at Penvale Manor was about.'

Boase made the tea and the two men sat at their desks.

'Do you remember, sir,' Boase began, 'when Algernon Hatton said to Annie Bolitho "It's in your handwriting" and "If my mother had found out what you did..."?'

'Yes, I do.'

'Well, I thought that Annie Bolitho must have done something bad and Hatton found out and started threatening or blackmailing her to the point where he got her right where he wanted her. Anyway, when you were talking to him about your gloves, I looked on the desk and there was a writing tablet with heavy indentations in it so I just quickly took the top sheet off and put it in my pocket. Putting two and two together, I wondered if it was connected to what Hatton had referred to when he said 'it's in your handwriting' and that's why I wanted her to write something down for me to compare.'

'Hence the rubbish about the sixty-minute boil fruit?'

'Exactly – although Mrs Rowe did promise me the recipe, so I wasn't exactly lying, I just hoped Annie would be there to write it down for me.'

'You're good, Boase, very good – I'm impressed.'

'Thank you, sir – shall we have a look at this then?'

He laid the paper with the name of the cake on it in front of Bartlett, then put the seemingly blank sheet of paper next to it. They compared them.

'Did you notice how slowly she wrote, pressing heavily on the paper, sir? Small wonder it came right through the sheet.'

'Yes I did. Your eyes are better than mine,

Boase, read me this note you found.'

Boase, with difficulty, read aloud slowly:

Dearest Rupert
I'm in a spot of bother, old man – you know I've
had trouble with my landlady and my tenancy
is now up. I really must see you as I need your
help. I don't want anyone to see us as I know
you still want to keep us a secret. Meet me at
Swanpool – I shall be waiting at the western end
of the pool at eleven o'clock tonight (Monday).
Please, please come – I need you.
Yours always
Harry

Bartlett walked over to the window and looked out.

'That's incredible.'

'I think there's something else, sir.'

Boase pulled the note Freddie Giles had given him from his desk drawer.

'Look, sir, this note that Harry Watson-Booth gave to Freddie Giles – the one threatening him and Rupert Hatton. It's the same handwriting too.'

Boase laid the three pieces of paper on the desk side by side. Bartlett couldn't believe what he was seeing.

'So, you think that Algernon Hatton murdered his brother because he was having a homosexual affair. He arranged to get Watson-Booth out of the way and got his brother

272

alone at Swanpool. What's more, he used Annie Bolitho to help him. That washbag you saw in the Hatton motor garage must have been his, Boase. Looks like his swimming skills came in handy that night. I want you to get Annie Bolitho here – or go to see her wherever she lives. We need to talk to her.'

'I think she lives in, sir.'

'Then get someone to bring her here.'

Chapter Thirteen

At four o'clock Annie Bolitho sat in the lobby of Falmouth police station. She looked nervous. Constable Penhaligon had brought her in. It was her half day and she wouldn't be missed. Bartlett came to the door of his office.

'Come in, Annie, would you?'

The girl nervously went into the room and stood, timidly fiddling with her handbag. Bartlett offered her a seat.

'Don't be nervous, Annie. I hope you're going to be able to help us – you're not in any trouble. I want to talk to you about Mr Hatton. Is that all right?'

'Yes, sir. Am I goin' to prison?'

'Whatever gave you that idea? Of course you're not going to prison. Boase, fetch Annie a cup of tea.'

Annie stared at the floor and refused to look at either Bartlett or Boase.

Bartlett pulled his chair from behind his desk and sat next to the girl.

'Look, Annie, you're not in any trouble, I promise, and what I'm going to talk to you about is very important. We saw you this morning when you were with Algernon Hatton and we need to know what you were both talking about. There's nothing to be afraid of. Now, do you think you can tell us what's been happening?'

'I'll try.'

Boase brought Annie a strong cup of sugary tea and she sipped it gratefully.

'Well, you see, sir, it's like this. I'd got into trouble – money trouble. There's a tally man that comes to the house every fortnight and all the servants usually buy something from 'im. With our bad wages it's the only way most of us can afford to buy anything at all. Anyway a month or two before Christmas I wanted to get some little things for me ma an' da. They 'aven't got much money an' I've got three younger brothers an' two younger sisters. Well I couldn't see 'em go without on Christmas day so I bought a few things – just some toys for the children, a scarf for me ma, an' a new tobacco pouch for me da. Anyway, I didn't know 'ow much it would all come to, an' when I couldn't pay enough, it just seemed to keep going up so I could never afford to pay it off.'

Annie stopped and rummaged in her bag for a handkerchief. She continued, 'I only wanted to give them something special for Christmas – they never 'ave nothing, honestly they don't. I give 'em what I can each week but that don't come to much. Anyway, Lady Hatton knows we use the tally man and she's quite 'appy about it, but she don't like us getting into too much debt – she says if we buy things we must pay what we owe.'

'That's easy for her to say,' muttered Bartlett under his breath. 'Go on, Annie.'

'Well, one day, I was cleaning the mistress's dressing table and I saw something shining on the floor under the window. I picked it up an' saw it was 'er lovely gold bracelet which she thought she'd lost months before. She never thought she'd see it again so I didn't think she'd miss it if I took it – it would've solved all me problems. Anyway I was stupid an' I got caught by Hatton with it in me pocket. 'E said I could go to prison but 'e wouldn't tell as long as I 'elped 'im with something. I 'ad no choice, did I? Anyway, all it was was writing a couple of letters – I don't know why 'e wanted me to do it, but I did it. Still, I 'ad to give the bracelet back, saying I found it on the floor, an' now I still owe all that money an' I shall get into terrible trouble. Lady Hatton will probably ask me to leave. Oh, the shame for my parents. I don't know what I'm goin' to do, really I don't.'

Annie was really sobbing now and Bartlett put his arm around her shoulder.

'Everything will be all right, Annie, I promise. Now, did you write these?'

He showed her the letters.

'Yes, sir, I did.'

276

'Thank you, Annie. Now, you finish your tea and you can go – mind, don't tell anyone at Penvale that you've been here, all right?'

'All right, sir, I won't.'

Annie left and Bartlett slumped down into his seat.

'Looks like we've got our man, Boase. We'll get him in, then the court can decide. He still maintains though that he didn't have anything to do with Ivy Williams.'

The next morning, Algernon Hatton was brought into the police station on suspicion of his brother's murder. Bartlett went down to see him in his cell.

'Well, well, Hatton, this is a bad business isn't it? Are you going to cooperate and tell me what's been going on?'

'I suppose I've got no choice – I'll bet any money that meddling Bolitho girl had a hand in this, the little thief.'

'Where we get information from is really none of your concern. What I would like is the truth – and I suspect that only you can tell me the real truth.'

Algernon Hatton, all at once, leapt to his feet and began shouting at the top of his voice. The constable present tried to restrain him but he was very strong. He shouted more and waved his arms frantically.

'All right, kill me, go on – see if I care. I've got nothing to live for. Go on, you might as well do it now. I'll admit anything you want me to. None of it matters any more.' The constable and Bartlett finally overpowered him.

Sobbing with exhaustion after his outburst, Algernon sank to his knees in the corner of the cell. Bartlett thought how pathetic he was.

'Constable, fetch Mr Hatton some tea, will you?'

The constable obliged and soon Hatton was sitting quietly drinking his cup of tea. His hands shook as he held the cup.

'What can you tell us about the murders?' Bartlett studied the aristocratic features opposite him and waited for some answers.

'I'll tell you about my brother – I've got nothing to hide now. You want to know if I killed him? Yes, I did. He ruined my life from the time I was four years old. It was always Rupert – Mummy and Daddy's golden boy. Algie could do nothing right. I was always the bad one. Rupert always covered up for me and I hated him for it. He always had to do the right thing. Rupert told me to help Frank Wilson out over the blasted court martial – I would have let him get what he deserved. Of course, my brother was so reasonable about everything. Years ago, when we were young, he was the boring one, I, the adventurous. People who didn't know us very well thought we were alike, but no, we were not alike in any way. When I fooled around with Maude

Mockett, Rupert told me to leave her alone. She was frightened and I knew I was playing with fire but I encouraged her and, well, you know the rest. I ruined everything with my stupidity. I always wanted to have a nice wife and children. It's too late now, I know. Rupert was different. All he wanted was a nice boyfriend. He made me feel sick. I knew about his disgusting ways for years but he kept it from my parents. We used to laugh because our father didn't know which of us had fathered Maude Mockett's child – we knew Rupert would never be seen near a woman. I suppose my parents never thought that there was anything unusual about him – he had girlfriends, of course, but nothing serious.'

Algernon paused to light a cigarette.

'Rupert told me to pay Ivy a lump sum of money to help her out when she started blackmailing us. He said it was the least I could do, but no, I wanted to get rid of her. I didn't do it though. I didn't kill her.'

Bartlett stood up and walked to the other side of the cell. He didn't know what to make of this strange man.

'Carry on, tell us about Ivy's death.'

'Well, I know I said I always wanted children, but, not like that – in that sordid way – and with a servant girl.'

'Well, she was good enough for you when you needed her, wasn't she?' Bartlett was growing irritated. Hatton ignored this last comment.

'Ivy Williams, or whatever her name was, was becoming very difficult – she threatened to tell my mother everything if we didn't pay her more.'

'But why didn't you take your brother's advice and pay her off?'

'I was fed up with the whole thing – I just wanted to be rid of her.'

'So, what did you do – did you kill her?'

'I promise you I didn't. I arranged for someone to do it. As usual, Rupert was telling me not to, but I couldn't take it any longer; especially when she threatened to tell my mother.'

'In fact, your mother had known all along.'

'It seems that way now, yes.'

'So, you didn't need to kill her.'

'I tell you I didn't kill her. I arranged for Frank Wilson to do it – he owed it to me for getting him out of that scrape in '17. I asked him.'

'So, are you saying that Frank Wilson is responsible for murdering your daughter?'

'I thought he had – until Christmas. He turned up at the house threatening us and asking for money. He said the job was done but he hadn't been responsible for it. It was all very strange but he said he didn't know who had killed her.'

'Do you believe him, Hatton?'

'I don't know. There's nothing more for me to be afraid of now. I can't believe that I tried to have my own flesh and blood murdered. My own child – how could I?'

Bartlett didn't know whether to feel sorry for Algernon Hatton or not. He walked over to him.

'There's something you should know. Maude Mockett gave birth to twins.'

'Twins?' Hatton was astounded.

'Yes, twin girls. I've just met the other, Gloria.'

'You mean ... I've still got a daughter? Where is she? Can I see her?'

'Not at the moment, no. We've got a lot to sort out first. Also, she might not want to see you. One more thing – if Frank Wilson didn't kill your daughter – who do you think did?'

'I've really absolutely no idea. No idea whatsoever.'

The evening came and a heavy rain had descended on Falmouth. Boase had gone to bed early but couldn't sleep. He sat up in his bed and looked at his watch – a quarter past eleven. This was no good. He wondered whether he could be bothered to go for a walk; it might just do the trick. He peered out of the window, it was raining harder now. He thought for a moment. Yes, he'd go anyway. He dressed and put on a mackintosh and heavy boots. Quietly he left the house and headed for the beach. He walked and walked. Surely, sleep must come when he finally returned home? It was just after one o'clock now. Thoughts were churning around in his head, the Hattons, Ivy Williams, Gloria Hesketh, Frank Wilson and his money – all these things and then, of course, Irene. Lovely Irene. He hadn't seen her for several days and she was very much in his thoughts.

Boase walked until he felt himself drawn to Pendennis, just as before. He made his way down the little cliff path towards the old wooden boats. He sat down on the wet grass and watched them for a while. He had made himself so comfortable and sheltered against the wind, that he must have fallen asleep for a few minutes. He awoke, his head feeling heavy and disorientated. Something had woken him. He listened. He could definitely hear voices.

He looked down at the boats; there was a light on board one of them. It looked like an oil lamp or a candle. As he watched, the light was extinguished. He continued his vigil and presently he heard a noise like a door slamming shut. He sat up. A dark figure came up from the direction of the boats. Someone was coming along the path towards him. What should he do? He didn't want to be caught. He didn't even know who this was - it could be someone dangerous, even armed. The figure was coming nearer. Boase managed to slide his body along a few feet to a hollow in the side of the cliff. He arched his back, covered his head and hoped that the stranger wouldn't notice him in the darkness. The footsteps were closer now. Closer still. The stranger was here now. Boase didn't move – not even when a heavy foot trod on the corner of his mackintosh. He remained in his position for what seemed like an age until he was sure the footsteps had disappeared. Slowly he lifted his head. All clear. Just what was going on here?

It was still raining. Boase couldn't see his watch and had no idea of the time. He thought perhaps it was about two o'clock. He walked down the footpath and made his way towards the boats. He hadn't been this close to them before. He could see the one from which the noise and the light had emanated. The name was just visible along the side in white paint. Boase looked and, with difficulty, just managed to pick out the name of the boat. *St Piran*. He could still hear a sound coming from inside. He hurried back up the path and made his way home. The rain was falling harder now and, arriving at the house in Melvill Road, he realised that his clothes were absolutely soaked through, right to his skin. He dried himself off and got into bed. A last look at his watch confirmed the time. It was half past three. Boase was extremely tired.

A very bleary-eyed Archie Boase turned up for work the next morning. Bartlett, already at his desk, looked up when his assistant walked in.

'You look a bit rough this morning, Boase. What have you been up to?'

'Didn't sleep much, sir.'

'You need to see someone about this not sleeping business – you don't eat properly, you don't sleep properly. It's not good for a man of your age I tell you. Is this murder affair upsetting you?'

No, sir. I don't really know what it is. I'm all right though. Cuppa?'

Bartlett knew that if work wasn't bothering Archie Boase it must be a woman. And as far as the older man knew, Irene was the only woman for him. Bartlett knew the signs all too well – he had felt exactly the same years ago. Still did, come to that. If Caroline was away, Bartlett didn't eat or sleep without her. He knew just what was wrong with Boase. The younger man returned with two cups of tea.

'Fancy coming round for supper tonight, Boase?'

'That's very nice of you, sir. Yes, I would, thank you.'

'That's settled then – seven all right?'

'Yes, thanks.'

Boase unwrapped a large slice of pork pie with a hard-boiled egg in the centre of it. He laid it on his desk while he decided how to negotiate it. He took a mouthful and sat back in his chair. Eventually swallowing it, he looked across at Bartlett.

'Something strange happened last night, sir.'

'Oh, yes?'

Bartlett put down his cup.

'I was walking out at Pendennis quite late and I heard noises from those old boats.'

'Not this again, Boase. No wonder you're tired.'

'No, listen, sir. Someone was on one of them – the *St Piran*. There were at least two people. I heard them talking and I saw a light. One of them came up the path and walked right past me – he even trod on my coat. I think there's something funny going on there, sir, really I do.'

'All right, I believe you – but even if someone is there, it's probably nothing. Just kids or something. Perhaps we'll have a look down there tomorrow if we get a bit of time; maybe send Penhaligon or that new youngster to take a walk up there – it's obviously bothering you. Now just put it out of your mind.'

'Right, sir. Thank you. How did you get on with Algernon Hatton yesterday?'

'He's guilty all right, Boase. Admitted killing his brother. Some old rubbish about

285

hating homosexuals. He did it and now he's going to pay the price. It's Lady Hatton I feel sorry for – no husband and, soon, no sons. What I still do not understand is about Ivy Williams. Hatton swore blind that it wasn't him. He wanted her dead, hired Frank Wilson to do it, then when Wilson turned up at Penvale Manor on Christmas Day he said he hadn't killed her – what's going on, Boase?'

'Well, he would say that, wouldn't he, sir? I mean, he's not going to admit it. I think we just have to find him and question him about it. Seems he was hired to do the job, the job was done – who else could it be?'

'Hmmmm. Maybe.'

As a storm was threatening to blow up in the bay, and the wind began to come in across the sea, Boase was making his way to the Bartlett home for supper. He couldn't wait to see Irene again. Arriving at the house, he walked up the path and knocked at the door. Irene opened it.

'Hello, Archie. You look nice – cold too. Come on in.' She pulled him into the hall and gave him a big kiss on the cheek. He looked at her. She was lovely and he kissed her in return, on her lips. He looked down. There was Topper, waiting to be acknowledged. Boase patted the dog on the head and Topper, satisfied with this, returned to his master. Bartlett and his wife were about to sit at the table. Caroline offered Boase a chair next to hers.

'Hello, Archie. Sit down. It's only a cold supper tonight – is that all right?'

'Of course it is,' he replied. 'Thank you very much.'

The four ate their supper while Topper sat under the table, lying across his master's feet and waiting for any morsel which might come his way, intentionally or otherwise. As they ate, Boase relaxed while Bartlett regaled them with stories about the City of London Police and the Metropolitan, along with his recollections of being a young police constable and chasing Jack the Ripper.

'As true as I'm sitting here, I nearly had him. I was that close.'

'Don't exaggerate, George,' implored his wife.

'Don't mock, Princess. Don't mock. I tell you I nearly caught him and I'm certain unto this very day that I knew who it was.'

'Go on, tell us, Dad.'

'Irene, don't encourage your father. He doesn't need it.' Caroline began to clear the table. 'Anyway, part of the fascination is that no one knows who Jack the Ripper was, not even you, George, so don't try to spoil it.'

Bartlett lit his pipe, disgruntled.

'Well, I do know. So.'

Archie Boase and Irene were in fits of

laughter. They had to admit knowing the identity of Jack the Ripper would somewhat spoil the legend.

Boase spent the rest of the evening with the Bartletts and left their house at about half past ten. He always felt sad to be leaving Irene. One day though, he wouldn't. He'd made up his mind that one day he would never have to leave her and go home. He couldn't wait.

Chapter Fourteen

Norman Richards was upset. Kitty could always tell when there was something wrong with him, and today she was concerned.

'Norman, what's wrong with you – you've been on pins all morning. Calm down. Look, it's almost eleven – why don't you go out the back and 'ave a nice cup of tea? Go on. Leave one in the pot for me while you're there. When you've done that, go out for a quick fag. Mrs Williams won't be back for at least three-quarters of an hour an' it'll do you good.'

Norman obeyed and shortly returned, a bit of colour now back in his cheeks.

'Tell me what's botherin' you Norman. Go on, you know you can talk to me.' Kitty was always sympathetic where Norman was concerned.

He sat down on a small stool.

'Last night, a policeman followed me, nearly all the way 'ome. Why would 'e do that, Kit?'

'What one earth are you talking about?'

'Like I said, 'e followed me an' I didn't like it.'

'Well 'ave you done anythin' wrong?'

'No.'

'So, there's no problem then, is there?'

'S'pose not. I'm still goin' to tell my friend though. 'E'll know what to do. 'E told me what to do when the gangsters were after me – my friend sorted all that out.'

'Well, 'e sounds like a very good friend to 'ave, Norman. An' there aren't too many of those about these days.' Kitty smiled. Poor Norman, she thought. Even the gangsters had been after him. Too much time at the pictures, that was Norman's trouble.

At eight o'clock that evening, George Bartlett knocked on the door of Boase's lodging house in Melvill Road. The landlady called him and Boase ran hurriedly down the stairs. 'Hello, sir. What're you doing here? Hello, Topper boy.'

'Topper and I were just passing and we thought we'd have a walk round to Pendennis to have a look at those boats of yours. Coming?'

Boase grabbed his hat and coat and the two men and Topper walked out towards the sea front. Topper was enjoying the fresh night air and stopped to sniff at every opportunity. At Pendennis he could smell rabbits and was hoping his master would let him off his lead so that he could chase some. Bartlett had often wondered what Topper would do if he ever caught a rabbit – he was such a big, soft, lump of a dog with not a vicious bone in his body. He often chased them but they were always too quick.

As Bartlett and Boase rounded the bend in the road that led them onto Pendennis Point, Boase grabbed the older man's arm. He pointed to a figure descending the cliff path towards the boats. The figure stopped suddenly and lit a cigarette. The silhouette came and went, came and went, as the wind twice extinguished the stranger's match.

'Look, sir. Someone's going down there.'

The two men and Topper walked across the road and looked down the bank towards the wooden boats. They could clearly see a man walking quickly down the narrow, winding path towards the sea. As he changed direction, he looked back up the bank and, in the half-light, Bartlett thought he recognised him.

'I bet you any money, Boase, that's Frank Wilson.'

'You're kidding, sir. That's the last person I expected.'

'Me too. I don't think he saw us so we'll come back tomorrow without Topper. If what you've been telling me is true, he's been here a while anyway – he'll be in no hurry to leave. He's probably made himself quite comfortable here.'

'Are you sure, sir?' Boase was worried. 'What if he runs away?'

'He won't, Boase. He won't.'

Gloria Hesketh answered a knock at the door of the house in Avenue Road; she had rented the entire five-bedroomed house as she didn't want to share with anyone. Still, she had plenty of money, so it didn't matter what she spent. As she opened the door, she was surprised to see Bartlett and Boase standing on the step.

'Inspector Bartlett and Constable Boase, how lovely to see you both – but how unexpected. Do come in.'

The two men followed Gloria Hesketh through a long hallway and into a neatly furnished parlour. She was dressed, as usual, very glamorously.

'Are you just going out, Miss?' Bartlett enquired.

'What? Oh, no.' Gloria straightened the front of her dress. 'But I never think it does any harm to try to look half decent in one's own home – or in this case, one's own lodgings.' She smiled at Boase.

'As a matter of fact, gentlemen, I was just about to have some tea – will you join me?' Bartlett walked back from the window where he had been admiring the garden.

'Tea would be very nice. Thank you.'

'Well you both make yourselves comfortable, the kettle's just boiled. I won't be a moment.'

She soon returned with a large tray bearing a pot of tea, milk, sugar, and an enormous plate of cakes. Boase stared at the plate. Come to think of it, he was beginning to feel quite hungry.

'Tuck in now, both of you. There's fruit cake, vanilla slice, apple turnover, or fruit tart.'

'Unfortunately, a man of my mature years and ample stature cannot afford to indulge in such luxuries,' began Bartlett, 'however, I am sure that Boase here will not disappoint you. In fact, I would be surprised if there's anything left in the house by the time we depart.'

Gloria Hesketh giggled a charming giggle and the two men smiled, Bartlett glad to have her, seemingly, on his side. He was going to ask a favour.

'The last time we saw you, Miss...'

'I told you, please call me Gloria – everyone does.'

'All right, Gloria, when we saw you, you said you would be happy to help us if you could.'

'Yes, I did.'

'Well, there is something you can do, but you might not be happy with it, so I'd like to make sure you fully understand before you agree. Boase and myself have come up with an idea – it's possibly not the greatest plan we've ever had but, if I'm honest, we really need to go for this bald-headed to be in with any chance of success. This isn't your problem, Gloria, but the head of my station will call in detectives from London within the week if I don't sort this out – and that's the last thing I want.'

'Your plan sounds intriguing,' the girl replied, handing round the teas.

'Our main suspect for the murder of your sister Ivy disappeared on the night of her death and we haven't, I should say, hadn't seen him since. That is, until last night. We think we've spotted him in the town and we want to question him – that's where you come in.'

'You want me to question him?'

'No. No, we don't, but we do want you to help us apprehend him. You see we feel that if you could come with us to where he's been staying and pose as Ivy, it might enable us to find out the truth.'

'You mean, frighten him?'

'Well, in a way, perhaps. Seeing you might bring it all back to him. It might give us more of an idea about what's been happening.'

Gloria looked pensive.

'But, well ... of course, if you'd rather not,' Bartlett sounded disappointed.

'No, I didn't say that. Will it be safe?'

'Yes, Boase and I will be with you the whole time, don't worry about that.'

'All right then, I'll do it.'

Bartlett put down his cup and walked over to Gloria.

'Thank you very much, Gloria. This, I'm sure, is going to help us – you're doing this for Ivy, just you remember that. Now, we'll come and pick you up at, say ten o'clock tonight? Here's a description of what your sister was wearing the last time anyone saw her – if you could match this, as closely as you're able, then I think that'd help. Is that all right?'

'Yes, of course.'

'All you have to do is follow our instructions and everything will be all right. So, we'll see you tonight – and thank you again, this will be such a big help to us, I'm sure.'

Bartlett and Boase left Gloria to prepare for the evening and returned to the police station to go through their plans.

Half past nine came and Gloria Hesketh was feeling nervous. She had been ready for almost an hour. She had managed to dress much the same as her sister had, although Gloria's clothes were much finer and well made – it was impossible to replicate the cheap fabric and the worn-out look that Ivy had become accustomed to. She felt sad and guilty that Ivy had had nothing. She had already learned that her twin had been a prostitute and felt very unhappy that the poor girl had had to earn a living that way.

At five minutes to ten there was a knock at the door. Gloria went to open it. There were Bartlett and Boase.

'Hello, come in.' The two men followed the girl into the house. Bartlett stared at her; the likeness was striking.

'I'm sorry, you startled me a bit. You look so much like her,' Bartlett explained.

'Well, we were twins.'

'Yes, of course. I was just a bit shocked that's all.'

'Have I dressed all right?' Gloria spun round.

'Just right, I'd say – wouldn't you, Boase?'

'Yes, most definitely.'

Bartlett handed the girl her bag – even that looked just right. Gloria had really done a good job.

'Now remember, Gloria, there's nothing to worry about – Boase and I will be with you all the time. We're just trying to entice your sister's killer; he's got nothing against you and he'll know straight away that the game's up. All right?'

'All right,' replied Gloria, nervously.

The three left the Avenue Road house and prepared for anything that might happen. Although it was a short distance, Bartlett had brought a car. It was a cold night and he didn't want Gloria to be uncomfortable – she was doing them a very big favour. Within a few minutes they were at Pendennis Point and Bartlett parked the car. The three got out, Gloria looking all around her and feeling worried. Bartlett squeezed her arm. They walked across the road to where they could see the *St Piran* along with the other wooden boats. There was a light showing again. Boase led the way down the footpath, followed by Gloria, then Bartlett. As they got closer they heard voices and music, Bartlett thought it sounded like a gramophone. They stood on the edge of the cliff and watched the boat which was gently bobbing on the water.

'I'm going on board, Boase,' Bartlett whispered to his assistant. 'You wait here with Gloria.'

'That's a bad idea, sir, we're coming with you, just in case.'

'All right, but keep that young woman behind you at all times, do you hear me?'

'Right-oh.'

The three stood at the edge of the cliff and Bartlett jumped the short gap from land to boat. He turned and offered his hand to Gloria. He was thankful that she had worn sensible shoes. She too jumped across to the boat and Boase followed. The music was louder and clearer now; there was some sort of jazz playing. Bartlett held his hand up to Boase to indicate that he must wait, then made his way around the deck. He tripped and an empty bottle rolled across the wooden

planks. He listened; the music had stopped –
someone must have heard him. He turned
and Boase was right behind him.

'You all right, sir?'

'Yes, but it looks like they've heard us.'

Suddenly, a small hatch opened up in the
deck a few yards away and a head peered
through. Its owner pulled his body up and
stood facing the three visitors. It was Frank
Wilson.

'Who are you, what do you want?'

Bartlett stepped forward.

'I know you're Frank Wilson. I'm Inspector Bartlett, this is Constable Boase, and
this young lady – well, you may recognise
her.'

Gloria stepped forward and Frank Wilson
gasped. In the half light he could clearly see
Ivy Williams – but how...?

'We'd really like to talk to you, Frank. We've
been looking for you for a long time. Don't
try to run, we've got the place surrounded.'

'I'm not going anywhere, but there's no
point standing up here in the dark. Come
down below, we can talk there.'

Bartlett, Boase, and Gloria Hesketh followed Wilson through the hatch, down a
short ladder and into a small room below. An
oil lamp lit the scene. The smell was quite vile
– a concoction of oil, stale food and general
unpleasantness. The four of them sat down,
each finding a place amongst an assortment

of stool and barrels.

'Why are you hiding away down here, Frank?' Bartlett thought that now, surely, he had to come clean.

'Because I knew you were after me – and I haven't done anything wrong.'

'We suspect you have.'

'You think I killed Ivy Williams and Rupert Hatton – well, I didn't.'

'We know you didn't kill Rupert Hatton – we know that for a fact, but you were the last person to see Ivy Williams alive and we understand that you had a motive.'

'Oh, and what would that be?'

'The Hattons told us that they paid you to get rid of Ivy.'

'They tried to, but I didn't do it. Anyway, I'm still waiting for you to tell me who this woman is – there's an uncanny resemblance.'

Gloria spoke for the first time. 'My name is Gloria Hesketh; I'm Ivy Williams's twin sister.'

'That explains it then.' Frank smiled at her. She smiled back, she thought he looked like a film star. Frank sighed. 'I suppose you've got it in for me too?'

She didn't answer.

'Look, Inspector Bartlett, I don't know how long I thought I could live like this, but there were a couple of things I had to see through before I could get away – and I was going away because I haven't done anything. I just don't know how I can prove it to you.'

'Neither do we,' piped up Boase.

The four looked up as suddenly footsteps could be heard up on the deck; the person was running. All at once the hatch was lifted and two feet appeared on the first rung of the ladder.

'Frank, Frank. The police have been following me; you've got to 'elp me Frank.'

Bartlett and Boase stood up to welcome the visitor.

Chapter Fifteen

The owner of the feet appeared in his entirety. It was Norman Richards. He was startled to see Bartlett and Boase. As Gloria stepped forward into the light cast by the single oil lamp, Norman looked horrified. He screamed and ran to the ladder as fast as he could. Boase lunged forward to grab his ankles but Norman was too agile. He scrambled his way to the top and out through the hatch. Boase ran after him. The two men were now on deck. Norman backed away.

'What's she doing 'ere? That woman – where did she come from? Back from the dead?' Gloria had now appeared through the hatch and she walked towards Norman. He was sobbing now.

'Keep away or I'll kill you. Stand back, I've got a gun.' He pulled the weapon from his pocket and pointed it at her. Boase had crawled across the deck while all this was happening and was now standing behind Norman.

'Put the gun down, Norman. You're going to get yourself into a lot trouble otherwise.' Bartlett was watching now from the hatch.

'I'll shoot, I will.'

As Boase suddenly lurched forward towards Norman, in an attempt to knock the gun from his hand, Norman stepped back, his foot getting caught in a rope which was laying across the deck. He tripped, dropped the gun, and fell over the side into the water. Boase looked into the sea; it was dark but he thought he could just about see Norman being taken on the tide. He wasn't moving or shouting. Boase dived in; the icy water made him gasp. He started to swim but he could hardly breathe, so cold was the water. He could hear Bartlett shouting to him from the boat.

'Boase, he's just in front of you – you're almost there.'

Boase carried on swimming. He could see Norman's head now. One final stroke and he had him. He grabbed him and began to swim towards the boat. As he almost reached the rocks, a strong arm grabbed the boy from him; it was Frank Wilson. He pulled Norman up on to the rocks then gave Boase his hand. Frank, unaided, and with one motion, dragged Norman and Boase up onto the boat. Bartlett had never seen a man exhibit such strength. Boase was shivering. Gloria had found two old blankets below deck and she wrapped Boase in the first one then Norman in the second; Norman was unconscious.

'He must have hit his head on a rock,'

observed Bartlett to Frank. 'You must be frozen, Archie; here, take my coat.'

'No, really, I'm all right but I think we should get Norman to hospital.'

Bartlett, Boase, Gloria Hesketh, and Frank Wilson, carrying the unconscious boy between them, made their way up the cliff path and back to the car. The car was, fortunately, large enough to accommodate all five of them and they shortly arrived at the Falmouth Hospital which was situated at the top of Killigrew Road. The hospital was open for emergencies even at this late hour and soon Norman Richards was in the capable hands of the doctor and nurses.

Frank Wilson looked at Bartlett. 'Can I go now – if that's all right with you?'

'Yes, it's all right, but don't you try running off – do you hear me? I need a lot of questions answering. Try running away and I'll catch up with you.'

Bartlett had a strange feeling that they might have been wrong about Frank Wilson. He looked at Boase who still seemed to be shivering.

'You should be out of those clothes. Come on, I'll just tell the matron we're leaving and I'll get you home. I'll come back and see the boy here tomorrow. You sure you're all right, Boase?'

'I'm fine, sir, just incredibly cold.'

'Tell you what, you come back to the house

with me – you can stay the night. I know Caroline won't mind.'

'Thank you very much, sir.' Boase was feeling so cold and unwell that he didn't really care where he went. The freezing sea had taken it out of him. Bartlett bundled his assistant into the car and they drove the short distance to Penmere Hill. They were soon in Bartlett's kitchen and the older man had brought some spare pyjamas from upstairs.

'Here, put these on, I'll put your clothes on the range. You can sleep in the small room – but not before you've had a nip of something. You sort yourself out and I'll go into the parlour and get us a drop. It's almost two o'clock, we'll be abed shortly.'

The two men sat and had a warming drink.

'Do you think Wilson'll stick around, sir?'

'I know he will, Boase. He's got a lot to tell us, I think. You were very brave tonight, my boy; I'm proud of you. Now come on, you're all in. Let's get some sleep.'

By the time Boase woke up in a strange bed, Caroline and Irene Bartlett had already cooked breakfast and as he came down the stairs a welcoming smell pervaded the house.

Bartlett had been up earlier and brought the dry clothes into the bedroom. Boase entered the parlour.

'Good morning, Archie – we didn't expect

to see you here this morning,' said Irene smiling and handing him a cup of tea. 'Dad told us what happened – you're so brave, jumping in the water like that. Bacon and eggs?'

'That would be very nice, thank you, I am quite hungry actually.'

Bartlett and Boase tucked into two large breakfasts before leaving for the station. As the two men walked up Penmere Hill the rain began to fall steadily.

'You feeling better now, Boase? I thought we'd be better off walking – you're still looking a bit pale, the fresh air will do you good.'

'Yes thank you, sir. That breakfast helped.'

'Good. Now since we're going past the hospital, I don't think it would do any harm to look in on that young Norman – find out what was going on last night.'

They arrived at the hospital about ten minutes later and asked to see Norman. The matron said that they could spend five minutes with him, but no more as he had not long since regained consciousness. They went into a small room where he was lying in a bed. He looked up at them.

'Hello. Thanks for comin' to see me. I really must talk to you.'

Bartlett and Boase couldn't believe how ill the boy looked.

'There's something you should know; please listen, it's important. I killed Ivy Williams.'

Bartlett sat on the edge of Norman's bed.

'Now, now, young man, you don't know what you're saying – you had a nasty bang on the head last night – would've drowned too, if it wasn't for this man here. You try and get some rest and I'll come and see you tomorrow.'

'No, please don't go, please. I did kill 'er. I didn't like 'er. You ask Frank Wilson – 'e's my friend an' I bin stayin' with 'im for a long time. I tell 'im ev'rything – always 'ave done. 'E's bin looking after me since I was about six years old; there isn't nothin' 'e don't know about me an' 'e knows I done it. You've got to believe me, I...'

Norman Richards's body suddenly went rigid, he clenched his fists and tried to breathe but he couldn't. Bartlett leapt to his feet.

'Norman, *Norman* – Boase, quickly fetch the matron. Quick!'

The matron and a doctor came and ushered Bartlett and Boase out of the room. They were in there for quite some time. Presently they emerged. The doctor came over to Bartlett.

'I'm very sorry, sir. There's no more we can do to help him. It didn't look very good for him last night but we still held out some hope. I'm sorry.'

Bartlett sat down on a chair under a window. He felt warm suddenly. He pulled out his handkerchief and mopped his brow.

'You all right, sir? That was a bit of a shock wasn't it? Poor kid. Come on now, sir. You need some fresh air.'

Boase led the older man outside and into the garden. A fine rain was still falling and Bartlett began to feel refreshed. He hated to see anyone die – especially a young man.

'I'm sorry, Boase. A few memories came back to me then and things went round in my mind all at once. I just thought about my boy John for a minute.'

Boase never heard Bartlett speak about his son – this had really shocked him.

'Come on, sir. Let's take a walk down the station and I'll make you a nice cup of tea. We can't do any more here now.'

The two walked down Killigrew Street to the police station. Bartlett sat down in his office. Boase brought him a strong, sweet cup of tea and the two men sat in silence. A knock at the door made them both jump. Constable Penhaligon came in carrying something in a bag.

'Sorry to bother you both. A message that Frank Wilson is coming in to see you at eleven and, also, one of our men picked this up from the *St Piran* this morning.'

'Thank you, Penhaligon, that will be all.'

Penhaligon handed the bag over to Bartlett and left the room.

Bartlett put down his cup, opened the bag

and, throwing it down on his desk in despair, looked across at Boase.

'I feel like crying, Boase, I really do.'

Boase came across the room and picked up the bag. 'Oh, no!'

Inside the bag was a small, toy gun, the sort one might find in a boy's Cowboys and Indians game.

'He died for nothing, sir. And it's all my fault.'

'No it's not, Boase. How could you tell that it was a toy in the dark – and how could you know he would hit his head? Put it all out of your mind for now. Perhaps Frank Wilson'll have some answers for us.'

At five minutes to eleven, Frank Wilson was shown into the office of Bartlett and Boase. He sat down and lit a cigarette.

'I suppose you've both heard about poor Norman? I've just been to the hospital on my way here. I'm devastated, I can tell you.'

Bartlett nodded and listened.

'You were quite close I gather?'

'Yes, he was like a kid brother to me.'

'Can you tell us everything you know? Going right back to the beginning?'

'Yes, I've known Norman Richards for about twelve years. He was a bit backward, due to something that went wrong with him and his mother when he was born. The odds were already stacked against him, as far as I knew – his mother was about fifty when he was born and the doctors had advised her not to have any more children, but, well, I suppose it's one of those things. It happened and Norman paid the price. Anyway, my parents knew his parents and when Norman was about six the family moved near where we were living. Norman used to follow me around all over the place and I used to give him sweets. He was such a kind kid.'

Frank Wilson looked upset. He lit another cigarette.

'When Norman got older, the other kids used to take advantage of him. They used to make him steal from shops – even a collection box in a church once. They never gave him anything. He used to want to be in their gangs but they just used to laugh at him. He would always try to buy things for them – or steal things to give them, just to be in with them. I can tell you it used to really upset me. Anyway when Norman turned fourteen he left school. His parents had both died the year before and my mother took him in just until he could fend for himself, so to speak. I managed to get him a job in Mrs Williams's tobacco shop – she owed me a favour and he was a very good worker. Of course, when he got his own money every week he used to spend it on daft comics and going to the pictures – he loved films. He was quite literally a simple boy, Mr Bartlett, and I shall miss him terribly.

'Well, what about his older siblings?'

'I think he lost touch with them – they were never really interested in him. I think the previous child must be getting on a bit now. Norman was born much later on.'

'Can you tell us more about Ivy?' Bartlett didn't tell Frank about the confession he had just heard from Norman before he died.

Frank stood up and walked over to the window and looked out onto the street below.

'I was very fond of Ivy Williams – in love with her I suppose you might say. We'd been knocking around together for a few months. I just felt sorry for her at the beginning but then I began to see the real Ivy. She was actually a very sweet girl. No one liked her – they always said mean things about her and she was really quite sad. We'd planned to go away together, start a new life. I didn't really have anything to keep me here and I was a bit lonely, if I'm honest. Anyway, you may know that Ivy had been asking the Hattons for money after having found out that one of them was her father?'

'Yes, we know, go on,' urged Bartlett.

'Well, I'd been with them in France during the war and I suppose they thought they'd done me a favour. I was implicated in a murder and Algernon Hatton helped me through it. I didn't have anything to do with it anyway, but he convinced everyone that I didn't and luckily nothing more happened. Anyway, Hatton came to me, saying I owed him a favour and that he wanted Ivy got rid of – if I didn't do it they would drag up the whole murder case and everything, just when I was starting to make plans to expand my business and to get on in life for a change. She was starting to cost too much – mind you, it was the least they could do after the way they treated her mother and then put her in the workhouse to die. Well, on the night Ivy was killed, I arranged to see a slip of a girl called Ruby Pengelly – she was sweet on me and I thought that I could use her as an alibi for what I was about to do. Norman was very friendly with her – with all the Pengellys, in fact, and he saw her waiting for me. She was very upset because I didn't turn up. He later saw me with Ivy. He told me after what he did.'

Frank sat down again.

'Do you think I could have a glass of water?'

Boase fetched him one.

'Apparently, Norman saw me on the beach with Ivy. I knew I couldn't kill her. I had taken her there and then, all of a sudden, I couldn't believe what I had actually agreed to do. Naturally I didn't tell her about any of that but I told her I had just remembered that I was supposed to be somewhere else and that I couldn't stay. I arranged to meet her the next day and then I just ran off and left her. I didn't want to hang round in case the Hattons had someone watching me. Norman told me later that he had been following us and when he saw her alone on the beach he hit her on the head with a rock. His mother had always told him that prostitutes weren't nice women and that they broke up families. He hit her – to please Ruby Pengelly, can you believe? Then he couldn't stop. He didn't want anyone to recognise her. He was a strange young thing – very protective of the girls. He often followed them around, especially at night because he had some mad idea that they might be in danger. Sometimes he was just looking out for them, other times he could be quite wicked, well, mischievous; he'd actually follow a girl just to frighten her – he thought it was funny, they never did. Sometimes he'd call out their name or jump out at them from behind a bush. There was never any harm intended, I know. Norman was the most likeable kid I ever knew.'

Ah, that explains a lot, Bartlett thought. I'll let young Norma know she wasn't imagining things.

'Do you believe his story, Frank?' Bartlett asked.

'Yes, I'm afraid I do, you see, I know it's

true. I had got up onto the cliff path after I left Ivy and then I thought that I should go back for her. I felt I shouldn't leave her alone like that. When I got back Norman was still standing there with the rock in his hand, paralysed with fear. I looked down and saw Ivy and I just didn't know what to do – I could see she was dead. I didn't know whether to give him the pasting of his life or to help him. I don't mind saying, I could have killed him with my bare hands there and then, but then I looked at the state he was in and I just knew I had to sort it out for him. As much as I loved Ivy, Norman was like flesh and blood to me and I had to stand by him. He stayed with me on and off, on board the *St Piran*. I kept low because I knew I was your prime suspect. Norman kept me stocked up with food and drink and visited me after dark. I had planned to get away – maybe take Norman with me.'

Bartlett looked at Frank Wilson. So, all along he had been a good person, just helping out a simple kid. He didn't mention the toy gun and neither did Boase. There was no point now, it would only make Frank feel worse than he already did – if that was possible.

'I think you should go and get some rest now, Frank. It's been a long night for all of us and a big shock for you.'

'What about the rest of it, sir? The blackmailing and all of that business with the Hattons?'

Bartlett let out a long sigh.

'Well, you were rather stupid there, if you don't mind my saying so – but, I haven't got the stamina or the inclination to bother with that just at the moment.'

Frank picked up his hat and coat. He shook Bartlett's hand and the older man patted him on the shoulder.

'Just one thing, Frank – why didn't you pick up that money from the cemetery?'

'I got there, saw one of your men and ran as fast as I could in the other direction. It wasn't worth five hundred quid to get caught. I knew you wouldn't believe my story, and, if it wasn't for poor old Norman, I don't suppose you would now – I'm guessing he confessed to you? Goodbye, Inspector, goodbye Boase.'

Boase sat down in his chair.

'Trust Penhaligon to get seen.'

Constable Ernest Penhaligon knocked at the door of the Pengelly's flat in Killigrew Street. It was getting late and he was on his way home. The door was opened by Ruby.

'Hello, Ernie. What you doin' 'ere?'

'I'm afraid I've got some bad news – can I come in?'

Ruby led the way into the parlour. It was about a quarter to ten and Bill and Jack had already gone to bed in preparation for their long day ahead. Rose was sitting in her armchair.

'Mum, it's Ernie Penhaligon.'

Rose got up from her chair.

'Hello, Ernie, what brings you here at this time of night – ev'rything all right?'

'No, I'm afraid it's not. I thought you should know that Norman Richards died this morning at the hospital.'

Rose slumped down into the chair and Ruby ran to her. 'You all right, Ma? She's got a bad 'eart, she don't need a shock like this.'

'I'm all right, Ruby. I can't believe it, that poor boy – dead? We only saw 'im a couple of days ago. What 'appened Ernie?'

''E 'ad an accident and was knocked unconscious; he came round briefly but apparently it was all too much for 'im. I thought you ought to know.'

'Thanks, Ernie,' said Ruby, 'I'll show you out. I can't believe this – does Kitty know?'

'I don't think so, Rube. I only came to tell you since I was comin' by your front door.'

''E was very friendly with my sister – she'll be so upset. I'll go an' see 'er tomorrow, I know she's 'avin' a few days off. Goodnight, Ernie.'

'Night, Rube.'

Norman Richards's funeral took place on the nineteenth of March at the Falmouth Parish Church. Frank had paid for it and, to any onlooker, it seemed that no expense had been spared. It was a sunny spring day and, after the service, the funeral cortège made its way to the cemetery at Swanpool. Norman would have been surprised at how many friends he actually had. They stood in the sunshine around the newly dug grave. They were all there. George Bartlett, Archie Boase, Frank Wilson, the Pengellys, the Rashleighs, Mrs Williams sobbing her heart out, Gloria Hesketh, Mabel Roberts and the Berrymans. There were so many flowers too. Norman would have been pleased that all these people cared so much.

As the mourners left the cemetery for the Seven Stars where Frank had paid for a magnificent wake, Bartlett walked over to Gloria Hesketh. She was putting flowers on Ivy's grave.

'You all right, Gloria?'

'Yes, thank you, I'm fine. I wish I'd known her. I should have made the effort sooner; she didn't even know I existed.'

'You know that your father has been asking to see you?'

'Yes, Inspector, I do, but I've decided I don't want to see him – is that too awful of me? It would bring everything back – Ivy, my mother, all of it.'

'It's entirely up to you, a decision only you can make. No one will think any less of you. What will you do next?'

'I suppose I shall go back to London now. I haven't really got much else to do here.'

Bartlett saw Frank Wilson waiting by one of the cars at the top of the cemetery.

'Are you quite sure there's nothing here for you?' he nodded in Frank's direction. 'Go on, he's waiting for you.'

Gloria ran quickly to the car and Frank kissed her on the cheek. Bartlett smiled. As the couple stood talking by the car Bartlett nudged Boase with his elbow. They both looked up the road. Coming down Swanpool Hill was an enormous car, chauffeur-driven. It stopped by the cemetery gates. The chauffeur got out and opened the door behind his. He leaned forward to help the passenger out. It was Lady Cordelia Hatton. She stood in the sunlight looking around her for a moment, then she spotted Gloria with Frank. She walked over to where they were both standing.

'Hello, my dear, you must be Gloria Hesketh. I'm Cordelia Hatton – your grandmother.'

Frank already knew who this was. He took a step closer to Gloria.

'I hope you won't tell me to go away, although I wouldn't blame you if you did. I just wanted to let you know that you're the only family I have left now and I'd very much like to keep in touch with you – you and your young man, that is.' She looked at

Frank and he felt sorry for her. It wasn't her fault that her two sons had turned out the way they had. Now she had nothing left. Gloria leaned forward and kissed her on the cheek.

'I'd be very happy to keep in touch with you, very happy indeed.'

Bartlett and Boase made their way up the hill and walked to the Seven Stars on the Moor to have a drink for Norman Richards. They were enjoying the spring sunshine. Within the hour they had returned to the police station. Bartlett thought he'd go home early tonight, Topper would enjoy a walk along the cliffs. Yes, he'd ask Boase if he'd like to come over and see Irene too. No doubt tomorrow would bring something new for them to worry about – it always did.

The publishers hope that this book has given you enjoyable reading. Large Print Books are especially designed to be as easy to see and hold as possible. If you wish a complete list of our books please ask at your local library or write directly to:

Magna Large Print Books
Magna House, Long Preston,
Skipton, North Yorkshire.
BD23 4ND

This Large Print Book, for people
who cannot read normal print,
is published under the auspices of

THE ULVERSCROFT FOUNDATION